MW01195603

Wildefell

Wildefell

✝✝✝

H.B. Diaz

CEMETERY DANCE PUBLICATIONS

Baltimore
2024

Wildefell Copyright © 2024
by H.B. Diaz
All rights reserved.

No part of this book may be reproduced in any form or by any
electronic or mechanical means, including information storage and
retrieval systems, without permission in writing from the publisher,
except by a reviewer who may quote brief passages in a review.

Cemetery Dance Publications
132B Industry Lane, Unit #7
Forest Hill, MD 21050
www.cemeterydance.com

The characters and events in this book are fictitious.
Any similarity to real persons, living or dead,
is coincidental and not intended by the authors.

Trade Paperback Edition

ISBN:
978-1-58767-992-6

Cover Artwork and Design © 2024 by Kealan Patrick Burke
Interior Design © 2024 by Desert Isle Design, LLC

Prologue

August, 1992...

*D*ARKNESS CONSUMED the old cellar like maggots on a dead sparrow, feasting slowly but inexorably, until the trembling moonlight revealed only the room's creaking bones. Shadows played along the rafters and bled out from beneath the cold dirt floor. Outside, they swayed to and fro on the branches of the great oaks and rattled their ponderous chains against the fence gate. One hundred years of night slept comfortably here, undisturbed.

Sara ducked beneath the storm hatch and crept down the stone staircase, mortar crackling underfoot. A propane lantern, held high above her head, swallowed up the murky darkness beyond.

"Sara, this is stupid," her younger sister whispered behind her.

"You afraid?" Sara asked over her shoulder.

"You know all the stuff you read in those goth books isn't real, right? There's no such thing as ghosts."

"Gothic," Sara corrected.

"Whatever. Let's just go. There isn't anything down here."

As Sara stepped onto the packed earth floor, her lantern illuminating the ghostly figures of furniture enshrouded in linen, a stone of dread rolled up into her throat. Her sister was wrong. There was something down here. She could feel it.

Hundreds of mason jars, their contents unknown, lined the shelves against the wall. Webs veiled the handwritten labels and bridged the space between the glass, trapdoor spiders making hasty retreats into their tunnels. Mice and cockroaches alike fled from the light, burrowing into crevices and skittering behind barrels of potatoes moldered to dust.

"Ever wonder why Grammy won't let us down here?" Sara asked, swallowing the lump. Her sister swatted something out of her hair with a squeal.

"Because its crawling with roaches and black widow spiders."

Sara rolled her eyes. "Middle schoolers are so lame."

"You were a middle schooler like two months ago."

"Shut up."

The wind blew curtains of rain down the stairs. The hatch door could not hold against the storm, and it slammed shut with the ferocity of a gunshot. Both girls screamed, embracing each other in the dim light. After a moment of stasis, Sara pushed her sister away. Cassie tried to snatch the lantern, but Sara held it tight, this small orb of safety.

"Did it lock?" Cassie whispered. Behind her, the lantern light fell upon a rocking chair draped in a moth-eaten sheet, like the ghosts in cartoons. The rocker only needed eyeholes and a voice with which to moan, *Boo!*

Sara sat the lantern on a stack of potato crates and the light spilled onto the floor, chasing shadows to the edges of the room. Dropping her backpack beside it, she unfastened the side pocket and removed an antique mourning broach.

Behind glass and tarnished silver inlaid with emeralds, a lock of golden hair caught the light.

"You shouldn't have stolen that from Grammy, Sara. It's like her prized possession."

"I didn't steal it," she said. "I'll give it back once I turn in the paper."

"Okay, but you could've picked Dad's cane or something. Wasn't the assignment just to find out the history of a family heirloom or something?" Cassie shivered and crossed her arms tightly around her chest. "Why'd you pick something so creepy?"

"Grammy only has two rules, right?" she said, brushing the pad of her thumb over the broach.

"Don't go into the cellar, and don't open her jewelry box," Cassie replied. "I don't want to be here anymore, Sara. I'm telling Grammy."

"Oh, come on, Cas," she said, grabbing her arm to prevent her from escaping. "It doesn't bother you these are her *only* two rules?"

"You could just ask her about it."

Sara had asked, and Grammy deflected her questions every time, making it even more intriguing. This assignment was a good excuse to get to the bottom of it.

"I'd rather ask the lady this hair belongs to," Sara said.

"Grammy told us not to try to communicate with them. She'll teach us when we're older. Come on. Let's go."

"I'm in high school. I'm old enough."

A bitter draft stoked the flame of the gas lantern, throwing wild shadows across the room. Sara's eyes fell again upon the form of the rocking chair.

"Is there anyone here with us?" she whispered, her fingers tightening around the broach.

"Sara—"

"I've seen Grammy do it before. It won't be that hard."

"But Grammy—"

"If you're here with us, give us a sign," she continued. The light did not flicker. Icy fog did not fall from their mouths as it did in the movies, but the crickets stopped chirping.

The rocking chair pitched forward, tossing the sheet onto the ground. It held there, suspended on the front rockers as if someone leaned in for a closer look at them, and then sprung back, crashing against a support beam. Cassie launched herself toward the stairs with a scream. She heaved open the latch and disappeared into the sodden night. Sara was alone.

The chair rocked.

A single drop of water fell from its worn arm and disappeared into the dusty fabric beneath, followed by another. The scent of the stagnant marshes came in all around her as filmy water poured from the seat, soaking the sheets, the puddle creeping ever closer, but Sara could not move.

You are lost and gone forever
Dreadful sorrow, Clementine

The voice crawled over the lyrics, spidering through Sara's mind without ever passing her ears. The lantern sputtered. A woman appeared out of the darkness, perched on the edge of the chair. She clutched a blanket to her breast as if it were an infant, weeping into its damp folds, stagnant water soaking a gilded era dress fastened at the throat with an emerald broach.

The woman lifted her head, frayed darkness gathering in her worm-eaten eyes. Snails clung to her nose. Algae discolored her face and bloomed across her sunken cheeks. Her mouth opened. Leeches wriggled on her tongue, fastened tight, sucking and sucking as she tried to speak.

Sara fell backward.

The woman's voice came as if from underwater, flooded with agony.

Come home.

Chapter 1

Present Day...

$\mathcal{S}$ARA WALKED alone up the moss-slicked steps, her phone's flashlight shivering in her hand like a guttering candle, strangled near to death by the viscous dark. Each flicker fanned an ancient terror in her chest, one imploring her to flee, but she did not heed it.

Wildefell Manor was not a place to be casually visited. It was generations of madness and untimely ends. It was sorrow and heartbreak and everything she'd left behind. Cassie knew that.

You need to come home.

Her sister hadn't answered the texts Sara sent in reply to this enigmatic message. Only voicemail answered her calls. It was as if she and Grammy had simply vanished. Annoyance morphed into anxiety in the car, followed closely by stomach churning panic. Her heart galloped in her chest as she hesitated at the final step. Afraid somehow standing eye to eye with the ancient structure might challenge it, she averted her gaze to the ground as one approaches a wild creature. The horses in the stable whinnied, and then, somewhere far away, a fox screamed.

The house knew she was home.

Sara dialed Cassie's number one more time as her phone battery died, the light blinking out. Though no lamps shone from within, the muffled ringing of her sister's phone sounded inside.

You've reached Cassie. I probably won't call you back, but you can leave a message if you want. Bye.

Something was wrong.

Sara reached for the door. Her fingers closed around the brass and came away slick with blood. She could smell it.

The door swung wide into the yawning dark, and Sara stepped inside.

The pull chain of the antique tiffany lamp, which sat upon the table beside the door for half a century, and might remain half a century more, clanked gently when she tugged it. Soft light blossomed into the room, revealing a dark set of footprints on the polished oak floor. She called her sister's name again. Her voice echoed off the walls, shimmered against the crystal chandelier, and then died in the vaulted ceiling.

Wildefell held its breath as Sara followed the gruesome path into the dining room and flipped on the light. Blood freckled the scarred table and smeared the glass of the china cabinet. Inside, Grammy's pewter pitcher shimmered in the weak moonlight, quietly nestled among the crystal.

She'd never seen so much blood in all her life. It seeped from the walls, from the floorboards and the rugs, as if the house itself was dying.

Sara did not cry out when her eyes landed at last upon the mutilated corpse of her sister. Neither sound nor breath escaped her lips, but the darkness crept in. It leached consciousness from her until she slipped into the merciful black.

- - -

RAIN SHIVERED AGAINST the windows, dragging Sara upward toward wakefulness. She resisted, but the storm raged on, and so when she woke at last with her cheek in a pool of blood, she believed perhaps she hadn't yet woken up at all. A nightmare, nothing more. In a moment, she would wake in her apartment in Savannah, alarm heralding the new day.

She tried to stand, but the blood was slick beneath her, and she cracked her head against the hardwood. Her memory returned in shards.

"No, no," she muttered, ghostly orbs of light darting in and out of the edges of her vision. She shut her eyes tight as murky dawn lit the room.

She did not want to see.

Outside, curtains of Spanish moss brushed against the window like the phantom skirts of a long dead belle. Sara drew in a ragged, foul breath and lifted her head toward the fireplace. Her sister's body dangled from the chimney, her torso bent at a grotesque angle against the grate, neck broken. A deep latticework of bruising covered her swollen face and shoulder, the flesh so hideously mutilated that Sara knew her only by Momma's silver necklace, which hung down into her hair.

Arranged painstakingly on the bricks were three long tresses of gray hair, bits of scalp still clinging to the roots.

Sara leapt to her feet. She knew where she would find her grandmother, and although her recognition of this fact propelled her inexorably forward, she could not recall exactly how she knew it.

All at once, she found herself on the back balcony, leaning over the splintered wooden railing. Rain soaked her blouse and fell upon the corpse of her grandmother on the stones below.

The grandfather clock inside tolled, but Sara did not count the hour.

Minutes passed away, ages, until the old rotary phone in the hall shrilled through the house. Sara backed away from the balcony and stepped silently into the house. She lifted the phone to her ear but did not speak. Words felt foreign, as if they existed on another plane altogether.

"Hello?" Someone said. She knew the disembodied voice, but she could not recall to whom it belonged. "Cassie?"

The sound of her sister's name snapped some hinge in her mind. Sara dropped the phone as if it burned her.

The screaming wouldn't stop. She covered her ears and fell to the floor as the rain blew through the doors, a shimmering curtain in the dim light. A moment later, or perhaps an eon, she heard another voice, and then felt someone's hands on her wrists.

"Sara!" the voice cried. "What happened? Is this your blood?"

But Sara couldn't speak. Arms gathered her into an embrace and rocked her. She recognized the voice at last.

"Lucy?" she whispered.

"It's me. The police are on their way."

■ ■ ■

THE MORNING SUN drew Sara's shadow down the pier, toward the house. She supported herself against the railing with the oily salt marsh at her back, unable to form a single cohesive thought but the feeble and disarticulated urge to run.

When she'd moved away from this place, she hadn't left an empty room in an empty house, waiting silently for her return. Instead, she'd left a vacancy into which the dark had crept to take her place. It withered the thick curtains of Spanish moss and curled the leaves of the ancient oaks. It peeled back the climbing ivy to expose naked, crumbling brick and thrived in the hedgerows where vines of poison ivy strangled the boxwoods and the yellow roses.

Sara had been away from this house for a very long time.

Not a house. A graveyard without a keeper. Crime scene investigators strung their police tape over the back door. Sara turned to face the water, the oppressive August weighing already upon the surface of the rotten water.

When footsteps sounded behind her, Sara did not turn around. Let them come. Let them ask their questions. And yet, even as she steeled herself for the reliving of the night before, something in the steps gave her pause. She knew the rhythm, knew the slight scuffing of the left heel.

Adam.

The very molecules comprising her existence recognized him, and her chest ached.

"Sadie?"

Something inside her cracked apart at the sound of his voice, different now, deeper, but still *his*. She could not turn to face him, not like this.

"Lucy said you'd be out here," He stepped closer and carefully set a large cup of coffee beside her hand. Goosebumps prickled up her arm. "Thought you might need some caffeine."

"Why is it you're always around when someone in my family dies?" she said, the words choked with decayed bitterness. She didn't like the taste of it.

"Sadie, I—"

"Don't call me that."

She could not suffer the sound of her childhood nickname on his lips, not after all this time. Not after she'd so resolutely abandoned her.

"Will you look at me, please?" he whispered, but she couldn't. "I'm the lead investigator. I'll need to ask you some questions when you're ready."

His steps on the pier faded away. Inside her throat, where his name ought to have been, was only a gnarled, foreign mass, so she did not call after him.

Sara could not gather the will to move. She could neither throw herself into the mercy of the marsh nor take a single step toward the house. Managing only to look over her shoulder, she watched as this man from her other life approached a tight circle of investigators, gathered like vultures around the body of her grandmother.

Nothing felt right.

An eddying thought took up residence in her head, but she couldn't keep it still, couldn't see it yet for what it was.

Her sun-bleached boat shoes clapped against the warped boards, her pace quick in defiance of the grief. Wood became grass beneath her feet, and then stone. No one attempted to stop her as she shouldered her way between the investigators. When she at last reached her grandmother's ruined body, she prepared herself for pain, but nothing happened. Inside, where there ought to have been a freely bleeding wound, she found only an aching chasm. She stood at its edge, waiting for someone to either push her over or pull her to safety. No one moved.

Sara stared at the stained bricks and the yellow evidence markers, at the scattered pearls and Grammy's wide, sightless eyes. Her throat was cut so deeply and with such violence that the cervical vertebrae separated, her bones gleaming white in the sun. Rainwater settled in glimmering, scarlet puddles on the flagstones.

Beyond, beneath the shade of the balcony, Adam Contreras crossed his arms tightly over his chest. He stiffened when a woman in uniform approached him. The four stripes on her sleeve marked her as the captain, and it took Sara a moment to recognize her.

Eva Mauk.

The same Eva Mauk who'd cornered her in the bathroom after English Lit, called her a devil worshipper, and then threw her grandmother's book on Spiritualism into the toilet. It was a 1922 limited edition copy, and they were never able to find a replacement. Sara held onto her grudge with a ferocity rivaling hatred.

"This place gives me the creeps," Eva said in a low voice, brushing away dark bangs with a hooked finger. "Always has. It's just, it's always been so... unchanging. How are the trees the same size as they were in high school? The iron gate never rusts. The ivy never dies or grows. It's just spooky."

"Have you considered the possibility that they actually take care of the property?" Adam asked, barely looking at her. "Or that the trees look the same because we grew, too?"

"Say what you want." She waved him off. "There's something not right about it."

"You don't know them like I do, Eva," Adam answered. He rubbed his eyes and then dragged his hand across his chin.

"It's *Captain*," she said. "Somehow you always forget that." When he didn't reply, she added, "Do you need me to assign this case to someone else?"

The muscles in his jaw clenched tight, and instead of answering her question, he asked, "How long before the coroner can take the bodies?"

"An hour maybe, but it's going to take some time to get this one—" she nodded toward Grammy "—in the van. Her head looks like it's about to roll right off. The lady was as cracked up as the rest of the bunch, but it's horrible."

The apparition inside Sara stilled. She no longer felt the heat of the day on her back. The metallic tang of blood in the air dissipated into a strange memory.

"Horrible to relate," she whispered, bringing her fingers to her temples and shutting her eyes. She could not lose her hold on this thought, this same indistinct idea that led her to Grammy's body last night. She followed it now at a dead run across the patio, into the house, and up the staircase toward her childhood bedroom, vaguely aware all the while of Adam following just behind.

"Sadie," he called. "You can't be in here."

She passed family portraits in the hall, their gilt frames dulled by dust, and crossed the threshold of her bedroom with her heart in her throat.

White linen draped the roll top desk, the Victorian wing chair, the night table. It hung from the bookshelves and covered the vanity. Each item she had so lovingly chosen those many years ago slept soundly beneath its dust-laden covering. They did not belong to her anymore, but to the house.

Losing her hold on the gossamer thread that compelled her here, she tore the sheet away from the bookshelf. Motes of dust swirled up into streamers of sunlight, taking the forms of ghosts.

"What are you doing?" Adam breathed. She had forgotten him.

"Help me," she said, running her fingers along the collection of hardbacks.

"You're not being coherent," he said.

"Get out of the way if you're not going to help."

"Help you what?"

"Which one is it?" she muttered. She couldn't find it, couldn't remember.

Finally, her fingers brushed a volume of tales by Edgar Allan Poe. In one moment more, she located the passage. She shoved the book into his hands, her fingernail marking the text. Adam looked at her, eyebrows knit, but then resigned and read it aloud.

"'A search was made of the chimney, and (horrible to relate!) the corpse of the daughter, head downwards, was dragged therefore; it having been thus forced up the narrow aperture for a considerable distance.'"

"And here," she said, pointing to the following paragraph.

"'The party made its way into a small, paved yard in the rear of the building, where lay the corpse of the old lady, with her throat so entirely cut that, upon an attempt to raise her, the head fell off.'"

"See!" she said, snatching the book from him. He attempted to take her by the arm, but she pushed him away so forcefully that he stumbled backward, sending the book crashing to the floor. Undeterred, he reached for her again.

"Don't *touch* me!"

Adam managed to pull her into his arms even as she pelted him with blows. Adrenaline roiled inside her, bubbling into her throat until it burst out in a cry of frustration.

"That's enough," he whispered into her ear, and the anguish in his voice drew the fight out of her. She fell against him, and when the tears stung her eyes at last, he held her tighter.

"They're gone," she cried against his shirt, balling it into her fists. "They're all gone."

Chapter II

*S*ARA WATCHED the coroner's van pull up to the house from her old bedroom window. Light rain blew across the marshes, blurring the faces of the medical examiner and her assistants as they removed two stretchers from the back of the vehicle. One of the assistants looked up at her and smiled tightly. She must have looked like Heathcliff's lunatic wife, peering down from her high window with her hair in her eyes and a shirt stained with blood. She did not recognize the faded reflection that met her eyes in the glass. The house took her image and remade it according to its own, with shadow and angles distorted by poorly refracted light. It wore her sister's blood as she did now. They had this in common, she and the house.

The coroner reappeared; this time carting human remains zipped tightly in black bags. Sara turned from the window. She had sequestered herself here for the better part of the day, listening to the hushed voices and the footsteps, waiting for someone to force her to leave. No one came, not even Adam. She had nowhere else to go.

A tapping sounded at her door. She ignored it, but he appeared after all, stepping softly into the room.

"Hey," he said, and she looked up.

The house reformed him, too. It morphed the lanky boy who'd taken her to prom into a man of great and terrible physical power, with a battle weary, military bearing. It weighed down upon him as he stood in the doorway, bowing his shoulders and darkening eyes moistened by sorrow.

"I'm sorry," he said, and she looked away. Too many years stood between them. Sara could not find her voice.

He stepped into the room, his stance vaguely threatening.

"You can't stay here," he said.

"I'll be fine," Sara replied at last, though her voice didn't seem to belong to her.

"That's not my concern."

"You can't force me to leave. This house belongs to me now." As she said this, she felt as if a coin had been tossed into the depths of her chest, sinking, sinking, until it landed in the pit of her stomach. The window screen shivered behind the glass and one of the shutters on the main floor banged against the brick.

The house didn't belong to her at all.

"It's a crime scene, Sadie," Adam said.

"I told you not to call me that."

A door closed downstairs. Sara sat down on the bed. If she left this house, this room, it might never allow her back inside.

"Look," he continued, running a hand across his jaw. "I know I'm the last person you want to see right now, but you have to leave."

Why wouldn't he just leave her alone? She needed more time. She needed to think.

"I could use a cup of coffee," she said. "Then I'll go."

He shook his head, and then walked toward the door.

"Hey," Sara called after him.

He turned, the desolate ghost of a smile playing across his lips. "I know. Cream, no sugar." And then he was gone.

When she could no longer hear his footfalls on the stairs, Sara rose and walked again to the window. The rain left a greasy sheen across the lawn, and with the exception of a wayward gust of wind shivering in iridescent puddles, all fell still. The whole world scarcely moved at all, and here she stood at its dark and churning core, stranded.

Lucy tapped gently on the door.

"How are you, sweetie?" she asked. When Sara didn't reply, she sat down on the bed and rubbed her swollen eyes. "God, this is so terrible."

On another day, Sara might have sat down beside her old friend and let her cry. She might have rubbed her back and recalled the happy memories of their youth, but she could not. Today, she could only manage the kind of tight smile reserved for passing strangers in the street. Lucy dabbed her eyes, swiping running eyeliner back into place.

"I ran into Mr. Buchanan on the way over," she said. "He wanted me to tell you not to worry about Salem and Poppy. He's found replacements for this week's carriage tours."

Sara closed her eyes. Cassie's horses. She'd completely forgotten them.

"He has the stable key," Lucy continued. "He'll make sure they're fed and watered."

"Thank you," she replied, and then added, "I'm not very good at this."

"No one is. Certainly not me."

Sara's memories of Lucy were inexorably intertwined with her sister. The longer she looked at her, the more unbearable her presence became, if only because it made Cassie's utter absence so impossible to ignore.

"I'd like to be alone, Luce, if that's all right."

Lucy took a quivering breath and nodded. "Of course." And a moment later, Sara was alone again. Muffled voices rose up through the air ducts of the old house, and if Sara listened closely, she could make out disjointed phrases.

A woman saying, "Let's pack it up."

Adam's voice mumbling, "I'm not sure we're equipped to handle this."

Sara! Sara, where are you?

Cassie. Cassie!

Sara sprung from the bed, gaining the hallway and swinging herself around the banister to bolt down the steps. It was all a mistake. It hadn't been Cassie's body after all! She crashed into Adam at the bottom of the stairs, and the coffee mug in his hand shattered onto the floor.

"What's wrong?" he asked, taking her by the shoulders.

"Where's Cassie?" she cried. "Where is she?"

"Oh, sweetie," Lucy said behind her, and Sara couldn't suffer the intensity of pity in her eyes, so she looked away.

"I heard her voice!"

Why wouldn't they get out of the way? Why wouldn't they let her see her sister?

"Cassie?" she called, standing on her toes and looking toward the door. It remained closed. A skeleton crew of investigators emerged from the dining room to stare at her, expressions of grim sympathy on their faces.

Adam walked her to the door, his arms tight around her. Sara called out for her sister again, but she was gone.

● ● ●

SARA WATCHED THE ceiling fan blades spin sluggishly overhead. The scent of copper lingered on her hands and in her nose, despite showering. The house remained with her also. She felt its eaves and its bricks filling up the emptiness inside her, walling her off like Montresor.

The pull chain of the fan tapped against the globe in regular intervals, lulling her either into dreams or into madness. It was too early to tell which.

Clink. Clink. Clink.

The sheets smelled of lemongrass. The shirt she wore smelled of him.

Sara did not remember arriving here. She had no recollection of walking through the door, except for the vague awareness of Adam's body near hers, and Lucy's voice whispering that everything was going to be okay.

A kind lie, but a lie, nonetheless.

She could still hear them talking. Every few minutes, one of them said her name.

"We should have taken her to my place," Lucy said, her voice hushed. "She's not going to know where she is when she wakes up. At least she's been to my house before."

"I wasn't going to drive her all the way to St. Helena, Luce. It's too far."

Someone put a dish in the sink. Lucy said something in Spanish. Sara always intended to learn, but the years slipped by.

"You're exhausted," Adam replied. "Go home and get some rest. I'll be here if she wakes up."

Don't leave me, Lucy, Sara thought. *Not with him.* Exhaustion darkened the corners of her vision. The ceiling fan spun round and round. If she could just close her eyes for a moment, she could fall away from all of this.

Don't sleep. You can't sleep.

"No offense, *primo*," Lucy continued, "but you're not exactly on her list of most trusted people. You two have a complicated history."

"You think I'm not aware of that every time she looks at me? If she even looks at me at all?"

Sara closed her eyes at last. The conversation faded away, followed closely by the remains of her consciousness. When the creaking of the door jolted her awake again, darkness had fallen fully across the room.

"Hey, it's just me." Lucy peeked inside. "We brought you to Adam's_"

"I know." She felt him everywhere; in the simplistic décor of the room, in the scent of the pillows and in the color of the curtains. Hunter-green, his favorite since childhood.

"Listen, I've got to go. I'll have the guest bedroom all ready for you tomorrow, okay?"

"They'll have the house cleaned up by then," Sara murmured. She swung her legs over the side of the bed and gathered her hair into a bun.

"Adam made arrangements with the cleaning company, but—" she stepped into the room, hugging herself. "But, Sara, you can't stay there. Not after... not with everything that's happened."

"I belong there," she answered, but the simplicity of this resignation did little to comfort her. Lucy's tears glistened in the glow of the streetlight.

"Cassie was my best friend," she said, her voice splitting apart. "We're family. Please let me help."

"I know. I'm sorry, I just... I'm not..."

Heavy, excruciating silence settled between them. Only the locusts outside continued the rhythmic dialogue.

"Let's talk more at Blackbird's tomorrow?" Lucy asked.

"Sure."

She left the room and Sara fell back onto the sheets with her hands over her face. Adam appeared in the doorway a moment later.

"Do you need anything?" he asked.

"I just want to be left alone."

"10-4." Adam closed the door without another word. She returned to her study of the ceiling fan and waited.

When the moonlight shone in through the window and stretched onto the bed, Sara sat up, listening. A tree frog cheeped in the crepe myrtle outside the window and locusts sawed all around, but inside, the little house slept.

She crept out into the living room. Adam snored lightly from the couch, a quilt patterned with blue orchids tucked around his chin. She slipped out into the humid night without incident.

As she walked, dodging low hanging branches and mosquitoes, she pondered how he had planted his roots only a quarter mile from Wildefell. There was perhaps no significance in this observation, but it was the safest place in her mind, safer than what she was walking toward.

Dried flower blossoms and withered tendrils of Spanish moss whispered beneath her feet as she approached the gate. Silence governed this hour before dawn, and it felt somehow grotesque in the aftermath of such violence. The house stood proud and dark, as it had for over one hundred years, and held this crypt hush close. Sara slipped through the gate.

As her shoes crunched on the gravel walkway, she stole a look at the second story windows, which drank up the early morning dark. The night before she'd left for college, she and Grammy had looked out across the lawn and talked for hours.

"You'll come back home, baby doll?" Grammy had asked.

"Yeah," she'd answered, but knew even then it was a lie.

"We'll miss you. The house will miss you."

"Will you stop with that, Grams? It's just a house."

Grammy had laughed. She believed their ancestors kept watch over them as the generations passed, the old house retaining their sentience until it took on a life of its own. Sara, after many years of study and searching, came to the necessary and only conclusion that it was all nonsense. It had to be nonsense.

"Do you know why the house chose you?" she'd asked.

"Because I'm pretty."

Grammy smoothed her hair and planted a kiss on her cheek. "It's because you can see it."

"See what?"

"You see the house for what it truly is. Behind the rumors and the tourist literature. And you can see everyone in it."

"I don't see them," she answered. "At least, I don't want to. They're not real."

"When you get to be as old as me, you'll be glad for visits from old friends every now and again."

Sara had only been back a handful of times after that night, for obligatory family functions or to pick Cassie up without ever going inside. But Sara knew now that no one ever really left here. Even after all of her fighting and striving for another life in Savannah, here she was. Back home. She wondered briefly, irrationally, if one of her ancestors had made some foolish bargain with the devil, if their great family fortune was ill begotten and they'd all been cursed to die here. Why, then, had she alone been spared?

Had she been spared?

Her car, a sensible Toyota Corolla, sat silently beneath the willow where she'd left it, unlocked, moonlight glinting off the windows. She opened the passenger door and ducked in to retrieve her wallet and cell phone from the console. A padded yellow envelope sat on the seat.

Sara picked up the package and examined it. On the label above the address was her full name in elegant, type written script: Sara Imogene Wilde. Curious. She never used her middle name. In fact, to her knowledge there were only three people still alive who even knew it, and one of them was sleeping soundly on his couch. The others were Lucy and the family attorney.

Carefully, she tore open the seal and tipped the envelope. A copy of *A Study in Scarlet* by Sir Arthur Conan Doyle fell out onto the seat.

She picked it up, frowning.

Tucked in between the copyright and title pages was a small note, which appeared to have been written on an old typewriter: *My condolences.*

Sara regarded the note for a long while, tracing her fingers over the edges of the book in the dim interior light. She recognized this font somehow, but regardless of how long she studied it, she could not recall how she knew it.

Her phone chimed, and she retrieved it from the console. Seventeen missed calls. Sara set the book on the dash, tucked herself into the seat, and held the phone to her ear with her head tipped back against the headrest. Nine voicemails, mostly from John.

Sara, are you all right? You weren't at work. Call me when you get this.

It's John. You missed our dinner tonight. Did something happen?
And then an hour later, *I saw the news. Please call me.*

Her boyfriend's voice troubled her. She had changed already, reverted to a version of herself that could not survive in Savannah, and so the sound of this man speaking her name in his honeyed accent felt foreign, despite their yearlong relationship. She deleted these messages with a pit in her stomach and listened to the others, which were from her editor.

He'd seen the news too, and had reassigned all her stories to Midge Wallace, who couldn't even write her way through a horoscope. She'd have to call him back to set it right in the morning. Sara had no intention of staying here long enough to see Middling Midge take her bylines. As this determination crossed her mind, the darkness inside the house shifted.

She lifted her eyes in time to see a tall figure glide by Cassie's bedroom window.

Still clutching her cell phone, Sara launched herself out of the car and ran toward the house, climbing the porch steps and ripping off streamers of police tape. She inserted her key into the lock as boldly as she could manage and stumbled through the door into the murky half-light of morning.

To her right, cavernous dark bled out from the dining room. Inexplicably drawn to it, she stepped forward, but the image of her sister's mutilated corpse rose up from the depths of her mind with such violence that adrenaline dumped into her blood. She paused with a muted sound of protest and turned on her heel toward the staircase.

Footsteps sounded on the floorboards upstairs.

Sara, is that you?

Cassie's voice traveled down the stairs, reaching her as if from under water.

"You're gone," Sara muttered, but her feet carried her past the yellow evidence markers and bloodied boot prints, and up the stairs. She was no stranger to madness, and she knew when she'd opened the front door last night, another had opened as well, one she'd locked many years ago. Behind that door, windowpanes shivered, spider's webs veiled memories dulled by time, and the disembodied voices of those who had come before her echoed inside the walls like the scratching of rats. But her sister's voice didn't sound like the others she'd heard before. No, her words were just the same as they'd been in life, and this fact disturbed her. She had always been able to tell the difference between the spirits and reality. Something had changed.

This was how it happened with Momma. Grammy said the grief of losing the love of her life had been too great. It broke her apart and let the ghosts inside. Eventually, there wasn't room left for anything else, not even Sara.

Sara?

She found herself standing before Cassie's door, tears streaming down her face. The house seeped into the cracks inside her as her hand closed around the cold doorknob. No footsteps sounded beyond. No light shone from beneath the door. When Sara opened it, the house held its breath. The shutters held soundly against the stone. Curtains hung as still as a photograph. The songs of the locusts outside hushed to a whisper.

Despite the aching feeling she was now only a guest in this place, Sara stepped inside and turned on the light. Blurred by tears, shapes materialized into forms she recognized. The sheets were bunched in the unmade bed, as if Cassie had only just rolled out of it, her hair a mess, eyeliner from the night before smudged beneath her eyes. Their mother's childhood teddy bear rested on the pillow, where Cassie lovingly deposited it every morning since childhood. Dirty laundry covered the old rocking chair she'd had taken from the cellar when they were children.

Sara ran her fingers over the worn wood, remembering the night they'd taken Daddy's lantern and Grammy's broach into the cellar. It was a strange way for children to pass time, but the house's sordid past bored through their family tree with as much ease as a woodworm, leaving behind only the labyrinthine dark, fit for discovering with bated breath.

The apparition that appeared to her that night came to her many times after, always on the property—her very own Lady in White. No one else had ever seen her. Now, as she averted her eyes from the chair Cassie had dragged out of the cellar in some childish attempt to torment her, she wondered if the woman had been trying to warn her all this time.

Sara pondered the portents too late. Ruin had already laid claim to her family, and the apparition did not appear to admonish her as she lingered near the chair.

Perhaps she'd only imagined the figure in the window, as she'd imagined Cassie's voice. The hush within the room remained undisturbed, except for the quiet beating of her own broken heart. She approached the window to look out over the lawn, the marsh a smear of darkness beyond. Boat lights shone like will-o-the-wisps upon the surface of the water.

Behind her, Cassie laughed.

She closed her eyes, summoned her courage, and turned to look. The room, like all the others at Wildefell, was empty. She returned her gaze to the window.

Over her shoulder, her sister's face peered back.

Sara could not turn around again to confirm this presence. She met the reflection of Cassie's eyes in the window, knowing in her heart she was still alone in the room.

"Where are you?" Sara whispered. Cassie did not reply but continued to look at her with the same ornery expression she'd worn in life. Sara closed her eyes again, and when she opened them, Cassie had gone.

Although her sister's laugh faded back into the depths of the house, another sound emerged. Sara waited, listening.

Crickets.

Not outside, but all around her, in the walls, in her head, sawing and chirping in unison. A bell chimed, and then she heard the gentle swish of a fan blade.

Oh, I'm sorry, a woman said, her voice airy, somehow metallic. *We're closed.*

Sara's heart pumped adrenaline into her limbs. She covered her ears, her own reflection in the windowpane a visage of horror.

"No, no," she whispered, and then rose her voice to address the house. "I'm not her anymore. I'm not Sadie."

Then the woman screamed.

Sara gasped, spinning on her heel, searching for the source of the sound. It came from everywhere, from nowhere. The cloying scent of lilac overpowered her.

Please! The woman begged, gagging and gasping for air. *Stop!*

"Where are you?" Sara cried, her hands in her hair. Something shattered, not the shivering chime of breaking glass, but the quick, hollow cracking of clay. Then silence.

No longer able to withstand the weight of her own body, Sara collapsed onto the bed. She could accept neither the possibility of her own madness, nor the appearance of her sister's ghost, and so she simply shut her eyes and willed it all away, Cassie's old teddy bear clutched against her chest.

Chapter III

ESPITE THE suspension of her consciousness in a pitch-black sleep, Sara woke fully aware of all that had befallen her. No merciful period of confusion spared her from the utter devastation hollowing out her insides. Adam's voice reached her from far away, but she could not answer him.

"Are you here?"

She was not. Although Cassie's sheets enveloped her legs, she felt so dissociated from her own body she might have been a ghost herself, lingering still in the places she'd haunted in life. Adam's footsteps sounded on the stairs, down the hall, and finally stopped outside her own bedroom door, where they had spent all those summer nights together. He knocked.

"Sadie?" she heard him call.

"In here," she managed, and Adam's footsteps continued on down the hall until he reached Cassie's room. He peered inside. An army green messenger bag hung from his shoulder.

"Jesus, what are you doing here? We've been looking everywhere for you."

Sara extracted herself from the sheets and sat up. She heard the front door latch. Hushed voices reached her from the foyer.

"We?" she asked, eyebrow raised.

"Your attorney's outside." He paused, and then added, "and the grief counselor."

Sara rolled her eyes.

"I know, I know," Adam said. "Just talk to her. Maybe it'll help."

"Like they helped my mother?"

When she slid off the bed, Sara discovered she was still wearing his old Beaufort High t-shirt and a pair of rolled up sweatpants. She hadn't brought a change of clothes, not even a toothbrush. Adam crossed the room and opened the closet, exposing Cassie's sundresses and boho skirts to the light. Sara stepped forward as he flicked through the hangers.

"What are you doing?" she began. "Those are my sister's things."

"No, they're not," Adam answered. He selected a floral maxi dress and tossed it at her. "Half of these are yours anyway, right?"

Sara's lip shook as she held the cotton between her fingers. It was indeed her dress, snatched from her closet and never returned. Sorrow grabbed ahold of her throat again, squeezing and squeezing until she could no longer breathe and the tears burst forth from eyes shut tight. Adam touched her shoulder, but she shied away.

When she became master of herself again, he had left the room.

Sara stepped into the dress Cassie had claimed as her own and drew it up over her hips like a shroud, hiding herself beneath folds of soft fabric. With it, she veiled the fear throbbing deep inside her chest, and concealed the crushing loneliness. As she slipped her arms into the sleeves, she left Sara, hotshot investigative reporter, behind in Savannah. The house, she knew, would not suffer a false double of her to exist.

"Sadie?"

Adam called her name from the kitchen, and with his voice came the scent of strong coffee. She followed both down the stairs, and he met her at the threshold of the dining room, mugs in hand. He smiled at her in his old way, with one corner of his lip higher than the other. Sara felt ill.

"Still fits," he said.

"Barely," and she tugged down the hem, which felt too revealing despite it reaching her knees. The vibrant fabric had just enough stretch to be forgiving of the last fifteen years.

"Last time I saw you in that—"

"Grammy was teaching us how to read tarot," Sara interrupted, but she remembered the warmth of his breath and the roughness of his hands. She remembered Gram's knowing smile as she left them alone on the pier.

The expression Adam wore now revealed plainly that he shared this memory, but behind the sharp glint in his eye, she saw only mourning.

"And the grief counselor?" she asked, accepting the proffered coffee with heat in her cheeks.

"Sent her away," he answered, clearing his throat. "Mr. Delaney, too."

"Thank you." Sara lifted her eyes over his shoulder to glimpse the fireplace, the stone stained the color of rust. Blood congealed on the grates. Sara could smell it. His body blocked the rest of the dining room from view.

"I'm trying to find a contractor to replace the stonework," Adam said, following her gaze. "The cleaners will be here today, but I don't know what they'll be able to do with it."

"It's the original fireplace, though."

Momma would have fainted.

Adam ignored this and motioned toward the front door with his coffee mug.

"We can't be in here. I have to ask you those questions now," he said, and Sara resigned, following him to the door. They stepped onto the front porch, the air already dense and fragrant with lilac. Locusts sawed in the willow, and beyond the wrought iron fence, banners of steam rose from the street as morning dew burnt up in the sun.

They sat together on the bench her grandfather had built; the hand-carved cameo of Grammy now smoothed to a ghost. Sara sipped her coffee and wrapped both hands around the mug, despite the heat. She leaned on the armrest, as far away from him as possible.

"What do you want to know?" she asked.

"Everything. Start at the beginning."

A news van drove into the cul-de-sac, slowed at the gate, and then continued on. The old tree offered enough cover that they wouldn't be visible from the street, and Sara was grateful. She hadn't brushed her hair since she left Savannah.

"I got a text from... my sister," she began, finding herself unable to speak her name aloud. *"You need to come home."*

"Where were you when you got the message?"

"In my apartment, getting ready for bed."

"Were you alone?"

Sara glared at him. "Are you serious? You want to know if I can verify my whereabouts?"

"It's SOP, Sadie. Persons of interest need alibis. You know that."

"I'm a person of interest?"

"The person who—" he paused, clenched his jaw. "The one who finds the bodies is always a person of interest."

Sara chewed on her cheek, the taste of coffee sour in her mouth.

"Just tell me what happened next," he said.

"She wouldn't answer any of my calls. So I came."

"And when you got here?"

Sara motioned toward the door. Someone had cleaned the knob. "Were there any prints?" she asked.

"Just yours."

She nodded. "I should've been more—"

"It's ok."

"Look, you know the rest. I came into the dining room and saw her, and then I found Grammy." Still in denial about the strange events of last night, or perhaps chalking it up to exhaustion, she chose to leave that part out of the tale. Instead, she added, "Just like in Poe's story."

"I want to know more about that."

"So, you believe me now?"

"I just want to know more." He took the hardback book from his messenger bag and handed it to her. Irritated he'd had the gull to take it without bothering to ask, she snatched it from him, and then opened it as reverently as if it were an ancient text.

She ran her fingers over the worn leather spine and finally flipped the pages to *The Murders in The Rue Morgue*. Now she'd been given the opportunity to prove her theory, but she didn't know where to begin.

"I loved this story," she said at last, almost to herself. "It inspired Sherlock Holmes. Did you know that? It was the beginning of everything."

Adam waited.

"Can you really read this and tell me it's a coincidence?" she said at last. "Didn't you see the way... the way she was pushed up into the chimney?"

After a long moment, Adam asked, "You think this was a message, then?"

She did not answer this question despite the ardent *yes* she felt inside her chest. Quietly and entirely without her consent, a laugh rippled from Sara's throat. It grew in intensity until Adam looked at her the way they'd all looked at Momma.

"Do you know who the actual murderer is in this story?" she asked him, clutching the book to her chest. He shook his head. "An orangutan." She continued to laugh as the nausea burned in her throat, as the porch began to fall out from beneath her and she felt herself sinking down into the house's depths. Adam set his hand on her shoulder and the laugh died away, but the sensation of falling remained.

Footsteps sounded on the gravel, and she lifted her head to find Lucy standing in the drive with a bouquet of sunflowers, a gift-wrapped box, and an expression akin to horror.

"Sara," she breathed, setting a palm on her chest. "Oh, it's you. It's you."

"Your cousin was just watching me lose my marbles," Sara answered, standing to greet her. "Are you okay?"

"It's just... you're wearing Cassie's dress," Lucy said. "I thought I heard her laughing."

Sara could only answer, "This is my dress."

"Oh," Lucy nodded, and she sat the flowers on the steps, avoiding Sara's eyes. She would not come any closer. "Well, you know how much she loved sunflowers..."

Sara gathered them and held them to her chest with a smile, but the nausea returned.

"Oh," Lucy said, passing her the gift box. "This was left for you out by the mailbox. It doesn't say who it's from, but it must weigh 10 pounds."

"One of Old Mr. Peabody's watermelons, I bet," Adam offered.

Sara sat down on the stairs with the box balanced on her lap. She untied the large blue ribbon, and then removed the lid.

"Oh my God," she murmured, casting the box away. It fell down the stairs as she stumbled backward into Adam, the corpse of a small terrier tumbling across the stone and landing at Lucy's feet.

"Jesus," Adam whispered, his hands on Sara's shoulders. Lucy scarcely appeared to see it. But for her gaping mouth, she stood stone still.

"It's Petey," Lucy mumbled, tears welling in her eyes.

Adam asked, "What?"

"Mr. and Mrs. Wilson's dog. He was 17 years old."

Before anyone could move to inspect the poor creature, Adam's phone chimed.

"Contreras," he answered, and then he became so still time might have ended all together. "Where?" Another pause, and then, "I'm on my way."

"What happened?" Sara asked, facing the house so she didn't have to look.

"Mrs. Hastings just found a body."

"What? Where?"

"The store. Don't touch the dog. I'll have someone over to get it. I have to go."

By the time Sara turned to ask him what she should do in the meantime, he was halfway down the drive. It didn't matter. Sara knew where he was going.

She was going too.

•••

THE STEERING WHEEL felt slick and cumbersome under her palms. Her legs felt too long, her back too straight. The quiet engine hummed beneath her, but she could not shift into drive. Biting her lip, Sara removed the keys from the ignition and stepped out of the Corolla, clutching the other key, the one she'd never been able to remove from the ring.

Her feet crunched over gravel as she walked to the garage, drawn by nostalgia and some other sensation she could not name. She wanted to sit in her father's car one more time, wanted to feel the worn leather and hear the turn of the engine.

Finding the garage door opener hidden in the same place as always, behind a stone under a thorny rose bush, Sara pushed the button and waited as the door slid upward. The car sat within, draped in a beige canvas.

She freed the 1965 Mustang from its dusty covering, motes of pollen billowing in sunshine that glinted off the shimmering red paint. As the debris settled and the canvas came to rest in a crumpled pile in the corner of the garage, Sara lingered. She traced her fingers over the sun-bleached ragtop, remembering the wind in her hair, Pearl Jam on the radio. She remembered the exhilarating sensation of freedom, and how quickly it had been stripped away.

Sara unlocked the door and sat down in the driver's seat, the smell of Cassie's lemon perfume overtaking her. Her Chapstick still sat in the cupholder, along with the pair of aviator sunglasses Sara had mailed her for her birthday.

Before the tears could well in her eyes, Sara jammed the key into the ignition and the engine roared to life, summoning a host of memories, among them the night she'd picked Adam up for prom. That night, like all the others, was stained with all that had come after it. She did not permit herself to dwell upon it for long, and instead focused her attention on opening the convertible top.

The smallest of smiles played across her lips as she navigated the car out of the garage, past the iron gate, and onto the street, but it fell away quickly. Sara Wilde, the reporter with too many pairs of black pumps, a nice boyfriend, and an apartment in the city, felt like a stranger. A different woman had driven up from Savannah, one who still believed she could make it out there on her own, who believed she didn't need her family's money to succeed. Now it was all she had left of them.

She guided the powerful car down Main Street slowly, against its nature. Curtains of Spanish moss glistened above her, discolored by rays of weak sunshine, and the antebellum houses with their grand porches and balconies sat among the ranks of Wildefell, their morning silence sinister. This had all been full of wonder and magic when she was a girl, when she and Cassie would run down to the marina to see the dolphins bob up and down between the tethered boats, ice cream cones melting all over the pylons.

She wondered if she could ever love Beaufort that way again, if she could ever feel its magic or appreciate its quiet charm. It hadn't really changed. There were more retail shops and tourists, but those same inns and bridges that had been a fixture of the city for 200 years would likely stand for 200 years more, despite every storm Nature cast its way. Sara, though, hadn't been able to withstand the storms at all.

She'd left her family here to rot and so it had.

Her cell phone rang from its place in the center console. Her editor again. She answered it on speaker.

"Mr. Woodward," she answered.

"Sara? Boy, it's good to hear your voice. Are you all right?"

"I've been better, Chief," but it was good to hear his voice too.

"Listen, honey, I'm sending Midge up to get a few police statements, maybe an interview if you're up for it."

"You're what?" She inadvertently tapped her brakes, and the car behind her honked.

"I know, I know. Midge isn't my first choice on this, but my ace reporter is a little too close to the story."

"I'll cover it," she said, flipping off the driver as he swerved around her, horn blaring.

"The hell you will."

"You want an inside scoop, don't you?"

"Well, yeah, but Sara, it's too much. You need time."

"I *need* to find the bastard who did this. It'd be easier with the paper's resources."

"What about the police?"

"Let's just say I know the lead detective and the captain, and they might not be much help."

"Christ almighty," he sighed, and she could see him running his hand across his white beard. "Fine. Just tell me what you need."

"Thanks, Chief. I'll check in later."

Sara dropped the phone back into the console as she neared the garden shop, nestled on the corner between a quaint bed and breakfast and a Baptist church. It was already buzzing with investigators. Police tape hung limp across the lot entrance, so she parked on the street. An older officer approached the car, his weatherworn hand resting casually near his weapon.

"No press," he said.

Surprised, she squinted up at him. "But I'm not—"

"Kid, you've got reporter written all over your face. This is a closed crime scene." He hooked a thumb over his shoulder, toward the store.

"Lieutenant Contreras knows me."

"Sure, I heard he met Scarlet Johansen once but I ain't lettin' her in either."

"She's with me," Adam called from the front door.

The officer shrugged. Sara stepped out of the car, ducked under the police tape, and crossed the small parking lot. The skirt of her dress clung to her knees, her tattered boat shoes splashing through iridescent puddles. She wished she'd had the forethought to bring a pair of those sensible pumps.

"What are you doing here?" he whispered through his teeth, so close she could feel his breath on her cheek. He blocked the open door with his body.

"I assume this is a homicide investigation?" she asked.

"That's what it looks like, but I can't let you in."

"Adam, there have been three murders in as many days. I can help. You know I can."

Adam shut his eyes and cursed under his breath. "If Eva finds out, I'll be patrolling the mall on a scooter." He took her by the elbow and led her inside. "Five minutes. Are you sure you can handle this?"

No. Every cell in Sara's body hummed with the word.

"Yes," she answered, louder than she meant to. Adam set his hand on her back. She stepped ahead of him to distance herself and walked into the store, the conditioned air cooling her cheeks. She walked past the wind chimes, granite garden gnomes, and stained-glass flamingoes. A great pressure had begun to build in her throat, pulsing in the hollow between her collar bones, but she ignored it.

A glass door provided access to the greenhouse, and as they entered, a small bell jingled above them. Hoses snaked across the floor, some spraying little fans of water with a hiss. Ceiling fans spun rhythmically overhead. Lilac perfumed the dense air.

Sara saw her eyes first; wide open and fixed upon the glass ceiling, mahogany irises already clouding over. In life, this woman must have been strikingly beautiful, with neatly cropped raven hair and olive skin, faded now to a pallid gray. She clutched a sprig of wilted white flowers.

There was violence in this killing, but not of the sort that had claimed her sister and grandmother. This had been quiet and quick, almost merciful in comparison, a strike of lightning instead of a hurricane. The only evidence of it welled internally in the woman's corpse, appearing as dark bruises around her mouth and neck. Investigators milled around the body, snapping photographs and setting down yellow evidence markers. Adam stood close, but did not touch her. This reassured her, if only because he was near enough to catch her should she collapse.

"You should go," Adam muttered. Sara couldn't speak. "I mean it, Sadie. Eva will be here any minute. This is obviously unrelated."

Sara wasn't convinced. While she wanted nothing more than to flee this place, the flowers in the woman's hand gave her pause. It wafted through her memory like a faint fragrance in a disused room. She looked at the body, at the surrounding foliage and display tables. A clay pot had fallen to the ground, perhaps knocked over in the struggle, and Sara remembered the sound of it as her heart tumbled into her stomach.

I'm not Sadie anymore, she said inside, her internal voice desperate and unconvincing. *Not anymore. Not again.*

Plants of all kinds lined the shelves, except in places where rust rings marked the metal. These pots were missing. No, they'd been moved and rearranged on the shelf below. Sara read their labels to herself. Fox Glove, Lily of the Valley, Narcissus. Bella Donna. All poisonous except for one, a small blooming bush labeled *Hawthorn*, whose flowers matched the sprig in the woman's hand. An idea began to form in her mind, but it developed slowly, like a storm cloud.

"Who is she?" she asked, her voice barely a whisper.

"Elisabetta Amello. 19 years old, lives on St. Helena Island. Don't know much more than that right now."

"Do you know how she died?" Sara asked.

"First glance, I'd say strangulation."

"That's not right," she muttered. She approached the body, knelt, and examined the bruises surrounding the woman's mouth. Something glistened behind the girl's teeth.

"Sara, you can't—"

"What's in her mouth?"

Adam knelt beside her and leaned in. He slid his right hand into a latex glove and opened the girl's mouth, exposing her tongue. Sara turned away as he extracted an ivory pill box from the back of her throat.

"What is that?" Sara asked, but Adam did not reply. The box popped open with a click. Inside, a single white tablet sat atop a folded slip of paper. A forensic technician appeared then, evidence bag at the ready.

"Run this through mass spec., will you?" Adam said to him, and he turned on his heel with a curt nod. Sara turned her attention to the paper slip as Adam unfolded it. She knew the font, recognized it from the note in the Sherlock Holmes book. She'd nearly forgotten about it.

Sara opened her mouth to read the single sentence aloud but could not.

She herself had become the deadliest poison in existence. Poison was her element in life.

She stood up so quickly she felt faint.

"Hawthorn," she murmured, and grabbed Adam's shoulder to steady herself.

"What is it? Do you know what this means?"

"It's just another message."

"To who?"

"Me."

Chapter IV

*S*ARA PRESSED her palms into her eyes, elbows sticking to the grimy picnic table outside the shop. If she could only make the world stop spinning for a moment, she could find her bearings.

"Talk to me," Adam said. He sat down across from her and waited.

"Did you read Rappaccini's Daughter in Mrs. Walden's class?" she murmured without looking up.

"You know I didn't."

"Well, that's what it's from… *Poison was her element in life*." She gathered enough strength to lift her head and fold her arms, squinting at him in the bright sun. "Rappaccini raises his daughter to tend his garden of poisonous plants. She develops a resistance to the toxins but absorbs them herself and becomes poisonous. She had a lover…"

"Naturally."

Sara ignored him. "He finds an antidote for her so they can be together, but it kills her."

"Sounds charming."

"It's written by Nathaniel Hawthorn. That's the name of the flower your victim is holding. Hawthorn. Order an autopsy if you want, but you're going to find she was poisoned."

Sara couldn't tell by his reaction if he believed her or not. In fact, he gave her no reaction at all; just listened with his gaze tilted toward the table. Even to her, it sounded like little more than a string of bizarre coincidences connected by an overtaxed brain.

"Sara," Eva said over her shoulder, startling them both. Her lean shadow stretched across the table and cast them both in shade. "I wish we could have reconnected under different circumstances."

"Likewise," Sara replied with as much sincerity as she was offered. Eva still wore the same tiny cross pendant she'd had in the tenth grade, still kept her chestnut hair bound up in a bun, but it had taken a great deal of striving, even with all her connections, for a woman to become captain. Sara could see the weariness in her eyes. Aside from this, the years had little effect on her high school bully, except perhaps to grant her even more power.

"Lieutenant," she said. "A word?"

Adam slid off the picnic bench with his lips pressed into a line and followed his superior beneath the shadow of a white oak. Sara, an eavesdropper by nature and profession, listened.

"What is she doing here?" Eva whispered.

"She's connected to all of this," he answered. "There's evidence this is linked somehow to classic literature, just like the Wildefell murders."

"Did she tell you that?"

"She noticed it, yes." Adam crossed his arms, his shoulders tensing.

"And you believe her?"

"Is there a reason I shouldn't?"

"She's looking for answers. Seeing Jesus in toast, just like her grandmother."

"I disagree. Do you have any officer on your force who can recognize these connections? We need her knowledge of the literature."

Eva lowered her voice, so Sara only caught pieces of the sentence. "I'm not— procedure, I'm talking about you digging—should stay buried."

"That's not what this is about." But Adam averted his eyes.

"*Please.* I know a lovesick puppy when I see one, trust me. I need your head in the game."

Adam looked over at Sara and she met his eyes. He sent her a nervous smile, said something to Eva, and then returned to the table.

"How much of that did you hear?" he asked.

"All of it," she answered, taking a small amount of satisfaction from the momentary horror in his expression.

"I'm surprised you haven't taught yourself to lip read."

"Who says I haven't?"

Adam ran his hand through his hair in his old way, pausing at the back of his neck and stretching the muscles. He'd never grown out of that, apparently. The nostalgia tasted bitter though, so she swallowed it.

He began, "About what Eva said..."

"She doesn't believe me," she finished, though she knew he wasn't referring to Eva at all. "I'm not surprised."

"I believe you," he said, lifting his shoulder. "But, Sadie, I'm not sure this is a good idea. You need to grieve."

"You don't get to tell me what I need."

"Look, I know how much you hate me, but—"

"You really don't."

This barb landed so squarely that he closed his eyes as if physically struck. "*But,* if you want to be involved in this at all, you've got to cut me some slack."

Sara shook her head. "I have to go. Your cousin and I were supposed to meet for coffee half an hour ago."

"Sadie—"

"I'll call you."

She felt his eyes on her back, and she walked across the parking lot, heat mirages rising up from the pavement like specters.

●●●

SOMEHOW SARA HAD forgotten her grandmother was a regular at Blackbird's Café. She had forgotten, every Tuesday morning, Grammy arrived here at precisely 8 o'clock and ordered a cheese omelet with an extra biscuit and did tarot readings for the waitresses. Did they know? Would she have to tell them?

Sweat dampened her palms as she pulled open the door, heralded by the jingle of a bell. Lucy stood up from a table tucked in the corner by the register, crossed the small space, and hugged her.

"I told them. I hope that's okay," she said in her ear. "I asked them not to say anything to you."

Some of the tension went out of Sara's shoulders, but she felt it ten-fold in Lucy. She didn't know how long her sister's best friend had been waiting here, shouldering her burden, but it had taken a toll on her. She could see in it her eyes, and in the smudged mascara darkening them.

"Thank you," Sara said, but the words did little to express her gratitude.

A waitress approached with a steaming pot of coffee as they sat.

"Lissa," Sara said, smiling. The waitress's face gathered a cluster of long forgotten memories, now tainted by grief. One in particular came to her, of Grammy performing a séance at her house on Halloween. The whole neighborhood showed up, but Grammy was unsuccessful in reaching anyone on the other side. The kids at school started calling her Crazy Miss Connie after that.

"It's good to see you," Sara added.

"Well, Lord love a duck," she replied. "You're all grown, aren't you?"

"Sure am."

Lissa took a breath as if preparing a long speech, but then Lucy caught her eye.

"Coffee smells great," Lucy said quickly, and Sara was grateful for her.

"Just brewed it," Lissa replied, filling their mugs. "It's our dark roast. That still your favorite, Miss Sara?"

"You know me well," Sara shrugged, but the effort required for small talk exhausted her. When Lissa had taken their orders and returned to the kitchen, Lucy leaned in and took Sara's hand.

"Is it true?" she asked. "Was someone else murdered?"

Sara nodded. She didn't want to talk about this. She pulled her hand away and reached for the silver pitcher of cream.

"You're going to stick your nose in the investigation, aren't you?" then, upon Sara's look of surprise, added, "I know that look. Cassie had it too whenever she was about to do something *totally insane.*"

"It's not insane. Adam wants me to consult."

"He *what?*" Lucy set her mug down on the table loudly. A few forks clinked against plates in the café.

"I can't really talk about it..."

"No, go back to the part where my cousin wants you involved in this nightmare."

"I'm connected to it, Lucy. I can't pretend I'm not. He thinks I can help." Sara busied herself with stirring her coffee.

"He thinks if you team up like the fucking Scooby gang and find the killer, maybe you'll forgive him."

"What are you talking about?"

"He's never forgiven himself for what happened," Lucy said, leaning toward her. "You know, with your dad."

"Well, that makes two of us."

Lissa arrived with their food and another round of coffee, but Sara had lost her appetite. She picked at a biscuit and watched it crumble on the scratched plate.

"Those are the best biscuits in Low Country," Lucy said. "You're wasting it."

"Help yourself." She handed it over and Lucy frowned but accepted it.

"You know, Sara," Lucy began, washing down a hunk of biscuit with a swig of black coffee. "Adam's a good man. If you took some time to get to know him again, maybe—"

"I don't need to get to know him, Lucy. My dad would still be here if it wasn't for him."

"You know that's not fair."

"What's not fair is him shipping himself off to the army and leaving me to pick up the pieces of my life." The other diners in the restaurant fell quiet again as her voice rose.

"What else was he supposed to do? You ran too."

"There wasn't anything left for me here."

"What about us? We're your family." She motioned to the waitresses and the diners, and to the owner who had been eavesdropping and smiled at her, nodding.

Lucy continued, "Adam's family, too."

Slowly, the people in the diner resumed their conversations. Sara wanted to change the subject. Unable to think of a way to do so smoothly, she simply asked, "I was kind of expecting to see your mom around these last few days. Is she all right?"

"I'm surprised Cassie didn't tell you," Lucy replied, accepting the transition as gracefully as ever. "She moved back to El Salvador last year."

Sara had neither expected this news, nor the effect it would have on her. The absence of Mrs. Contreras, who had been like a surrogate mother, was a great loss indeed.

"Adam and I are grown," Lucy continued, lifting a shoulder. "No grandkids to speak of. Her brothers wanted her to come home. She asked if you needed any help making arrangements?"

Sara shook her head. "I spoke with Moleworth's Funeral Home and they e-mailed me their... packages." The word felt comically wrong. "I don't know when BPD will released their bodies."

Lucy patted her arm, tears glistening in her eyes. "You'll let me know how I can help?" she asked. Sara nodded. "Have you told your mom?"

"It's next on the docket."

- - -

ROBERT JOHNSON PLAYED over the loudspeakers in the visitor's room at Saving Grace Mental Health Institute, loud enough for the lyrics to be plainly heard, but not so loud it concealed the moaning from the room down the hall. Sara tapped her foot against the chair, waiting, listening and trying not to listen. Dread slipped across her heart and into her throat. She fought the urge to cover her ears, afraid they might make her stay, might mistake her for a resident.

"Not this song," she muttered behind her teeth.

I got to keep movin', I got to keep movin'
Blues fallin' down like hail, blues fallin' down like hail
And the days keeps on worryin' me
There's a hellhound on my trail, hellhound on my trail

Like the rattling of chains to herald the coming of a vengeful spirit, *Hellhound on My Trail* foretold tragedy in the Wilde household. It had played on the radio in the café before her father's death, and again nearly a year later before her mother's first suicide attempt. She thought she heard it as her car radio scanned stations the day before Cassie had sent her that text message, but she ignored it. Surely, it was just a coincidence. It couldn't actually mean anything, not anymore. She had her life together. She'd gotten away from that house.

She knew better now.

"Sara?" The nurse slipped through the swinging door and smiled at her, but she could not return the gesture despite having known him most of her adult life. His beard, which had grayed in her absence, was trimmed short against his dark skin. He ran his palm across it with a grin.

"Somehow I turned into an old man, but you're just the same," he said.

"How are you, Charlie?" she asked, standing.

"Doin' fine, honey. You can come on back."

I can tell the wind is risin', the leaves tremblin' on the tree
Tremblin' on the tree
I can tell the wind is risin', leaves tremblin' on the tree

All I need's my little sweet woman
And to keep my company

Sara rose and followed him with as much trepidation as if she were climbing the Tower of London. Maybe this had been a bad idea. The last time she visited, four nurses had to restrain her mother to prevent her from bashing her head against the window. She couldn't remember what had triggered the episode… a question about the weather or the mention of a particularly offensive flower, it didn't seem to matter. Maybe Momma wouldn't even remember her this time.

They arrived at room 236, and Charlie slid a keycard into the door, and then peeked his head inside.

"Miss Imogene, someone's here to see you." He turned to Sara and stepped aside. "You can go on in. Dr. Walsh has been adjusting her medication to help with the hallucinations, so she's been a little out of it. Seeing some improvement though."

"Thanks," Sara said, stepping inside.

"You holler if you need anything. I'll be right outside."

He closed the door and Sara turned to her mother, who sat in an old wing chair facing the window.

"Hi, Momma," Sara said quietly, afraid she might startle her. "It's Sara."

Her mother made no move to acknowledge her. Sara sat down quietly in the chair beside her. The sun showed her age, every worry line and dark spot. Her eyes glistened as if she'd been crying.

"How are you, Momma?"

"Cassandra came to see me yesterday."

Sara shifted in her chair and tried to breathe through the ice pick in her chest. She inhaled to speak, but her mother continued still, her eyes empty and far away.

"She's dead now," Momma said. "Mother too. They're all dead."

"Who told…" but before Sara could finish her question, she spotted a newspaper clipping on the table beside her mother's chair. "Where did you get this?" she asked, snatching it up.

"What's that, dear?"

"My article from the Beaufort Times, where did you get it?"

It was her first byline, a poorly written analysis on Sherlock Holmes as an anti-hero.

Her mother took it from her, examined it closely, and then smiled. "Oh, your father brought it to me yesterday."

"Mom…"

Sara retrieved the Sherlock Holmes article from her mother, who grabbed for it.

"That's mine," she cried.

"Mom, I need you to think. Who told you about Cas and Grams? Who gave you this article?"

"My daughter wrote that, give it back!" Her mother seized it at last, clutched it against her chest, and began to sob.

●●●

SARA FOUND ADAM in the first place she looked; a local diner named Miss Mae's, which had always been a favorite haunt of his. The owner, a member of the church board, believed she was a bad influence, so she rarely went inside. Adam looked up from a corner booth as she stepped through the door. She ignored the greetings of the hostess behind the counter, and stormed over to him with fire in her blood.

"How dare you," she spat, standing above him. Adam looked up at her with a forkful of apple pie halfway to his mouth.

"I'm sorry?"

"Little late for apologies, don't you think?"

He sat the fork gently on his plate and swiped a thumb across his lip. "I meant, I'm sorry, but I have no idea what you're talking about."

Sara slapped the clipping of her article, which she'd eventually pried from her mother's hysterical clutches, onto the sticky table.

"What's this?" he asked.

"You told my mother?"

"What? I didn't."

"Bullshit."

"Look, if you're going to accuse me of something, you might as well sit down." He pushed his plate away and took a final sip of coffee before leaning back in the booth and waiting for her to launch her attack. Sara dropped down in the seat across from him.

"Then how do you explain how she already knew about Cas and Grammy? And why would you give her this? She was in hysterics." She stabbed her finger at the clipping.

"Sadie, I haven't been to visit Mama Wilde in weeks."

Something about the way he said her mother's name completely disarmed her.

"You visit her?"

"You may have left, but we're still family." Then he asked, "Did she tell you how she knew?"

Sara settled back against the vinyl booth and bit her cheek, still angry but reasonably certain he was being honest with her.

"She said Cassie came to visit her," she said with a smirk.

"Is that so far outside the realm of possibility?"

"Oh, don't start that with me. Grammy was bad enough with all her talk of ancestral ghosts and prophesies. You always believed all that crap."

He looked at her as if she'd wounded him. "So did you."

"Yeah, well I grew up."

Adam set his jaw and straightened in the seat. He leaned forward and leveled his eyes on her, his gaze so intense he might have been looking at her through the scope of a rifle.

"No, you didn't," he retorted. "You're still just a scared little girl running around in your sister's dress."

Seething, Sara replied, "This was *my* dress."

Adam didn't reply, just shook his head and raised his hand for the check. Sara crossed her arms over her chest.

"What about my article?" she asked.

"That I can't explain. For all we know, your mother's had it all this time and was just reading it before you got there."

Sara raised an eyebrow. "That would be quite a coincidence."

"Stranger things have happened," he answered. "Pie?" He moved the plate toward her, but Sara pushed it back.

"I'd rather eat a cactus. Why are you being so cavalier about this?"

"I'm not being cavalier. Your mom isn't exactly a reliable source, Sadie. You have to know that."

"I need answers."

"I need them, too. Miss Connie and Cas meant a great deal to me."

The twinge in her heart moved into her right eye. She tried to blink it away.

"You know," Adam began, setting down his fork with a rueful smile. "I remember you writing that Sherlock Holmes article. You used up half your dad's bottle of White Out trying to get it perfect. Stood me up twice so you could keep clicking away at your old typewriter."

Sara stilled.

The *typewriter.*

Chapter V

*S*ARA'S FINGERS trembled as she closed them around the glass doorknob of her father's study, the copy of *A Study in Scarlet* tucked under her arm. The door creaked open, stiff after having been shut for so long. The cleaning company worked downstairs, scrubbing and bleaching, but the house could not be cleansed.

Little had been moved since his passing all those years ago. His model ship still collected dust on the fireplace mantel, his sailing books still lined the floating shelves behind his desk, and if she inhaled deeply enough, she could still smell his Old Spice aftershave.

Sara searched for the old typewriter, where she'd written her first headline, and where he'd written his. They'd always been connected in that way, though he'd gone on to freelance for The New York Times and she was still writing second page copy.

For thirty years, that typewriter sat on the bookshelf, wedged between a copy of The Old Man and The Sea and a collector's edition of Moby Dick, but it was gone.

"What the hell?" she whispered, running her fingers across the shelf. No dust. Someone had taken it recently.

Sara rummaged through her father's desk. In all of the copy he'd written on the typewriter, there must be one draft hidden among the tax documents and the ledgers. She dumped the drawer onto the floor and searched the papers, pushed aside the pens and paperclips, and closed upon a tarnished letter opener. Finding nothing else, she moved to the filing cabinet, jimmied the lock, and repeated the process until the contents covered the floor.

It wasn't her father's work she at last discovered, but her own. Twenty years ago, in a feeble attempt to be like him, she had written the draft about Sherlock Holmes. It ran on the seventh page of the Sunday paper alongside a review of Christopher Nolan's *Memento*.

Sherlock Holmes: Hero or Villain?

A poor headline, even for a fifteen-year-old, but her father had liked it.

Sara examined the document, with its faded typeface and yellowed edges, and placed it on her father's desk beside the recent note of condolences. The letter M on the typewriter had always tilted a little to the left. The documents were a perfect match.

Exasperated, Sara sat down in her father's chair and swiveled toward the window, away from the havoc she had wreaked upon the room. She watched the setting sun spill blood across the water. A shrimp boat headed back into the marina, a flock of gulls already swarming its hanging nets.

"What am I supposed to do, Cas?" she whispered. Her sister, wherever she was now, did not answer.

Sara sat until darkness descended upon the house, until its creaking bones settled down for the night with the slamming of doors and the groaning of floorboards.

Drafts, her father had explained. *That northerly wind blows right through these old stones.*

He had an explanation for everything, and she wondered what he would make of it all now. The marsh grasses did not bow to a breeze, nor did the silver oaks sway with any gale. No, the wind existed inside the house alone, shuddering as it breathed. As it lived.

Sara must have dozed. When her eyes flew open, the gray light of dawn was seeping across the marsh, and the desk lamp flickered. The tension in her shoulders spread to her throat and into her jaw.

She clenched her teeth, knowing as the rotting stench of the ocean flooded in all around her that she was no longer alone.

She heard the water at her back, trickling onto the papers she'd scattered over the floor.

Drip, drip, drip.

Sara inhaled the damp air, and it spread like ink into her bones, spilling down her spine and throbbing through her limbs until her heart struggled under the density of it. If she could only muster the courage to look, to face this phantasm, this old and derelict fear, perhaps she could vanquish it altogether.

Sara closed her eyes as the malodorous sea pooled around her feet, and then she turned.

The specter stood in the doorway, her head listing toward her shoulder like a scuttled ship. She swayed to and fro, clutching the sopping blanket to her chest, but her lips remained closed, turned down in an expression of great mourning. She did not hum her lullaby. No, it seemed whatever lifetime had passed while Sara was away, the apparition knew now her child was gone.

Sea worms and acorn barnacles clung to her salt-encrusted eye sockets. Kelp braided through hair floating gently above her, moving rhythmically, as if she were still beneath the waves. Sara willed away her own fear, but she had not steeled herself to bear witness to the hideous sorrow etched into the woman's face.

She opened her mouth.

Black water poured down the buttons of her dress, small fish flopping on the sodden carpet. Sara could no longer suffer the presence of such wretchedness. As she turned her back with tears in her eyes, the woman spoke.

Come home.

• • •

SOMEONE CALLED SARA'S name. Not her sister, nor the Lady in White.

A man's voice.

From her father's chair, she watched the dawn claw up over the horizon and stretch its arms along the glittering water, as beautiful as it was blinding. When the sun at last reached the window and poured into the study, it revealed no evidence of what she had seen the night before. The carpet and papers showed no signs of water damage, and the room smelled again faintly of her father, not the sea.

It must have only been a nightmare. Or a hallucination. The latter prospect frightened her more than the presence of any ghost.

"Sadie?" the man called again. *Adam.*

Her phone vibrated in the pocket of her dress, and she fished it out, but shut her eyes at the name on the screen. Drawing a deep breath, she answered, "Hi, John."

"Thank God," he breathed. "Are you okay? I've been trying to reach you for days."

Adam called her name from the hall, but she ignored him.

"I know, I'm sorry," she answered. "I'm fine."

"Do you need me to come up? I can be there this—"

"No," she replied, louder than she'd intended. "I mean, well, I— I'm not feeling like myself. I'm kind of a mess."

"We've been together for over a year now. Do you think I care if you haven't brushed your hair?"

She could barely fathom the idea of seeing John in this house. He did not belong here.

"You wouldn't even recognize me, Johnny," she said, for she scarcely knew herself.

"Jesus Christ, Sadie," Adam said from the doorway. He slid a hand through his dark hair, gaping at the mess she'd made. "What the hell did you do?"

"Is someone with you?" John asked over the phone. "Who is that?"

She met Adams eyes and answered, "No one. I have to go." Then she ended the call before he could say good-bye and dropped the phone back into her pocket.

"Who was that?" Adam asked. He picked his way through the scattered papers and upended cabinets. When she didn't answer, he said, "I'm getting really damn worried about you, Sara."

She could see it in the lines on his face, in all the years that had wrought them. It seemed as if he had been worrying about her all his life; she just hadn't been around to see it. Remembering all she had to tell him, Sara grabbed her article, and the book, from the desk.

"Look," she said, thrusting the paper toward him. "See the tilt of the M?"

"Yeah, so?"

"I saw the same imperfections in the message in the book. I knew I recognized it. It was written on my grandfather's typewriter, like that article."

"Wait, what book? What is this?" He took it from her, and the note fluttered to the ground, which he retrieved. "Who gave this to you?"

"I found it in my car. I figured it was a gift from a friend of the family, but—"

"Shit," he muttered, rubbing his chin. "Why didn't you tell me? We should have had it dusted for prints."

"I didn't think it was anything important at the time."

"Where's the typewriter?"

"It's gone." She nodded toward the bookshelf. "It's been there on that shelf for thirty years, ever since Poppop died. Someone's taken it."

"Have you touched anything?"

Sara looked around. She'd touched everything. Adam drew in a heavy breath and set the items on the desk as she dropped down into her father's chair.

"You can't keep doing this," he said at last, sitting on the desk.

"Doing what?"

"For starters, your constant trespassing on active crime scenes."

"Are you going to arrest me?"

"That's not the point," he said, crossing his arms. "You need to grieve. Get out of this house. Brush your hair. Eat."

"And you suddenly know what's best for me?" Sara stood up and picked her way across the room, tired of his company.

"Will you just leave the investigating to me?" he said, ignoring her. "You're out of your depth. This isn't healthy."

"I'm an investigator too in case you've forgotten," she retorted at the door.

"You're an investigative reporter. There's a difference. A big difference."

The nod Sara sent him was a lie.

Chapter VI

*S*ARA DROVE her father's Mustang around town for the better part of an hour, talking to her sister as if she were in the seat beside her and turning up the volume of the radio so no one could hear her scream. Her fingers clutched the steering wheel until her palms ached. The road blurred.

Get out, a voice inside her said, which sounded strangely like her mother's. *They'll never let you be.*

She pulled onto the freeway with every intention of driving south until she reached Savannah.

"Keep driving, Sara," she muttered to herself, her voice thick. "You are not responsible for this."

But she was. It was the jagged splinter in her heart. As the last lucid Wilde, she knew by the throbbing of the wound it created that it could only be her.

Swallowing the acid in her throat, Sara took the next exit and returned to Beaufort. The Wildefell curse had now branched beyond the family tree, and even if she had to paint lamb's blood across every door in town, she'd be damned if she would allow it to go on unchecked.

But, deep inside herself, Sara wondered if somehow this was all her fault, if she had angered some entity and it had escaped the dark rooms of the house.

So, armed with her father's stubborn streak and maybe a little of her mother's madness, Sara drove toward Wellness on Main, where Elisabetta's father practiced. She recognized the girl's surname because it hung in gold letters beneath the company sign.

R. X. AMELLO, DR. OF PSYCHOLOGY
LICENSED THERAPIST
NOW SCHEDULING

The office, like many businesses in town, had been a single-family home in the early 1900's. This one in particular still retained the original shutters, brickwork, and most of the exterior crown molding. Sara parked the car on the street, squared her shoulders, and somehow made it to the reception desk before her legs buckled.

"Do you have an appointment?" The secretary, a frail, bird-like woman with skin the color of parchment, flipped through an oversized calendar in search of Sara's name. The slightest hint of an English accent rounded her vowels. Too tired of human interaction to bother with introducing herself, Sara slid her business card beneath the Plexiglas partition and waited.

"Oh," the secretary cooed, staring at the card with narrowed eyes. "We take patient confidentiality very seriously, Ms.—" she consulted the card again, and then returned it "—Wilde. No reporters. Sorry."

"Is Dr. Amello in today? It's important that I speak with him. It's about his daughter."

"I'm sorry—"

"This is urgent. I've been sent by the police."

With a suspicious frown, the secretary sighed and said, "Very well. I'll ring him for you."

"Please."

The woman picked up the phone and punched a number with a short finger. Her nails were chewed down to the beds, pink polish and all.

"Doctor," the secretary said. "There's a reporter here to see you. She says it's important." A pause. "I don't know, should I ask?"

Sara rounded the desk and pushed through the door leading to the back offices.

"Dr. Amello," Sara said, opening the door labeled with this name. He stood immediately; his mouth open to admonish her for the intrusion. "My name is Sara Wilde. I'm here on behalf of the Beaufort Police," she lied. "I need to speak with you. It's about your daughter."

"My daughter is no longer my concern," he said, his mouth hard.

"Dr. Amello, please sit down."

The slightest expression of real concern creased his brow, and he sat calmly, eyes fixed on her.

"What has she done?" he asked. Sara sat across from him, where his patients would sit.

"Doctor, your daughter's body was found last night." Whether she dropped it on him like an atomic bomb or led him to it gently, the result was always the same, but he made no indication he had heard her.

"Doctor?"

"I warned her this would happen," he muttered to himself. His voice betrayed more disappointment than grief. Sara's mind ricocheted to her phone call to Momma that day after prom, when Adam guided the boat up to the dock, dripping wet and alone, her father nowhere to be seen. The reaching silence on the line haunted her still, laden with anguish, and followed by a single word, whispered: *No.*

Sara shook her head to clear the memory.

"Do you understand what I'm saying, Dr. Amello?" she asked, leaning toward him. "Your daughter is dead."

He pursed his lips, both of his hands splayed flat on the desk, but made no effort to speak.

"Was your daughter seeing anyone?" Sara asked.

"I don't know. I haven't spoken to her since she dropped out of school to work at that damn gardening shop."

"I take it you disagreed with her decision?"

"Elisabetta disgraced this family. I gave her every opportunity to be successful and she turned her back to me, to our religion, everything we are."

"Did anyone else in the family resent the decision?"

"Not enough to kill her. That is what you're getting at, isn't it?"

"Dr. Amello, I'm not interrogating you. I just want to find out what happened to your daughter."

"You are wondering why this is no surprise to me, are you not?" he asked, and then looked over at her with a weary expression.

"News like this isn't often handled with such calm."

"Have you ever lost anyone close to you, Ms. Wilde?" His voice softened slightly, his shoulders sagging.

Sara, stunned by the question, could not immediately answer. She felt heat in her ears.

"You have then," he said. "I can see your grief is fresh, still an aching wound. I have been grieving my daughter for years already. My injury is only a callus."

- - -

SARA'S ICE CREAM melted into a viscous soup as the sun drew long shadows from the pylons and the masts of docking sailboats. Gulls flew overhead. Children played on the lawn at her back, and a couple sat in the swing to her left, watching the sunset. A beautiful evening, by all accounts, but Sara did not see it.

She stirred the ice cream with a plastic spoon but could not eat.

Bitterness clung to her tongue from the morning's coffee, exacerbating the sourness in her stomach. Disturbing images flickered across her memory, the strange marbling of her sister's skin, Grammy's scattered pearls, and the sunken eyes of the sweet little terrier. When she brought the spoon to her mouth, her mind conjured up Elisabetta Amello's swollen tongue.

Her thoughts lingered on Elisabetta, and on the father who had disowned her. One of the driving forces of Sara's life had been to make her father proud, if he were still around to see what she'd become. It stood behind every story she wrote, urging her to do better, to be more. But now, as she looked out over the water, she felt only emptiness. It had all been for naught.

In time, her grief would morph and twist into a less recognizable beast; an anxiety attack with no discernible trigger, a nightmare lingering long into the day, or the sighting of a long dead ancestor. Sara knew these stages by heart.

"The prodigal child returns," someone said behind her. Sara turned.

"Mrs. Cunningham," she said, standing. Her stomach turned. From beneath the shadow of a pale-yellow sunhat, the pastor's wife glared down at her, and then suddenly sent her a tight, sympathetic smile, as if she'd just remembered it was the polite thing to do.

"Please accept my condolences, dear," she said, taking her hand. Her fingers were cold, the manicured nails digging into Sara's skin.

Sara answered, "Thank you," and the fingers tightened.

"I expect we won't be seeing you at church this Sunday," she sighed, and before Sara could answer, she added, "I thought you were the only one in that family to have any sense. We'd all hoped you'd found God down in Savannah, but here you are."

The woman released her hand, opened her pocketbook, and began rummaging around.

"I'm here to make arrangements," Sara replied, her cheeks burning.

"Of course you are, dear. That's always the way with the non-believers. You think you have to do everything on your own. If your family had only turned to the church—"

"Mrs. Cunningham," Adam called behind. He squinted in the sun as he jogged to them, took her hand in his, and pressed it. He had rolled up his sleeves to the elbows and three buttons of his shirt were open, revealing a dark patch of sweat-dampened hair. "You'll forgive me for interrupting. I need to borrow her for a moment."

Mrs. Cunningham extracted a rosary from her purse and handed it to Sara with a nod, pausing as if she expected it to burn her.

"Of course, dear," she said to Adam. "We'll see *you* at mass on Sunday."

She hugged him, and stage whispered, "Remember Leviticus 20:27. Take care not to fall under any unholy influences, child."

When the woman walked out of earshot, Sara said, "What's Leviticus 20:27?"

Adam didn't answer this, which was answer enough, and took a seat on the swing. He motioned for her to join him.

"I almost forgot how that felt," she said, sitting beside him.

"How what felt?"

"Being *othered*. I should be used to it by now, I guess. Journalism is a boys' club. But, being excommunicated always feels slimier." Sara dropped the rosary into her ice cream and watched it slowly sink into the viscous liquid. "You've always been a good catholic boy, you wouldn't understand."

"I think that's a pretty ignorant thing to say, all considering."

"Considering what?"

"I was the only Latino kid in our graduating class."

"That's different."

"Sadie, the football team called me Pedro."

Sara frowned. "You never told me that."

His gaze fell upon the sparkling water and followed ripples as fish surfaced for their supper. For a long while, he sat in silence, and Sara saw the past in his face. She saw the many nights they'd spent in this very spot, sharing ice cream cones and juvenile dreams. She saw his fingers slipping across the strings of his guitar but could not recall the tune of the song. Then she saw him tying off her father's boat, soaking wet and weeping.

"Did you need to talk to me about something?" she asked, resisting the urge to leave him there alone.

"The coroner finished the autopsies." he said finally, with nightfall in his voice.

"Oh," she muttered.

"You were right."

"I know."

He turned to look at her, an expression akin to wonder widening his eyes.

"They found *Atropa belladonna* in Amello's bloodstream," he said, but she couldn't meet his gaze. "A lethal dose."

Sara nodded with a mordant smirk. "That tracks."

"What do you mean?"

"Belladonna is Italian for beautiful lady. It's *Rappaccini's Daughter* played out in color."

"Do you remember anything else from the story that might be important, that might link all of these cases together?"

"I can reread the stories tonight and see if anything stands out. I feel like there's something I'm missing, some parts of the message I can't understand."

The muffled voice of the Lady in White swept through Sara's mind like a red tide, sickening her. She knew all of the intonations of her speech by heart, knew the syllables and the sounds, but did not understand. *Come home.*

"The same poison was found in the Wilson's dog," Adam continued, and Sara looked at him, surprised. "I had a hunch and ordered a necropsy."

"Can you release his body? I think the Wilson's would like to bury him." She had seen Lost Dog signs posted all across town. They deserved the truth.

"I don't think there'd be a problem with that, but there's more."

Sara waited as the tightness in her chest hardened to stone. She took a breath but didn't feel the air. Adam continued.

"Toxicology tested the pill in the ivory box. It's a birth control placebo pill." He removed a slip of paper from his pocket and added, "Specifically Lo Estrin FE."

"That's odd."

There were probably hundreds of women in the city who'd been prescribed this same contraceptive, but Sara found it curious. She'd been taking it for years.

Adam didn't appear to hear her. He went on, "I called her OBGYN," Adam continued. "He never prescribed it. According to him, she wasn't using contraceptives at all, wasn't even sexually active."

"Then where'd she get it?"

"It gets weirder. Tox screen came back negative. No birth control in her system. I'm going to talk to her father tomorrow. Maybe he knows something she didn't tell her doctor."

"He doesn't," she added quickly, averting her eyes from him. Now was as good a time as any. She straightened. "I already talked to him. They were estranged."

Adam cocked his jaw. "What did you say?"

"I said they were estranged. He doesn't know anything about her relationships."

His lip twitched, and then he put his fingers to his temple. "I think I misunderstood you. I thought you said you already interviewed him."

"I did." She lifted her chin slightly as the vein in his neck pulsed. His eyes closed for a brief moment, and she braced herself.

"I'm curious," he began. "Do you actually want to find the son of a bitch who did this?"

"Of course I do."

"Then quit interfering with my fucking investigation. You are not a detective. You're a reporter."

"And this is my story," she bit back.

"You're kidding, right? You're reporting on this?"

"Well someone has to. It might as well be me. I'm not asking for permission."

She could no longer tolerate his livid gaze upon her, so she stood.

"Hell, don't look at me like that," he said, grabbing her hand and pulling her back onto the bench.

"An unholy influence," she muttered, drained. "Mrs. Cunningham's right about me. I never should have come back here. Everyone I've ever loved is dead."

"Not everyone, Sadie."

He met her eyes, his intensity prickling the hairs on her arms.

"What is it you want from me, Adam? You want to reminisce about the good ol' days, or have some tearful reunion?"

"No." He sat so still he scarcely appeared to breathe.

"Then what?"

Adam didn't answer, just lifted his eyes to the water.

"What about Cas and Grams?" she asked, the silence too heavy. "Are their autopsies done?"

"Cassie's, uh—" He ran a hand down his face and drew a breath. "Cassie's official cause of death was strangulation. And Miss Connie, well—"

"It's ok, I know."

"It was just like you said."

Sara tipped her head back and looked at the sky, too clouded over for stars. A pale sliver of the moon appeared for a moment, but then faded to a ghost.

"I don't understand why this is happening," she whispered.

His fingers moved, as if he considered touching her.

"Can I walk you home?" he asked instead.

"I thought you said it was a crime scene."

"Not sure why that matters all of the sudden, but they're finished. The cleaners are done, too."

The thought of being alone in the house with the Lady in White filled the pit of her stomach with acid. Even if only by a small margin, Adam was better company than the dead. She shrugged and exhaled loudly before rising and turning to take her leave.

"Are you coming?" she called over her shoulder. He caught up as she made her way through the square. Outdoor string lights twinkled as the night cooled, draping patio bars and dimly lighting the faces of diners as they bent over their meals. A man played blues guitar on a small stage. The square came alive when the sun released its death grip, but Sara felt as alienated from it as from Adam, who walked in pensive silence beside her.

The music fell behind them as they walked along the street, becoming quieter by degrees until locusts and crickets suffocated it with their own melody. Watery yellow streetlamps illuminated the cemeteries flanking them, drawing sinister shadows from the crypts and tombstones. Cockroaches hissed and skittered into raised stone coffins as they approached.

"Sadie," Adam began, his hands in his pockets. "There's a lot I've wanted to say to you…"

Footsteps sounded behind them, whispering across the husks of Spanish moss and cottonwood leaves. She turned to look over her shoulder, but the cracked and buckled sidewalk was empty.

He continued, unaware. "The way we left things back then, I—"

"It's been fifteen years. We don't have anything to talk about."

She stooped under the still branches of a massive live oak, leaving him momentarily behind.

"We were friends once," he called after her.

"That was a long time ago. You don't even know me."

He walked again beside her, closer. "I know you, *querida*." His voice moved deep inside her bones. She clenched her teeth. "And you know me, the way only kids can—before the world tells us who we're supposed to be."

She stopped and turned to face him. "And who was I supposed to be, Adam? After all this time, was I supposed to end up right back here? All those years I spent trying to get this place out of me, all for nothing. Is that what you're saying?"

"What happened to you?" he asked. "You've forgotten everything."

They'd arrived at Wildefell's gate and Sara wrapped her fingers around the cool wrought iron. The branches of the willow stretched toward the overgrown lawn, tickling the grass, hiding all but the house's second story widow's walk from view. Inside, beyond the glass doors, Sara's blush-colored curtains fluttered, though the doors were sealed tight.

"No," she whispered, staring up at the house. "No, I haven't."

Chapter VII

*S*ARA'S FEET crunched on the gravel as she walked toward the house. Adam followed close behind, but she had nothing more to say. As the porch came into view, the figure of a man rose from one of the rocking chairs. She recognized him by the gleam on his head.

"Mr. Delaney," she called. The family attorney lifted his hand in greeting and met her at the bottom of the steps. "Did we have an appointment?"

The old man, bespectacled and bald as a mole rat, peered over coke bottle glasses, his starched Hawaiian shirt hanging from his thin frame. He enveloped her in as enthusiastic a hug as ever. She shouldn't have ignored his calls.

"How are you?" he asked, giving her one last squeeze and releasing her before adjusting the satchel over his shoulder.

"I've been better."

"I hope you can forgive me for dropping in so late like this, but I haven't been able to reach you and, well, we have quite a lot to discuss." He noticed Adam then and smiled widely. "Does a man's heart good to find the two of you together again."

"Adam was kind enough to walk me home," she said quickly as he took the attorney's outstretched hand. "We aren't together in any sense of that word."

Sara walked up the steps and unlocked the door, motioning for Mr. Delaney to enter. Adam turned to go.

"Ah, Mr. Contreras," Delaney said. "You should join us."

"He can't stay," said Sara.

"What I mean is, well," Delaney stammered, adjusting his glasses. "You see, these matters affect the two of you."

Adam frowned.

"The *two of us*?" Sara gawked. "There is no two of us. These are personal, family matters, Mr. Delaney. I'd prefer if we spoke in private."

Delaney took the lead then, shuffling into the house. Sara and Adam followed as he flipped lights on along the way, as familiar with the way as if he lived there himself. Finally, he turned on the dining room switch, and an antique floor lamp brightened the room. He paused at the fireplace with a deep frown.

"Sit, both of you," he said, motioning toward the table, but Sara hesitated at the threshold. Both Mr. Delaney and Adam drew breath to speak, likely to offer another meeting place, but she rushed into the room as if she'd been wound by a spring.

"This is my house," she muttered as she dropped into her usual chair, left of the head with her back to the fireplace. Adam, with all his usual gall, sat in her father's chair. She glared at him.

Delaney sat down across from her. He dropped his satchel on the table and unsnapped the buckles, and then removed a set of documents from a folder. Never before had the slowness with which he executed his existence frustrated Sara so much. She couldn't imagine what he could possibly have to say to both of them.

"That's precisely why I need to speak with you," he began at last. "We've all known each other a long time, so believe me when I say that this is all most... unusual."

"Please," Sara urged, gaze landing on the bowl at the center of the table. The cleaners had disposed of the fruit, but a single freckle of blood remained on the porcelain. She was going to have to throw it away.

Adam set his elbows on the table and said, "I second that, sir."

"Well, now, Sara… first and foremost, you've been granted sole ownership of the Beaufort Times."

Sara stilled. "Grammy told us she sold it after Dad died."

"That newspaper, as you know, was a point of great tribulation and pride for your family. I expect Miss Connie couldn't bring herself to part with it after so much history."

"But it's still in operation," Adam said. "Who's running it?"

"She appointed various editors over the years, financial officers, et cetera. She's been running it behind the scenes all this time. I would have told you, Sara, but I was sworn to secrecy. She said it was best if everyone believed another family owned it. Water under the bridge, she said. A clean slate."

Sara didn't know what to say. She assumed the newspaper was sold to Aggie Barlow, who'd been assistant editor for twenty years. Now it was suddenly hers? She stood up, unable to contain the nervous energy shivering through her limbs, and paced the room.

"How the hell am I going to run a newspaper from Savannah?" she said, but as the words left her mouth, she couldn't imagine returning to Georgia at all. Ever.

"I know this is quite a shock," Delaney said. He pushed his glasses up higher on his nose and shuffled his papers. "You've got another one coming, so it's best you sit back down."

With her heart in her throat, she did as he advised.

Delaney continued, "You well know how much your sister loved this house."

"She and I differed on that point," she answered.

"I believe she knew that when she made her will. As you know, your father left the house to both of you equally. You share the deed."

"Well, not anymore," Sara replied. Now the whole cursed pile of stone fell squarely on her shoulders. She could feel the weight of it even as she sat.

"That's correct, but Sara..." He paused to take a breath. "She left her half to Adam."

"*What?*" they said together.

"She didn't want to burden you."

"This is a mistake." She looked at Adam, whose gaze had fallen to the table. The muscles in his jaw clenched and released, and when he lifted his eyes, the lamplight glistened off his tears.

"You see why this couldn't wait," Delaney said. "I know you may be considering selling the property, but legally Adam has as much say in that decision as you."

Selling the house had never crossed her mind. She was as bound to it as the earth it stood on. It didn't belong to anyone but her, regardless of her long-standing denial of that fact.

"I don't understand," she whispered. "Why would Cas leave it to *him?*"

Delaney looked from Sara to Adam, and back again. He slid the legal documents across the table, snapped his satchel shut, and stood.

"Should the two of you choose to sell it, I have a number of interested buyers." He looked down at his shirt and cleared his throat. "Including my wife and I."

"What?" Sara asked.

"We've always wanted to open up a bed and breakfast when we retire..."

Sara shook her head, unable to process so great a quantity of information.

"I have another appointment," he added, though Sara knew he didn't. "You two have much to discuss. I'll be available for questions as they arise." He left the room, and Sara dropped her head into her hands when the screen door slammed shut.

"This house has been in our family for generations, and she just leaves it—" she lifted her head to look at him— "to *you?*"

"We've been friends since we were five years old."

"I don't understand." She walked to the window and looked out, her own reflection obscuring the view. Behind her, Adam pressed his thumb and forefinger to his eyes.

"Sadie," he began. "Cassie and I—"

She turned and glared at him. "Oh my God. Don't tell me—"

"We dated for two years. We stayed friends even after I broke it off."

"No. No, she would've told me."

"So you could take it the way you're taking it now?"

"Wait." Sara held up her hand and then buried it in her hair. "*You* broke it off?"

"Yes."

"Why?"

Adam stood up and turned his back to her, lingering near the fireplace with his hands on his hips. "Does it matter?"

"*Why?*" she urged.

He turned to face her, arms falling to his sides as though the motion spent the last of his strength.

"Because she wasn't you," he answered finally. "Okay? She wasn't you."

Sara stared at him, stunned. She knew by his expression he expected her to reply, to bite back at him with anger or even mock him, but all the words had gone out of her. It did not occur to her until this moment how utterly cruel she had been to him.

"Cas left it to me because she knew how much it meant to me," Adam said quietly. "I grew up in this house. We both did."

"But—"

"It's funny," he interrupted with a bitter laugh. "There's only one thing on earth you hate more than this house."

She looked at him, waiting. She did loathe this house. Didn't she? When he didn't continue, she asked, "Which is?"

He met her eyes and answered, "Me."

— — —

SARA POURED HERSELF another cup of coffee and leaned against the counter, all the weight of the day clinging to her. Humidity poured in from the window she'd opened, needing air, and the rhythmic song of crickets lulled her into a kind of trance.

"I guess we should pick out curtains or something," Adam said, walking into the kitchen. He nodded toward the coffee maker, and Sara slid out of his way with a devil-may-care gesture that said, *might as well help yourself.*

"Do you think this is amusing?" she asked as he poured the steaming coffee into her sister's favorite mug. He did so automatically, as though he'd done it a thousand times before.

"No," he sighed, hoisting himself onto the counter beside her. "I'm just trying to lighten the mood. This is a surprise to me too."

The scent of fresh acrylic paint wafted in through the window, and she breathed it in, feeling faint.

"Do *you* want to sell it?" she asked, walking to the other side of the kitchen, but the odor was stronger there.

Adam answered, "Not in a million years."

Sara thought she might have been relieved to hear this, but she wasn't. He owned a piece of her soul, and not just the part she'd given him as a teenager. She shook her head, willing away the vertigo. A deadbolt unlocked, and then a man's voice slid into her mind, one she didn't recognize.

I'm so glad you saw my ad in the paper.

"What the hell?" Sara whispered, rubbing her eyes.

"You okay?" Adam asked. The scent of turpentine overpowered her, corrupting her other senses until the room spun.

"Do you smell that?" she asked, but she didn't hear his answer. She heard instead the gentle brushing of paint over canvas, and then the clink of the paint brush against a glass cup.

I've been looking for a model for this piece for a long time. And then, *Please don't move. I've almost finished. What are you doing?*

Panic shivered around the edges of the man's voice. Sara's coffee mug shattered on the floor as she pressed her hands over her ears. Not again. This wasn't happening again. She reached blindly for Adam and fell to her knees, pain writhing inside her eyes like conqueror worms intent on expulsion. Her ears filled with the unmistakable sound of a blade slicing through flesh, nicking bone. Again. Again and again until the voice folded into itself, gurgling and wet. His fear stilled. He was thinking of his son. Blood vanquished the scent of turpentine. She could hear nothing but the drip, drip on the threadbare carpet. Bile rose up in her throat.

"Stop," she cried, tears streaming down her face. Adam's voice was far away, the sensation of his arms around her illusory, a memory from long ago.

The man was gone.

When the walls of the house rose up again around her, stone by wretched stone, she found herself clutching Adam's hand, her face pressed to his chest and his arms wrapped tight around her. She pushed away from him and tried to stand but stumbled. He caught her beneath the arms.

"You didn't tell me you still had the visions," he said, his voice grave.

"I'm not—" Sara murmured. She held onto him despite herself. He was the only thing tethering her to the earth. "I don't have *visions*."

The pain behind her eye slowly subsided, leaving an aching halo around the kitchen lights. Sara managed the few steps to the window seat. She dropped down onto it and leaned her forehead against the cold glass.

"You just had a vision, Sara," he said, making no attempt to approach her. "I've helped you up off the floor enough times to know it, even now."

"I never got them in Savannah," she said at last, defeated. "It's this house. It's diseased."

Adam walked to the medicine cabinet, selected a bottle of Motrin, and then sat down on the small seat beside her. His leg touched hers, but she didn't have the energy to move away. She took three tablets without water, and they scratched down her throat.

"Is it still just smells and sounds, or can you see now?" he asked.

She shook her head. "I never see anything. It's just gray, like fog."

"How's your head?"

"I heard Elisabetta's murder," she blurted out. Tears burned in her eyes. "I listened to her die."

After a fleeting expression of surprise, visible only in the twitch of his eyebrow, he asked, "Why didn't you tell me?"

"Would you have believed me?"

"Yes," he answered, and when she met his eyes, she knew it was so. He had always believed her, even when the school nurse referred her to a psychiatrist. "And now there's someone else?"

Sara nodded and raked her fingers through her hair. It fell loose from the tie, strands clinging to her damp palms. "A man. An artist. In a museum or a studio. I think the killer was posing as his model."

"Do you remember anything else?"

"The M.O. is different. He used a knife this time."

Adam stood and walked to the open window, his back to her. He inhaled through his nose and released it quickly through his mouth.

"We don't have serial killers in this town," he said.

"I'll call the security office at the history museum," she said, standing and slipping her cell phone from the pocket of her dress. "Can you get some uniforms to check out the studios?"

He shook his head. "I can't mobilize a team based on your clairvoyance. You know that. Eva will never go for it."

"Just say you got an anonymous tip. You don't have to tell her it was me. I know she thinks I'm a Satanist or something."

Outside on the sill, a cockroach hissed. Adam hesitated.

"I'm not comfortable with this, Sadie. I don't feel right involving you."

"Involving me? Look, my sister and grandmother are dead. I'm hearing these people as they die. I'm connected to this whether you're comfortable with it or not."

Considering the matter settled, Sara pulled up the museum's information on her phone and dialed the number. She left him in the kitchen with the intention of calling every art studio in the zip code. If it took all night, she was going to find this man. She was going to tell his son how much he loved him.

Chapter VIII

*A*DAM FELL asleep on her bed. They had gravitated to her childhood bedroom as the night wore on, her phone calls and his pleas with the intolerant Eva all for naught. Despite Adam's efforts to convince his superior of the urgency of the situation, he had only managed to secure a pair of officers for a welfare check in the morning. And the few studio owners Sara had been able to reach reported no suspicious activity, annoyed to be disturbed at so late an hour.

As Adam slept, his brow still furrowed, Sara removed the moth-chewed coverings from her abandoned belongings. Her desk, still cluttered with Grammy's hand-me-down crystals, smudging sage, Lip Smacker gloss, and the occasional Pearl Jam CD, remained exactly how she'd left it fifteen years ago. Anyone else might have packed these items away in boxes, but Grammy always believed Sara would come home.

She opened her closet and grabbed a volleyball jersey and a pair of stretchy sweatpants. It would have to do. In the morning, she would make the drive back to Savannah to pick up some of her clothes. Adam snored lightly, and it struck her how easy it was to accept his presence in this space. She was still reeling from the fact that they now owned it together, but despite how angry she was at Cassie for putting her in this position, she had to wonder if it had been deliberate. Her sister's last scheme.

He's family, Sara, she'd said. *You can't just cut him out of your life.*

Sara walked into the bathroom joining the bedroom with her sister's, closed the door behind her, and turned on the shower. She slipped out of the dress they shared, avoiding her own eyes in the mirror. Would the old house show her the woman she had become? Or would she see the girl she had been all those years ago, back when she believed in ghosts, before they told her she was crazy like her mother. Before she began to believe them.

Her life in Savannah almost convinced her she was normal. The house had no hold on her there. Its roots could not reach her. And yet, as she thought of her apartment in the city, of her office hung with Sherlock Holmes quotes and images of Lois Lane, it occurred to her how utterly false it all was. Here, in this house with this man, was the hideous truth that she belonged here.

The mirror clouded with steam as Sara stepped into the shower. She let the hot water soak her hair and ease some of the stiffness in her neck. Lathering with Cassie's shampoo, she breathed in the fragrance of honeysuckle and closed her eyes tight.

The reality of life without her sister descended fully upon her. There would be no more yearly pilgrimage to New Orleans, no more video chats or goofy Valentine's Day cards. No more late night therapy sessions when the world got to be too much. No more. She was gone.

The water was cold. She'd have to check the water heater in the cellar.

As she rinsed the conditioner from her hair, the decaying sea overpowered the scent of honeysuckle. The temperature dropped so drastically that Sara leapt out of the shower spray with a cry. Filmy black water bubbled up from the drain and pooled around her feet. She fumbled with the shower knob, the stinking water falling into her eyes and dripping down her legs.

Sara fell out of the tub, taking the shower curtain with her. The metal rings popped one by one until she dropped, entangled, onto the tile floor. In the mirror, the Lady in White rocked her baby, singing.

"In my dreams she still doth haunt me
Robed in garlands soaked in brine
Though in life I used to hug her
Now she's dead, I draw the line."

Sara tried to look away, but she saw her in the oily puddle on the floor. She saw her in the brass cabinet handles, and in the metal vase on the vanity.

The woman held something between her fingers as she swayed, dangling it above the blankets like a baby rattle. Sara watched in the mirror as she lifted it higher. A length of red string wrapped around her gangrenous fingers, tightening and tightening until it sliced through the decayed flesh. The woman lifted her head, a hideous moan cutting open the song, breaking it into syllables and reforming it into the phrase Sara knew in her heart. It fell from the yawning darkness of her mouth, sea slugs and leeches dropping onto the floor.

At last, Sara screamed. With all the force left in her body, she screamed.

Adam burst through the door, and she clutched the plastic shower curtain to her chest.

"Did you see her?" she cried, the breath burning in her lungs. He snatched a towel from the hook on the wall, Cassie's towel, and draped it over her.

"See who?" He knelt beside her, but did not touch her. By the time he followed her eyes to the mirror, the woman was gone. With her, the marsh receded, leaving only the chlorinated bathwater behind. "Are you hurt?"

Sara shook her head, though she could already feel a bruise forming on her hip. Pain shot through her elbows and down into her fingers as she attempted to disentangle herself. Adam took her hand, averting his eyes.

"What the hell happened?" he asked, turning his back as she peeled herself from the curtain and wrapped her sister's towel around her chest.

"Do you remember my Lady in White?"

"The one with the baby? You're seeing her again?"

She brushed by him without answering, shaking the water out of her hair, and he followed her into the bedroom. His eyes loitered on her a moment too long.

"I don't know what she wants. It's worse than before. She's... *suffering*."

This word did not adequately express the relentless anguish pouring from her apparition. Adam's phone rang in his pocket and he answered on speaker.

"Lieutenant Contreras."

"Hi, um," a young boy began. Sara's chest tightened. Inexplicably, she knew this voice belonged to the dead man's son. "You called earlier, and I told you my dad was working on a painting in the back studio... that everything was fine."

Adam disappeared for a moment into the bathroom. "Yes, I remember," he urged. He reemerged with Sara's jersey and sweatpants, tossed them at her, and turned away.

The boy's voice shook, a moment from cracking apart. "I was wrong."

"I need you to check his pulse for me." Adam said.

"I did."

"Don't go anywhere. We'll be there in 10 minutes."

There was a silence on the line, and then, "Can you... can you stay on the phone with me?"

Sara struggled into an old pair of underwear, two sizes too small, and grabbed her bra from the bathroom floor. Fully clothed, she followed Adam downstairs and into the kitchen.

"I'm going to give you to my friend, okay?" Adam said, searching for his keys. Sara handed him her cell so he could call for backup.

"I'm Sara," she said into Adam's phone. The boy sniffed. "What's your name?"

"Brian."

"Hi, Brian. I want you to hear something, ok? Are you with me?"

"Yes."

"Your dad loves you very much. Whatever happens after tonight, I want you to remember that."

Adam spoke with the dispatcher, rattling off an address. Sara slipped her bag over her shoulder, tapped him as she trotted by, and jangled her keys.

"Brian," she said, running now. Adam followed her out the front door. "Are you with me?"

● ● ●

SARA SMELLED THE blood from the sidewalk. The studio, a converted shotgun house on the south side of the art district, stood between a massive oak tree and an out of business art supply store. The evening's night collected in every open window except the attic, which glowed as if from the cover of a gothic novel. Sirens wailed in the distance.

"Are you here?" the boy asked over the phone, his face appearing in the attic window, phone pressed to his cheek.

"We're here, Brian." Sara answered. "Can you open the door for us?"

The boy vanished from the window, and Sara heard the creaking of stairs. Diffused light glowed in the other windows as he made his way to the front of the house, his breath labored. She ended the call once the deadbolt unlatched.

"Where's your dad?" Adam asked as blue and red light flickered across the boy's face. Wiry haired and no older than sixteen, Brian bore the shock of his father's demise in his eyes, which moved over them like a botfly, never landing on anything at all. The sirens silenced, and officers exited their squad cars with weapons drawn. Adam waved them back, and they stood down.

"In the studio upstairs," the boy answered. The paramedics, two young men with the fire department, arrived a moment later, carrying a gurney between them. Brian led the grim procession through the dimly lit house, pausing only to answer Adam's questions.

"I was playing God of War," he said over his shoulder. They passed a small kitchen with dishes stacked high in the sink; pale yellow curtains drawn at the window. "I didn't hear anything. He doesn't like to be interrupted when he's with a model, so I usually stay down here."

He led them around a pull-out sofa, toward the staircase. Peculiar paintings hung on the walls, depicting the emaciated forms of men and women clothed in furs, their bodies lifeless. None of them had faces.

"That was his funeral series," Brian offered. "The museum wanted to purchase them, but he turned them down, said they were private. They always creeped me out."

"He was working with a model tonight?" Sara asked, though she already knew the answer.

"I was out with friends until 9:00, so I didn't see anyone, but I heard him up there so I left him alone."

The stairs groaned and popped under the weight of so many visitors. A hanging bulb illuminated bone-pale wallpaper adorned with golden flowers that shivered as their shadows passed. The boy stopped at the top of the stairs, chewing on his thumbnail. Adam walked past him and disappeared into the hall.

"You should go downstairs," Sara said, setting a hand on his shoulder. "I'll be down to talk in a minute."

She left him on the landing as the paramedics passed, and did not hear him descend. The staircase opened into a loft lit by floor lamps and bulbs clamped to bare rafters. The corpse of Brian's father lay slumped at the feet of an easel, which held a nearly finished painting. A number of stab wounds opened up the flesh behind the man's ear. The vein there had bled out quickly and completely, pumping life-blood onto the floor until there was nothing left to drain.

Sara turned her head away quickly, eyes shut tight as if in reaction to a bright flash of light. A wave of vertigo swept over her and she reached out for something to steady herself. Adam caught her arm. He didn't speak, just stood close and steadfast by her side, waiting.

"I'm sorry," she murmured. Her stomach churned as she worked to free her heart from the barbed wire of her own grief. Adam's fingers tightened slightly on her arm, reassuringly. Once she was master of herself again, she opened her eyes not as Cassie's sister, Sadie, but as Sara Wilde, the reporter who'd seen her fair share of crime scenes without so much as a grimace.

The paramedics wheeled the gurney around her as Adam knelt beside the body, feeling for a pulse.

"No good, guys," he said quietly, standing. "Tell Scene of Crime to come on up on your way out." They left Adam and Sara alone with the dead man. Sara's eyes rose to the canvas, and the nearly finished portrait of the killer. The brushstrokes made up a slender man, clad in a tattered suit and draped over a sarcophagus made of stone. His face was only a featureless void, a puff of fog on a cold afternoon.

"That's convenient," Adam muttered, following her gaze.

She stepped forward, careful to avoid the coagulating pool shimmering crimson in the stark light. Attached to the canvas' frame with a woven red string, was a typewritten note.

"Adam," Sara said, her voice only a whisper. She read it aloud. "'He was trying to gather up the scarlet threads of life, and weave them into a pattern, to find his way through the sanguine labyrinth of passion through which he was wandering.'"

"What's that from?" Adam joined her.

"The Picture of Dorian Gray," she answered.

"How do you know?"

"Because it's one of my favorite books."

"What is she doing here?" Eva, leading a handful of crime scene technicians, stormed into the room, eyes leveled on Adam.

He lifted his hands in a gesture of surrender, the way one might ease a spooked horse.

"She's a consultant, Cap," Adam said. It was news to Sara. "It's cleared with HR."

"The hell it is."

"Eva—"

"It's okay," Sara interrupted, stepping around her and heading toward the door. She wanted to talk to the kid anyway. As she trod down the stairs, the argument escalated into a shouting match. She paused to listen.

"You know we don't have the budget for consultants. And *her*? Really?"

"Then find me someone else. Find me someone who can make sense of all this. Besides, she's not being paid."

"Just doing it out of the goodness of her heart then? If her goddamn family had left this town in peace, we wouldn't be in this situation at all."

"Her family was just murdered. Have some decency."

"They've been nothing but a plague on this town since they bought the newspaper out from under the Mauk family's feet. *My* family's feet."

"That was 150 years ago. You're being ridiculous."

Eva had likely been holding this grudge ever since her daddy told her the tale as a babe. If she found out a Wilde still owned the newspaper, she'd make Sara's life even more of a hellscape than it already was.

The slate wasn't clean at all, it had just been hidden away where no one could read it.

"That family is a curse, Adam. After everything you've been through, you should understand that better than anyone."

"I don't have time for your prejudice, Eva," Adam said. "People are dying."

"You're right about that, and they're dying because of her family. Because of her. If I see her at one more crime scene, you're done. Do you hear me?"

Adam did not reply to this, but his steps sounded on the floorboards, so she descended the remainder of the staircase as quickly and silently as possible. Her cheeks burned as much with anger as with humiliation. Years ago, she would have marched right back in to that room to tell Eva off, but now she wondered if she, like everyone else in this town, was right.

She found Brian in front of the TV, fingers working over Play Station controls, headphones covering his ears. She tapped him on the shoulder, and he whirled around with a muffled cry.

"Sorry," he said, pulling his headphones down around his neck. "I wasn't sure what else to do while I waited."

"May I?" Sara motioned to the couch, and he nodded. She sat beside him and stared for a long moment at the television screen. "Did you know my grandmother, Miss Connie?" she asked at last.

His eyes widened. "Oh shit, Miss Connie was your grandma?"

"Yes."

"I'm sorry for what happened to her. Everyone said she was crazy, but I always really liked her. She had the best decorations on Halloween."

Sara smiled, remembering the stack of boxes in the attic, filled to the brim with Styrofoam headstones, plastic skeletons, and tangled masses of polyester spider webs.

"It was her favorite holiday," she said. Behind all of the tacky decorations though, Sara knew Grammy displayed them largely to honor their original Pagan purpose: to ward off the gathering evil as the veil thinned. Sara felt it thinning even now, as the leaves died on the branches outside.

"I think what happened to her may be related to what happened to your dad," she said, and to her surprise, he nodded.

"I guess it would be too much of a coincidence to have two killers in town at the same time."

Adam reached them then and sent Brian a sympathetic smile.

"We're working as fast as we can," he said. "Do you have somewhere to stay tonight?"

"I can stay with my girlfriend."

"Good, we'll need to seal off the house for a little while. Do you have a security camera?"

Brian stood up and grabbed his laptop, decorated with stickers of bands Sara had never heard of, and powered it up. "Yeah!" he answered with enthusiasm. "Do you think it could've caught something?"

"Won't know until we look," Adam answered. He leaned over the back of the couch as Brian sat back down, fingers flying across the keys. An app opened on the screen, and a grainy image of the front of the house appeared, the low-quality camera struggling to adjust to the flashing police lights.

"You said you came home at 9:00?" Adam asked. He nodded. "And when did you go out?"

"I left around noon."

"Can you backtrack?"

Brian clicked on a thumbnail image, and pressed play.

"There I am leaving," he said, pointing. The timestamp read 12:11pm. He scrolled through the thumbnails until another figure appeared on screen, at 5:27. Brian played the footage, and they watched as a tall man, clad in a dark suit, limped into the frame, his face tilted away from the camera.

"Do you know this man?" Adam asked the boy, but Sara nodded. There was something unmistakably familiar about the figure's gait, about the squaring of his shoulders when he knocked on the door.

Brian shook his head. On the footage, Mr. Herman opened the door and invited the man inside. At 8:47, the man reemerged, limped back the way he came, and disappeared from view. Adam asked him to rewind the footage, and they watched the man exit again. The pit in Sara's stomach hardened to stone.

"We'll put a BOLO out," Adam said. "See if we can get any hits. Adult white male, suit and hat, limp. It's better than what we had before."

Sara shook her head. "I don't—it's not—"

"What's wrong?"

"You don't see it?" she muttered.

"See what?" he asked. "Do you know who this is?"

It couldn't be him. It wasn't possible.

Chapter IX

HE CLOCK struck the hour; once, twice, three times, its antiquated tune tolling from the mantel in the sitting room as it had since 1947.

"It's three AM, Sadie," Adam said, running a hand down his face. "Go to bed."

He sat in her father's favorite chair, the one Daddy always pulled up to the fireplace on Christmas morning, where he might have a better view of the unwrapping of gifts. Now, it sat beside the open window, heavy crimson curtains trembling in the coming storm. In the dim light, Adam looked nothing like the memory she harbored of him. His cinder-black hair, once slicked back and curling behind the ears, was now cropped short, a touch of silver at his temples. Crow's feet gathered at the edges of his eyes, and all of the mischief once gleaming behind them had hardened to amber.

"And what, you're going to sleep here on the couch?" she replied. She looked back down at her phone, the screen lighting her face as she examined the photo she'd snapped of the painting. Recalling the story this killing emulated, Sara saw Basil, Dorian's ever-faithful painter, stabbed to death and lying on the floor beneath the painting. And she saw the grotesque remains of Dorian Gray himself, nothing more than a putrescent mound of human flesh, bearing the full weight of several lifetimes' worth of corruption.

Adam answered, "If you want me to," but she scarcely heard him. Upstairs, a door gently latched. He stiffened. "Did you hear that?"

"It's only the house," she answered, rubbing her eyes. "Northerly wind."

Lightning flashed in the darkness outside, and Sara waited for thunder but it never came. She set her phone on the antique side table, 100 years of coffee rings and the imprints of a thousand letters adding to its charm. So Grammy had said, anyway. Sara always thought it was a piece of junk, like most of the Victorian furniture in the house.

Adam played the CCTV footage on his phone, emailed from Herman's son, for the 18th time.

"Find anything this time?" she asked.

He hesitated, and then rubbed the back of his neck.

"Herman's visitor reminds me of your dad," he replied on exhale, as if yielding to the thought exhausted him. For a moment, Sara couldn't speak. Hearing it outside her own head made it sound less ridiculous, and all the more distressing.

"He's dead," she managed.

"It's the way he walks…I could swear—"

"He's *dead*. You of all people know that."

"Yeah, I know." He nodded heavily, traced his tongue across his teeth, and then walked to the window. "Weather's changing."

Sara could not accept this change of topic. "You don't get to do that."

"Sorry?"

"You don't get to imply Daddy's still alive, and somehow involved in all this. And then change the subject to the fucking *weather*? What the hell?"

Adam held up his hands. "I wasn't implying anything, Sadie. I don't understand why the man in the video walks like your father, but it means something. It has to." He dropped back down into the chair. "Jesus Christ, I know he's dead. I watched him go down and never come back up."

"Just stop," she said. "I don't want to talk about that."

Adam shook his head, his fingers absently tracing the wrought iron cart beside him, used in eras gone by to bring coffee and cakes to the master of the house. He picked up the book Sara had deposited there after rereading it the night before.

For a long while, he didn't speak, just thumbed through the pages. The air between them, pregnant with topics neither of them could breach, settled into charged silence.

"A Study in Scarlet," he said at last, reading the cover aloud. "I can't figure why anyone would send this to you."

Sara stilled. A puzzle piece clicked into place with a sickening crack, like the break of a bird's bones. She stood, closed the space between them, and then snatched the book out of his hand.

"The scarlet thread," she said to herself.

"Come again?"

She flipped through the pages, and then returned the book to him, her finger marking the line. "Read this."

"There is the scarlet thread of murder running through the colorless skein of life."

"And the note on the painting said, 'He was trying to gather up the scarlet threads of life, and weave them into a pattern.' Adam, the scarlet thread is *murder*."

"But, what about Elisabetta Amello, and Cassie and Miss Connie?" he asked. "Why connect this murder to Sherlock Holmes, but not the others?"

Sara pondered this as thunder sounded at last across the bay.

"Well, the connection to *The Murders in the Rue Morgue* is blatant," she replied. "The character of Sherlock Holmes was directly inspired by Poe's character, Dupin."

"Fair enough," he said. "But what about—"

"The pill," she interrupted. "Look." She flipped through again, and read, "'Of the two pills in the box, one was of the most deadly poison, and the other was entirely harmless.'"

"I'm not following."

"Petey the dog, you said he was poisoned?"

Adam nodded.

"Sherlock Holmes poisons a terrier in this story to prove his theory. The dog dies. The other pill was nothing but sugar, like the one in Elisabetta's mouth. The note in the box said, 'She herself had become the deadliest poison in existence.' That's from *Rappaccini's Daughter*."

"*Híjole*. How the hell did you—?"

"It's a message for me. He knew I'd put it together."

"Because you know these stories by heart."

"Yes. Since I was a girl."

Adam looked up as the lights flickered. The storm. It was just the storm. Sara shivered.

"I let it out," she whispered, her hand over her mouth.

"Let what out?"

"The curse. Every single member of this family, going back generations, has met a violent and untimely end, but it was always confined to the house. Now it's out." Deep down inside herself, the things she locked away began rattling their iron chains. The dark memories of her childhood reared up, and she saw the fear in her father's eyes when he spoke of winds. She heard the hushed voice of her grandmother as she prayed, smudging the house in sage.

"I was supposed to keep it inside," she said, as the realization dawned upon her. All of Grammy's rituals and incantations, the tarot readings and salt sprinkled on the sills…"I always thought she was trying to protect us, to keep something from coming in, but she was trying to keep something from getting out. I let it out."

Lightning split the sky over his shoulder.

"Then I did too," he said.

"What?"

"They left us this responsibility together, Sadie. If you're going to shoulder it, I am too."

The lights dimmed, and then went out. She heard him rise. Thunder rolled over his curses as he rummaged in the table drawer at her side. He found a flashlight, but the batteries were dead. Sara set a hand on his arm as goosebumps prickled down her spine.

"Quiet," she shushed. "We're not alone."

Floorboards creaked above them. Somewhere upstairs, a child laughed.

"I don't have my gun," Adam whispered, but she shook her head.

"Your gun won't do any good here."

They waited, listening. Tiny footsteps sounded on the stairs, running up, up, until the sound dissipated into the skull of the house.

"What the fuck was that?" Adam asked, and Sara's fingers tightened on his arm. She knew what was coming next.

"It's Caroline," she breathed.

Before Adam could question her, a little girl screamed. The sound shivered along the walls, curling up through the chimneys and then dancing on the windows. Adam stiffened. Sara closed her eyes as the hideous cracking of bones reverberated through the floors.

Adam cursed again and reached instinctively for his hip, but his hand grasped air. He ran from the room in search of the sound. Sara followed, lighting the way with her cell phone. The pale white light cast a monstrous shadow before him as he stood in the foyer, wheeling about in a vain attempt to locate the child who'd fallen from the rails above.

"It's just Caroline," Sara repeated.

"Who the hell is Caroline? What's happening?"

"The railings broke," she answered, pointing up. "She died in 1927."

"Sara—"

"That was her death echo. I haven't seen her in a very long time. I thought she was at peace."

"Apparently not. Jesus Christ."

He's almost home.

Sara grabbed him again, holding tight to his arm, holding tight to anything real. Blood dripped on the floor at their feet. Together, they lifted their eyes to the balcony.

A small girl leaned over the rails above them, her pigtails swaying in the dim light. Blood streamed down the side of her face, the bones of her cheek and skull shattered, bound to her face only by ruined flesh. She put her finger to her lips.

He's almost home.

Her mouth moved erratically over the words, as if she spoke them a thousand times at once.

"Who?" Sara whispered, but she was gone.

"You're hurting my arm," Adam said, eyes still fixed on the second story. Sara released her grip on him.

"She's never said that before," she said.

Adam crossed himself. "In all the years I've known you, I've never once seen anything like that."

"They don't usually show themselves to anyone outside the family."

"Do you think they're angry?"

"No," Sara replied. "They're scared."

• • •

THE TINY CORPSE of Petey the terrier, sealed up in a cardboard box, weighed as heavily in Sara's arms as it did in her heart. She carried him down the drive of Wildefell, through the gates, and to the street. Cool, damp morning wind blew up from the marshes, a reminder of the coming autumn. She walked the remainder of the distance between the two houses with what felt like a stake in her chest.

The Wilsons had lived in the neighboring mansion for as long as Sara could remember. One of only three others on the street, the couple had a reputation for keeping the structure immaculate, despite their age. The porch steps did not creak as Sara climbed. No cobwebs collected debris in the windows or lingered in the eaves. The giant oak tree shading the house had shed its leaves, though they hadn't yet turned, a consequence of the summer's suffocating heat. They gathered at the edges of the drive and beneath perfectly trimmed rhododendrons.

Martha Wilson opened the door before Sara could raise her hand to the brass knocker.

"Sara," she said, clutching a string of pearls around her neck. "I saw you come up the drive."

"Hi, Mrs. Wilson," Sara began. Mrs. Wilson looked down at the box and tipped her head to the side. Her eyes widened. "I'm so sorry, but—"

"Oh," she murmured. "Oh no."

Mr. Wilson appeared over her shoulder.

"Sara," he said. "We're so sorry about what happened—"

Martha clutched his t-shirt and turned her face away. "Oh, Petey."

"I'm sorry," Sara repeated. "We found him on the front porch."

"What happened to him?" Mr. Wilson asked, lifting his chin even as tears shone in his eyes.

"The police say he was poisoned," she answered.

"Poisoned?" Martha's eyes snapped back to Sara. She released her hold on her husband's shirt and snatched the box from her. The dog's body shifted inside. "Who did this?"

"They think the same person who killed my sister and grandmother."

For a long moment, Martha remained quiet, her fingernails digging into the cardboard. When she spoke, frost hardened her voice.

"We've always been tolerant of your family's ... *secular* ways," she said. "We said nothing when your grandmother hosted those devil-worshipping parties—"

"The séances?"

"You've all communed with the dead so long it's infecting the whole town. Someone has to put a stop to it."

"Martha," Mr. Wilson said, a hand on her shoulder.

"No, Jack, enough is enough." She turned back to Sara, angry tears glistening in her eyes. "I'm calling Pastor Cunningham and the ladies at church. It's time this town exorcised its demons."

Martha slammed the door in Sara's face, leaving her on the flawless porch, alone.

- - -

THE BRIEF COOLNESS of morning evaporated with the rise of the sun. It fell down upon Wildefell like the glimmering sea, running off the roof and pooling on the lawn, sending shadows into the rose petals and under leaves of ivy, but Sara still felt the night in her heart. As her shoes ground into the warm gravel, Mr. Buchanan approached from the side yard. He hailed her, squinting in the sun as he broke into a jog.

"Ms. Sara!" he called. "Just need a moment."

She waited for him in front of the porch.

"I've been meaning to call you," she said. His face, perpetually tan, was more wrinkled than she remembered, undertones of clay revealing his years spent in the burning sun. His blond hair had burnt to ash.

"Likewise," he answered, his expression grim.

"I wanted to thank you for taking care of the horses. It's a great help. I'd like for them to continue with the carriage tours if you can manage it? I'll pay you, of course, for all your time."

"Ms. Sara, I have some awful bad news," he said, wiping his forehead with a yellowed handkerchief.

"Are the horses okay?"

"Oh, yes, they're fine. But unemployed."

"What?"

"The tour company was receiving complaints from the locals. Something about a curse. I tried to convince them to transfer the horses to the ghost carriage tour, figured it might help drum up some buzz, but the owner doesn't want the bad press."

"He doesn't want to be associated with us, you mean."

"Something like that."

Sara thanked him, and after an awkward embrace, they parted ways. Adam, she knew, was inside waiting with coffee in hand, but she headed instead toward the stable. She walked around the side of the house where a small, sandy pasture stretched out toward the marsh, the fenceposts only dark sticks in the glaring sun. The stable stood nestled in a cluster of gala apple trees. Honeybees and wasps, which fed upon the rotting fruits, fled as she approached.

She unbolted the latch on the barn door, and the horses nickered a greeting.

"Hey, guys," Sara said softly, stepping inside. Dust swirled in the sunlight as Poppy, Cassie's palomino mare, pawed the earthen floor. The black one, Salem, snorted at her, shaking his head.

"It's just me," she said to him, but it had been so long, she doubted he would even recognize her. "Looks like you guys are out of a job."

"Sara?" a man called from the house. The horse's ears flattened. A stranger.

John.

She lingered there, her hand on the door, panic throbbing in her heart. How could she find the woman he was looking for? She'd left her back in Savannah, with a hundred pairs of pumps and tightly fitting pant suits. Before Sara could gather up the pieces of herself, she heard Adam's voice.

"Can I help you?" he asked. His boots sounded on the porch. The screen door slammed.

"Oh," John stammered. "I must have the wrong house. Is this the Wilde residence?"

"Sure is."

Sara peered out the barn window, able to see John on the drive, but not Adam. John, just as she remembered, stood tall and straight with the bearing of a lawyer. A starched oxford shirt clung to his slender, but muscular frame, a physique she had once found attractive. He looked wan now, almost weak. He wore his press badge clipped to his belt loop, like always.

"I'm looking for Sara Wilde," he said. "Who are you?"

"Depends on who's asking," Adam answered. "Sadie and I own this house."

Sara winced. There were some things she would've like to explain to John before he'd arrived here. She should have just returned his calls.

"You must be family, then," John said, extending his hand. Adam came into view and shook it.

"Something like that."

"I'm John. She's probably mentioned me. I'm her boyfriend."

Adam shook his head with a tight frown, releasing his hand. "Nope, not a word."

"Ah." John looked at the ground, and Sara decided it was time to intervene before things got out of hand. She left the barn, letting the door slam behind her. Both men looked her direction, and she waved as she jogged over.

"Johnny," she said, the smile forced, foreign. "What are you doing here?"

He leaned in to kiss her, but she hugged him instead. Adam whistled under his breath.

"I've got some errands to run," he said. "I'll let you two catch up." As he walked by, he set his hand on Sara's arm and stage whispered, "Washed your favorite mug. Coffee's on."

"How very domestic of you," Sara muttered in reply, and then met her boyfriend's expectedly irritated gaze.

"I see why you haven't been returning my calls," he said plainly.

"Adam's an old friend, and he's being a dick," she answered. "I don't even have a favorite mug."

"Is he living here?"

They walked together onto the porch, but Sara hesitated at the door.

"You shouldn't be here, Johnny," she said instead, her eyes on the lower windows, where a heavy curtain gently swayed. They were watching.

John cupped her face in his hand, brushing the pad of his thumb across her cheek and drawing her eyes to his.

"Look at me, Sara."

She had always found the calm sea in his eyes, but now she felt adrift, shipwrecked in the slate-gray Atlantic.

"You're different," he said, lowering his hand.

"Yes."

Sara wanted to tell him to come inside, to have a cup of coffee and talk things through, but she didn't. She could not tolerate the idea of bringing him into this place, but when she tried to convince herself it was for his own protection, the excuse fell flat. There just wasn't any room for him here. He turned and walked down the steps with his hands in his pockets.

"I brought some of your things from the apartment. I'll bring them by later?"

"That'd be fine, thank you." Sara wrapped her arms around herself, suddenly cold. "Johnny," she called after him. "I'm sorry. I'll explain everything. I just need time."

He nodded, sent her a quick smile, and continued down the drive, his gangly shadow following close behind.

Chapter X

*S*ARA TURNED the copy of *A Study in Scarlet* over in her hands, alone, her back to the fireplace. The sun glared in through the kitchen windows, stark bands of light gleaming on the elbow-worn boards, smooth after years of disobeying her mother.

Elbows off the table, young lady, Momma had said, over and over, but Sara never paid her any mind. Somewhere in Savannah she had lost that streak of defiance. Perhaps she'd just become too weary for it.

She drank a third cup of coffee out of a mug she hadn't seen in years. Emblazoned with the Beauford Police logo, she'd gotten it from the summer camp they'd hosted for kids interested in a career in law enforcement. Before Sara had turned toward writing, she'd wanted to be a detective, just like Sherlock Holmes. It was true she had no favorite mug now, but back then, this had been it.

A barb of guilt startled her as her mind turned to John, and she wondered where he was. He'd probably gone back to Savannah. It was safer there.

Her phone vibrated on the table, and she glanced at the name on the screen. Her editor.

"Hey, Chief," she answered.

"Listen, honey, we need to talk. You and John are the best reporters I've got, and you're both gone. You've got that man in a tizzy ignoring his calls like you are. He can't write worth shit right now."

"I know, I'm really sorry. I saw John today. I think he'll be back in Savannah soon."

"HR wants me to put you on leave if you don't come up with that story soon. You've got to give me something. Have you made any progress?"

"There have been more murders," she said by way of answer.

"Shit, a serial killer?"

"Looks like."

"Do you have any leads?"

Sara drew a breath, her thumb tapping the handle of the coffee mug in time with the clock.

"Me," she answered at last. "Somehow I'm at the center of this, but I don't know where to start." A dense pause stretched across the line. Sara closed her eyes.

"Well, kid," he breathed. "Start at the beginning."

"I've been over these last few days in my head a thousand times."

"No, I mean the beginning of *you*. If it's important to the killer, it's important to the story. Start with where you've come from, then work your way out. Then come home."

Come home.

Sara thought of the night she and Cassie had summoned the Lady in White, the night the hinges of her life swung her out into the fringe.

"Did I hit on something?" he asked.

"I'll bring you two stories," she answered, surprising even herself. "The serial killer bit, and a heritage piece. It'll be about a woman who died in this house after the civil war, and her missing child."

Mr. Woodward grunted. "Can you have it to me by the end of the week?"

She winced and rubbed her eyes. "Give me two?"

"Two *weeks*? Midge'll have your desk by then, kid."

"Please, Chief. You won't be sorry."

"Right, well between you and me, Midge can't write copy on the back of a cereal box. I'm holding this one for you, but I need you back, Wilde."

Sara smiled. Something in the way he said her name reminded her that a world existed outside this house, outside herself. Despite the sinking sensation in her gut, the idea of this second story grew on Sara until a part of her came back to life. The identity of her Lady in White had been a mystery for too long. If exposed to light, would she shrivel like a fungus and finally leave her in peace? Sara ended the call with her editor and stood, momentarily rudderless.

Where could she truly begin? The answer came quickly, dragging the corpse of an old fear behind.

The cellar.

Before she could lose her nerve, Sara strode outside and rounded the west side of the house where the ivy climbed high, reaching its tendrils into the mortar between the stones. The storm cellar doors wore many coats of paint, most recently a peeled and blistered Victorian blue, exposing the scarlet red beneath, like a fresh wound.

For the first time since that fateful night with Cassie and her Grammy's broach, Sara forced the rusted latch and heaved open the door. She peered down into the stale darkness, all the fear of her childhood welling up in her throat. Swallowing hard, Sara stepped onto the staircase.

The rotting stairs groaned as she descended, her phone light illuminating the way. Rusted nails popped and creaked, heralding her presence. Cockroaches and house crickets fled into their holes. Spiders dangled from their webs, spinning wildly in the draft she let inside. The eye shine of a frightened field mouse gleamed in the thin cone of her light, revealing plainly the only perceivable monster here was her.

She reached the packed earth floor and felt frantically for the pull string dangling above, surprised and relieved to hear electricity hum through the bulb. Yellow light bloomed across the cellar, and Sara breathed through the dread gathering behind the hollow of her throat. Beyond the shelves lined with mason jars and preserves, in a mahogany hope chest, were the family portraits. Sara had asked only once why they were stored down here, subject to mold and flooding rain, and Grammy answered with an expression of mourning.

"Best to let them be," was all she said, and after Sara's ghostly encounter, she'd been satisfied to do just that.

Not today, not anymore.

Sara hoisted a box of old typewriter ribbons off the chest and swept aside a scattering of desiccated pill bugs. The lid creaked on its rusted hinges as she lifted it. Inside, wrapped in layers of plastic sheeting, sat 200 years' worth of family history, hidden away like the tell-tale heart. The plastic, once unfolded, was nothing more than a filmy shower curtain, its rings rusted and bleeding. She hesitated, fingers lingering on a leather-bound album labelled only with the year. *2005.*

It was the last album Momma had put together. Sara remembered her at the dining room table with a year's worth of memories scattered all around, scissors and glue sticks at the ready. That was the year before Daddy died, before Momma went away and the remembering turned cold.

She picked up the book at last. The cover cracked down the spine as she drew it back. A family photo greeted her first, the five of them on Daddy's boat, squinting in the summer sunshine. Sara traced her fingers over her own face, so remarkably like Cassie's in all but the eyes. Cassie had Daddy's eyes, as brown as the earth. Sara, like her mother and all the Wilde ancestors before her, had eyes the color of the angry sea.

As she flipped through the stiff pages, she watched herself transform into a woman. At the back of the book, the last photo depicted her in front of her father's mustang with Adam on her arm. Lanky and awkward, a cross around his neck, Adam grinned defiantly. What a rebel he had been, the good catholic boy going to prom with the pariah. The witch.

"I'm sorry, Grams," she whispered. Sara had left her own religion here in the house. Savannah had no space for the pagan rituals they practiced when she was a child, and in turn her ability to glimpse beyond the veil had been gratefully relinquished. It was a sacrifice she was happy to make, but now, meeting her own eyes in the photograph, she wondered if it had all been a mistake. She could imagine the look on Grammy's face as clearly as if she were still alive; disappointment nearing grief. Shame.

This incantation must be spoken with a pure heart, baby doll. You mustn't allow them too much control over you.

Her voice came into Sara's heart like a cedar stake. The memory fastened to it was pale and faded, as cracked as the album, but after a moment, she saw herself standing before an altar. Sage burned in a stone bowl on her right side, and on her left, Grammy lingered, her bony fingers striking a match. It gasped to life, and she held it to a white tapered candle.

Say the name of who you want to reach. The nightmares won't stop until you've allowed her to speak to you.

"I don't know her name," Sara said aloud.

Bring her face to the forefront of your mind. Push aside all else. Do you see her?

Sara had nodded. Grammy held her hand as she described her Lady in White, the one she'd conjured all those years ago in this very cellar. Grammy's hand had tightened, and then she blew out the candle. They never spoke of it again, and Sara had been too much of a coward to learn anymore. If the specter frightened even Grammy, as hardened to the supernatural as anyone could be, Sara had no chance against it at all.

She snapped the book closed, this curious memory enduring as she rummaged through the hope chest.

At the bottom, nestled between a tattered album and a stack of faded daguerreotypes, Sara found a rusted tin box, barely the size of a hardcover. She extracted it, knowing in her heart once this box was open, she could never close it again. The latch crumbled in her fingers. With the breath held deep inside her lungs, Sara lifted the lid. Atop a small scrap of silk was the old broach, the lock of hair more withered than she remembered. Sara picked it up and held it in her palm, marveling at how utterly this piece of jewelry had shaped her life. She closed her fist around it, and then tucked it into her pocket.

Beneath this, she found a small portrait, its gilt frame tarnished and scratched. The silver encircled a faded daguerreotype photograph of a woman, clad in the white dress Sara had come to recognize well. Her face, pallid and sunken, gave the impression of death, made all the more grotesque by the peculiar, nigh unnatural, tilt of her head.

The great vastness in the woman's eyes disturbed her, and Sara dropped the photograph into the tin as if it had stung her.

The woman in the picture was dead.

"Memento Mori," Sara murmured. She had heard of postmortem photography, which became popular in the Victorian era, but had never before seen one of these unsettling and horrible images for herself. Recovering, she took the portrait again in her hands, and turned it over. Pinned to the back of the frame was a newspaper clipping from 1893. The obituary of a Theodora Anne Wilde.

Theodora Wilde, of Wildefell Manor, died this Tuesday last. She is survived by her son, Stephen Anderson, and husband, Bennett Paul. Tragically, their infant daughter passed away in her mother's loving arms. The family, not being members of the church, will hold no funeral service. A private burial will occur in the family plot on the property on Sunday, April the first.

The family plot?

As far as Sara knew, there was no cemetery on the property. Grammy and Cassie would be buried in the churchyard down the road, where her father's empty coffin had been interred all those years ago. To what, then, did this refer?

"Theodora," she whispered, turning the frame over and running her fingers over the photograph. Sara knew the name of her great grandfather, Stephen. Grammy spoke of him often. This woman, her Lady in White, was her 2nd great grandmother, her stories lost to time, or perhaps as hidden away as the graveyard where she'd been buried.

Beneath her portrait, the tin held a collection of newspaper clippings, delicately pressed flowers, and opened letters. She selected the first item, an article from the Beaufort County Times, dated April 7, 1893.

WILDEFELL MANOR MURDER-SUICIDE – THE CURSE LIVES ON

Beauford, SC

The tragic murder-suicide of Theodora Wilde and her infant daughter has the town up in arms. Rumors have circulated these past decades of Wildefell Manor, gripped by a deadly curse, and the fate of the poor child must remind us all of the consequences of flirting with the powers of evil. The Wildes, owners of the property these hundred years, are known to practice witchcraft and are proponents of the new spiritualist movement now spreading like the plague across Europe.

The bastard child (fathered by a man this reporter has heretofore been unable to identify), was carried by her mother into the frigid waters of the bay after rumors circulated about an affair. Bennett Wilde, Theodora's husband, has not offered comment. Her suicide has left a young boy motherless, which will no doubt negatively affect the course of his life. We can only pray that this incident will turn him from the pagan influence of the Wilde family and bring him into the loving fold of the church.

Sara stopped reading. The article must have been written before the Wildes purchased the newspaper. Her ancestors never would have allowed this defamation. If she remembered correctly, Bennett Wilde had bought the paper in 1893, just a few months after the date of this article. Aside from murmured rumors from the elders in town, passed down no doubt by their parents before them, Sara knew for certain only that the sale was some kind of scandal. It caused a rift between her family and the Mauk's that existed still.

Still pondering this, she picked up a packet of letters wrapped in twine and selected the first in the set. Postmarked on June 8th of 1891, the letter was addressed to Theodora Wilde in elegant, albeit hurried, script, and had been sent from Whitby, England. Sara removed it carefully from the envelope and began to read.

> *Dear Thea,*
>
> *How I wish we could sit up in the picture window and talk through the night as we did in days gone by! This little seaside town is so beautiful this time of year, but so dreadfully dull without you to enjoy it with me. And we have so much to talk about. I can hardly stand to wait for your next letter.*
>
> *Freddie and I have only arrived a fortnight hence and he has already made friends with another newly married couple, the Stevensons, who are lodging in the house across the street until midsummer. We've had dinner with them twice, and I don't know if I can survive another visit. He and Paul, that's Mary's husband, rattle on so much about the hunting of guinea fowl that Mary and I are bored to tears. Somehow, I thought this honeymoon would be more exciting! We can dine with friends in any old place. I want to swim in the sea and wander that old cemetery up on the hill.*
>
> *Enough of my prattle. I want to know more about what you wrote in your last letter. Your assurance that Bennett leaves you be much of the day, and that this is as confidential a method of communicating as if we were whispering in our room, has relieved me some. We may speak freely then!*
>
> *In your last letter, you wrote me that you met a man. I've always made my feelings about Bennett plain, so you needn't fear any judgement from me. A cruel, covetous old sinner if ever there was one!*

Well then, Thea— Tell me everything! How did you meet him? When will you see him again? Rest assured at my secrecy. I shan't tell a soul!
All my love,
Clemmie

Sara chewed her lip, the dirt floor cold as she sat down and selected the next letter. Her fingers trembled. Someone had gathered Theodora's most valuable possessions and placed them in this rusted tin. All that remained now of a tragic life.

Dear Thea,
The news that you're with child has just reached me, from little Stephen no less! He wrote me a letter and posted it, I imagine, all on his own, begging me to come home. He said the baby in your belly is growing big and strong, but Daddy doesn't know.
We have been friends the whole of our lives, Thea. How could you not tell me?
What have you done?

The remains of a crumbled rose were pressed with the last letter in the stack. It had been read and refolded so many times the page tore down the folds.

Dear Theodora,
Our last meeting lingers with me like a ghost, my business unfinished. You begged me not to write or call upon you, but I can bear this misery no longer. I must see you again, Thea. My sweet Thea! If you ever loved me, even for a moment, pray, return my letter. You need not write at all, only enclose a lock of your hair, or the imprint of your lips on the page, or I am lost, my love. I am finished!
Desperately yours,
J.

"What happened to you, Theodora?" Sara whispered.

She knew what needed to be done. It was what she ought to have done from the start but had been too frightened to go through with it.

Returning the photograph and the letters to the tin, she held it against her chest and fled the cellar without bothering to turn off the light. She must have left the front door open, for it swung inward as if Theodora herself had invited her back inside. When Sara reached the door to Grammy's room at the end of the hall, she did not recall climbing the stairs. Smothering a pang of grief, summoned by the lingering scent of Grammy's Chanel no. 5 and smudging sage, she opened the door and stepped inside.

Sara could not pause at the sewing table, where her grandmother sewed dresses for her dolls and hemmed her prom gown. She walked by the vanity with its paper cup of bobby pins, and the mahogany dresser where Grammy kept photographs of her late husband.

Her altar, situated between the only two windows in the room, remained exactly how Sara remembered. Half-burned white candles and jars of herbs cluttered the surface. A pentagram, for protection, had been carved into the wood with a ritual knife still resting silently in a copper vase, alongside the dried husk of a rose.

"Grammy," Sara whispered, clutching the tin to her chest. "I wish you were here to tell me how I'm supposed to do this." She waited, staring into the mirror above the altar, but no one answered. No shadowy form materialized behind her in the glass. She was alone.

Sara set the tin onto the altar, and placed the broach beside it, trying to recall the conjuring incantations Grammy had taught her. She removed the image of Theodora Wilde and propped it against the mirror, lighting the candles with a murmur of uncertainty.

Finally, Sara closed her eyes.

"Theodora Wilde," she called, feeling for all the world like a fool. "Are you here?"

A hawk cried out across the marshes, but the house held its breath.

"You've been trying to talk to me for a long time," she continued. "I'm here to listen."

Sara opened her eyes and lifted them to the mirror, but it was not her face looking back. The Lady in White met her eyes. No putrescence poured from her lips; no snails clung to the protruding bones of her cheeks. She instead appeared to Sara as she had been in life, with a blush of rouge on her cheeks, and tragedy reflected in eyes Sara mistook for her own. Agonizing sorrow poured over her as she stared into the glass, and when the tears stung and she began to weep, so too did Theodora.

Tell him it's time to come home, she said. Her lips did not move in time with the words.

"Who?"

She gathered up the folds of her blanket and began to sing.

"In my dreams she still doth haunt me, robed in garments soaked in brine…"

"I don't know what it means," Sara pleaded, tears dropping onto the altar. "Please, I don't understand."

The woman looked up from her blankets, and Sara watched in horror as worms wriggled into her eyes. The flesh paled to blue and decomposed before her eyes, first green with algae, and then black with rot.

"Theodora?" Sara whimpered.

My baby, she wailed. And she covered her face with her bony hands, the blanket falling from her arms. *I had no choice. They gave me no choice.*

"Who?" she asked.

Theodora did not answer, but such a mournful cry echoed through the room that Sara lifted her hands to cover her own face. The woman reached toward her, through the mirror. Her cold fingers met Sara's forehead, and then the dark swallowed her whole.

Chapter XI

ENEATH THE silken black, Sara dreamed. At first, she heard only the gentle lapping of water against the shore, but footsteps soon joined, squelching through icy mud. She felt the chill around her ankles, and then her knees. The marsh filled up the emptiness inside her, the frigid water a welcome balm for the sorrow burnishing her heart. It seeped into her lungs.

"Sadie? Are you up here?"

Adam's voice reached her from under water. She gasped, gagging and sputtering as her eyes flew open. He was by her side in a moment, hands on her shoulders.

"What happened? Are you hurt?"

"She walked into the marsh," she murmured, wiping the tears away.

"Who?"

"Theodora. She couldn't bear it." Sara rose onto her knees and then sat down again on the floor, exhausted by the effort.

"Bear what? Who's Theodora?"

"The Lady in White is my 2nd great grandmother. Her name is Theodora. Something happened to her baby, and she committed suicide."

Gathering up her strength at last, Sara stood and approached the altar. She handed him the death portrait.

"This is her, then?" he asked. "Is she—"

"Dead." Sara took the photograph back, feeling suddenly uncomfortable it was out of her possession. "She's connected somehow to all of this, to this house, and the murders."

"How could she be connected to the murders?"

She shook her head. "I don't know, but I'm going to find out."

Adam stepped up behind her, and she met his eyes in the mirror.

"Did you... summon her?" he asked, eyes wandering over the altar and candles, which had somehow gone out. She nodded. "This stuff always messed me up a little."

"It's only frightening if you do it wrong."

"How did your family get into all this anyway? I never asked."

Sara inhaled and ran her fingers over the carving in the wood. "Grammy said we were spiritualists back in the early 1900s. She said it meant something I was so drawn to the gothic, to Sherlock Holmes."

"Why?"

"Well Doyle was a big proponent of the spiritualist movement. Anyway, there are diaries up in the attic from 100 years before that, from demonologists, witches, and conjurers. The Wilde family has always been pagan. They just gave us different labels as the centuries went on. It doesn't matter anymore."

"Why would you say that?"

"Because I'm pretty sure I'm just as crazy as my mom. None of this is real."

"You obviously don't believe that, or you wouldn't have tried to conjure that spirit. I admired that about you. It never mattered what people called you. You were just... you."

"Look where that's gotten me."

Then, noticing a pile of boxes and shopping bags dropped haphazardly at the threshold of the room, she asked, "What's all this?"

He accepted this change of topic, and walked past her, gathering up the items and placing them on Grammy's threadbare throw rug.

"Sit," he said, selecting a pink bag from one of the local clothing boutiques. "I got you some stuff. It'll save you the trip back to Savannah. I think these are your size."

Sara sat down, folding her legs as he dumped the contents of the bag.

"You got this for me?" She picked up a beautiful cotton dress, the kind she wore before the pantsuits, and let it unfold, holding it close to her body. "It even has pockets." He nodded with a shrug, selected a Walgreens bag, and dumped it as well.

Sara ran her fingers over a bottle of coconut hibiscus shampoo.

"I haven't seen this in years," she said, a smile tugging at the edge of her mouth. "I didn't think they still made it."

"I always liked the smell. And here—" he tossed her a travel-sized bottle of Coppertone SPF with a smirk. "Your pale ass is getting sunburnt."

Sara laughed, and it sounded like home.

"Found some of that Cover Girl stuff you used to use, too," he added, and pushed aside a bottle of conditioner to hand her a pressed powder compact.

"You found my old make-up?" she asked, at this point exasperated.

"Well, you don't need it," his eyes moved gently over her face, lingering. Heat bloomed in her cheeks. "I have the receipts," he added quickly, and withdrew a collection of papers from his back pocket.

"No, it's perfect," she answered. "It's all perfect, thank you."

She was so touched by this gesture of kindness, by this time capsule of toiletries, that she stood up and embraced him. She meant for it to end quickly, with a friendly pat on the back, but his arms pulled her close and Sara found herself enwrapped. She breathed him in, allowing herself this single moment of solace as the tears sprung up behind her eyes, as his palm opened on the small of her back and his whiskers brushed the curve of her neck.

Adam stepped backward, clearing his throat. "I uh," he stammered. "Lucy wants us to come over for dinner tonight." He looked at his watch, a simple, analogue clock with a worn leather strap. "In about an hour. You in?"

She nodded but couldn't speak. Her body hummed where he had touched her. He walked to the picture window with his hands in the pockets of his jeans and looked outside. For a long moment, he stood in silence, the warm sun enveloping him in ruddy light.

"I'm worried about all this, Sadie," he said. "Worried about you."

"I'm fine."

"You keep saying that." He turned to face her, brow creased. "Can you think of anyone who would target you like this? Maybe one of your stories pissed off the wrong person."

She lifted a shoulder. "I haven't written anything very hard hitting recently."

"What about the story you wrote a couple months back? That one about the string of kidnappings. Didn't you help put that guy away?"

Sara regarded him, surprised. "You read my work?"

"Well, yeah. Of course I do."

Unable to properly process this bit of information, Sara stashed it away for later analysis and moved on. "I did, but his trial was a month ago. He's in prison."

"Okay. And you think the killer is specifically targeting you to send some kind of message?"

"Ignoring the fact that Cassie and Grams were his first victims, the connection to the gothic stories *and* Sherlock Holmes is too much to disregard. It's *designed* for me."

"So aside from me, who else has been in your life long enough to know how important those two things are to you? And who has some working knowledge of your family?"

She shook her head. "I'm not the most popular kid in school, Adam. I'm sure there are a lot of people who would like to see the Wilde family gone for good."

"No, I don't think that's the motive. Otherwise, why branch out? Why not just kill you all and be done with it? The killer is tormenting *you*. This is personal."

Adam's phone rang, and he checked the screen.

"It's Eva. I'm holding off a press conference for you. Meet you at Lucy's?"

"Sure," Sara replied. When he'd gone, she held her new dress to her chest, the sensation of him lingering all around her.

- - -

THE MUSTANG'S TIRES crushed a blanket of acorns into the gravel, popping and cracking, until Sara rolled to a stop on the grass. Cool air ruffled her hair, smelling sweetly of cut grass and decaying leaves, and she was glad she left the top down. The windows in Lucy's house shone into an evening crowded by oaks and hushed by the chirping of a thousand crickets. The house might have belonged to a woodland faerie and not her sister's best friend.

Adam's car was already parked in the driveway, and she saw his silhouette in the kitchen window. It had been many years since she'd seen this place. Long forgotten memories overwhelmed her as she sat in the car, her hands still clenched around the wheel.

This house, in stark contrast with her own childhood home, had always been warm. There were no unexplainable noises, no bitter drafts or cold stone floors, just the smell of freshly made tortillas and soft carpet underfoot. It was watching romcoms in Lucy's room and stealing glimpses of Adam or chopping radishes with Mama Contreras for her prize winning chimol.

Fragments of his conversation with Lucy, who gathered dishes from the cupboard, reached her through the window.

"She's with someone?" Lucy asked, clutching a plate to her chest.

"A *gringo* from Savannah. Real stuffy. I met him today."

"Is he at least a nice guy?"

He shrugged as he set the table, then said something in Spanish and shook his head.

"As long as she's happy..." Lucy turned her back and opened the refrigerator, so Sara didn't hear the remainder of the sentence.

"That's the thing though, Luce. She didn't seem happy. She barely touched him."

An acorn dropped onto the hood of the car, startling her. Adam looked out the window, spotted her, and then yelled, "Are you going to sit out there all night?"

They had the table set and the food prepared by the time she walked into the house. Lucy had made her mother's pupusas, which had always been one of Sara's favorite meals.

"Everything's ready," Lucy said, all of her mother's warmth in her voice. "Sit anywhere you like."

"Smells amazing," Sara said, selecting the chair she'd always sat in, back when her biggest worry was catching Adam's eye from the other side of the table. She did so now as he sat across from her, and he smiled warmly. They chatted casually as they passed around a basket made of Gullah sweet grass, stacked high with pupusas oozing with cheese. For a single, lovely moment, Sara felt comfortable, at home.

"Are you guys going to sell Wildefell?" Lucy asked, dousing a pupusa in hot sauce and drawing Sara back into her mire.

"No," Adam answered, but Sara hesitated. John's appearance, and her editor's phone call, had reminded her how hard she'd worked to build a new life, a life separate from Wildefell. From Adam. How could she throw it all away? And Johnny. *Johnny.* He deserved more than this, more than a half-hearted promise for explanation and a casual dismissal. He'd driven all the way to see her, and she'd barely even bothered to look at him.

Adam glared at her. "Sadie?"

"It's just a lot to think about, okay? My editor wants me back at work soon."

"But there hasn't been a funeral yet," Lucy added.

"I don't even have their bodies," she replied.

"You're just going to leave?" Lucy wiped her hands on a napkin, resting her elbows on the table. Adam neither spoke nor ate, just looked at her, waiting.

"I'm not just going to leave," Sara answered, raising her voice. "I have responsibilities."

"Yes, to your family," Adam said.

"You don't get to talk to me about responsibility," she retorted, and then pushed her chair away from the table. "I need some air."

Sara retreated to the porch. The screen door slammed behind her as she dropped into a rocking chair and buried her face in her hands, stifling an angry cry. She scarcely had time to swallow it when Adam stepped onto the porch, his boots crushing a gathering of oak leaves. He walked by her silently, and stood with his hands on the rail, looking out into the night.

"I'm not good company right now," she said to him, but he didn't reply. His shoulders heaved as he drew a breath and, once released, he turned to her.

"You can't sell it," he said.

"I worked too hard to get out, Adam. My life is in Savannah now."

Adam rubbed the back of his neck, shaking his head.

"I mean you legally can't," he said. "Not without a lawsuit."

Sara's lips fell open, and when she lifted her eyes to him, resolve as hard as iron banded in the cords of his neck.

"You would *sue* me?" she asked.

"I won't let you take this from me."

"You can't be serious." She rocked forward in the chair, fingers clutching the armrests.

"Let me buy you out," Adam said. "Then our business with each other will be through, and I'll be out of your life again. That's what you want, isn't it?"

Tears bit at the edges of her eyes as she rocked in the chair. She pressed her clammy palms to her cheeks in a vain attempt to cool them. Nearby, someone lit a bonfire. She could smell the lighter fluid, and the wood smoke. It stung her eyes.

"I don't know what I want," she whispered.

"*Pues,* maybe your boyfriend can help you figure it out." She could not return this jab. Adam took her silence as an opening to land another blow. He met her eyes, his gaze too heavy for her to hold. "Does he know about the visions? About the house?"

"No, and he never will."

"You think that's a healthy way to be in a relationship?"

"Pretty funny, coming from you," she countered. The smoke thickened, overwhelming her before she even had time to cry for help. In a moment, she was blind.

She shivered as the cool night climbed her vertebrae, one bone at a time until it bloomed into pain and sprung into her right eye. She coughed, stumbling out of the chair. Adam yelled Lucy's name, and something in Spanish, but he'd already gone far away.

Sara heard the latch of the barn door, and a man cried out, his voice familiar.

Fire! he cried. *Save the horses!*

Heat swelled inside her skin until she felt she might split open. Her parched tongue clung to the roof of her mouth, and she could not utter a sound. A horse panted, snorting, and protesting. *Salem.* He whinnied over the hushed clink of the stirrups. Someone had mounted him.

What are you doing? The man cried. *Stop!*

He received no reply. The galloping of hooves thundered in Sara's head. The man ran. With the night tearing through her lungs, damp grass soaking her feet as the horse gave chase, Sara clutched her throbbing chest.

Hollow footfalls resounded down the pier, and the horse's hot breath blew down her neck. A swift blade struck bone. Sara collapsed on the porch, her face striking the smooth wooden boards, drawing her sharply back. Adam hovered over her.

"What is it? What did you see?"

"Fire," she said, but she couldn't speak loud enough for him to hear. Ignoring the blinding pain in her skull, she grabbed ahold of his shirt and pulled herself up. "Call 911," she managed.

"What do I tell them?" He already had his phone to his ear.

"Wildefell is on fire."

- - -

THE HORSES LOOKED at her curiously, ears flicking back as she stood on the straw covered floor, Adam at her side.

"I don't understand," she said. The naked lightbulb hung still above them, illuminating the unscathed stable and weakening the flashing lights on the firetruck in the drive. "Have you been able to reach Mr. Buchanan?"

"Not yet," Adam answered.

A fireman, clad in full gear, tapped on the door and then stepped inside.

"We haven't found any incendiaries on the premises," he said. He removed his helmet, revealing a shock of dark hair. He tossed it off his forehead with a flick of his head.

"Thanks, Nico," Adam said.

"Thank you for coming," Sara added. "I'm sorry for the trouble."

"Better safe than sorry," he said with a shrug. "Adam has my cell if you need anything."

When he'd gone, Sara sat down on a bale of straw and shook her head.

"It's never happened away from the house."

Its influence was spreading, hooking its gnarled claws into her back even as she turned away. But was it a vision at all? Clearly, there had been no fire. The possibility her overtaxed mind had conjured this hallucination brought acid into her throat.

"This is how it began with Momma," she whispered. The day-time nightmares, the vivid hallucinations. It was finally happening.

"Don't go there," Adam warned, and then held his hand out to her. "Come on. Let's go inside. It's been a long day."

Sara rubbed her eyes as sparks of light shimmered in her vision, a migraine encroaching like the scratching of a thousand feral rats. When she took Adam's hand, he pulled her into a hug.

"I believe you, Sadie," he said into her ear. "I've always believed you."

"I know." She inhaled the scent of him and closed her eyes, acutely aware of the warmth of his palm as he slipped it gently into her hair.

The familiarity of this gesture somersaulted inside her stomach. Sara stepped away.

"I was thinking," Adam began after clearing his throat.

"Never good," she joked, and his grin shone all the way into his eyes. Their impasse over the fate of Wildefell had been momentarily suspended.

"I was *thinking* I'd like to spend the night."

She looked up at him, unable to reply.

"If you have another vision," he added quickly. "I don't want you to be alone."

Surprised by the sensation of relief in her chest, Sara could only nod. They walked in silence together, rounding the house and climbing the porch steps. Nothing stirred inside as she clicked on the lamps, dropping her bag onto the floor beside the sofa. Even the mice in the walls were quiet tonight. Adam's presence had as calming an effect on the house as it had on her.

"I take it you need some ibuprofen?" Adam asked, pausing at the threshold of the sitting room.

"Please." She dropped down onto the couch, picking up the copy of *A Study in Scarlet* she'd left on the table. Drowsiness settled over her as she flipped through the familiar pages, searching for a meaningful passage.

"I'll sleep down here," Adam said, reappearing a moment later to set three orange tablets and a glass of water on the table beside her.

"There are four beds upstairs, don't be stubborn." She tossed the pills into her mouth and drank them down.

"I'll take the guest room then?"

"Half the house is yours anyway, you can have whichever room you want." Although she said this playfully, the ruefulness interwoven in the words reached him. Adam frowned and turned away to stare out the window, as was his wont.

"We're going to have to talk about this, Sadie," he said without turning back to her. "We own this house together, we need to figure out what to do with it."

"Can I bury my family first?" As she said this, she thought of the family plot, lost to time somewhere on the property. Tomorrow, she would go to the historical society to find the original deed.

"Fair enough," Adam answered. He sat down on the couch beside her and leaned his head against the wall, eyes on the ceiling. "Sometimes I think I'm just another one of Wildefell's ghosts."

Sara looked at him curiously, waiting for him to explain.

"I thought if I joined the Army, I could let it go. I spent six years in Afghanistan, and still ended up here, with a house down the street. Sitting on this couch with you. This house is all I ever wanted."

"But you still don't feel complete," Sara finished.

"No."

"You feel… used. Manipulated somehow."

He nodded. "But I can't figure out why."

"I know, I feel the same way."

He lifted his head and looked at her. "Maybe we're haunting it because we have unfinished business."

"Yeah." The weight of the day fell upon her, and she leaned against his shoulder, no longer possessing the energy to hate him. Adam rested his cheek on her hair with a gentle exhalation of breath, and in a moment, she closed her eyes and slept.

Chapter XII

THICK, BLACK smoke curled in through the open window.

Sara coughed. She lifted her head to find herself nestled on the couch with Adam, her body settled along the length of him as his chest rose and fell in sleep.

"Adam," she whispered, her hand on his chest. "Wake up. It's happening again."

She didn't feel the ice pick behind her right eye this time, nor were there any disembodied sounds vying for her attention. If Adam helped her focus, maybe she could stave it off. He awoke with a start, his hand grasping her wrist as if she held a knife to his chest.

"It's me," she said, pulling away. "It's just me."

"Sadie?" He blinked, and as consciousness returned to him, his alarm increased. She extricated herself from the cushions and stood. Adam leapt from the couch, coughing.

"Shit," he murmured, running to the window. Sara followed, eyes widening in disbelief as ash collected on the sill.

"Oh my God," she whispered. "It's real. This is real."

A horse screamed in the driveway, and Sara looked out to see Poppy pawing at the gravel and tossing her head. Sara was out the door before Adam could even dial 911.

The horse, somehow knowing her mind, stilled at her touch and allowed her to mount bareback. Without instruction, Poppy took off toward the burning stables, toward Salem. As they neared, though, Sara drew the horse back. Flames engulfed the entire structure, its black bones only moments from collapse.

The horse screamed, rearing up.

"Sadie!" Adam called. Sara wrapped her arms around Poppy's neck and held tight as she took off at a gallop toward the pier. The purple light of dawn poured down across the still marsh, and something in the dark water moved. Poppy tore through the reeds, saw grass slicing Sara's bare legs.

"Salem," Sara whispered, sliding off her mount and splashing into knee-deep water. The stallion swam a hundred yards off shore. She called for Adam, who ran toward her as the roof of the stable collapsed.

Algae clung to her arms and neck as she moved through the water, toward the horse. His head bobbed, nostrils flaring. She didn't know how long he'd been swimming, but his strength was waning.

"All the tack is in the stable!" Adam called from the bank. He coaxed Poppy out of the water and gripped her mane in his fist. Sara cooed at Salem as she approached, careful to avoid the powerful legs struggling beneath the water.

Sirens wailed as Adam splashed in behind her. He swam the distance quickly, reaching her moments later.

"Easy now," he said gently, hand outstretched to the panting horse. "I'm going to try to get behind him, nudge him toward shore."

"Be careful. Watch the legs."

Sara grabbed ahold of Salem's mane as Adam swam around them. Her legs screamed with fatigue.

"What the hell?" he cried, and drew himself backward. "There's something down here."

The horse began to thrash, splashing briny water into her eyes.

"Alligator?" She blinked, eyes burning.

"Shit, I hope not." They stilled, Salem following suit. "There it is again. Too soft to be a gator."

"Let's just get out of here."

With excruciating slowness, they led the horse toward Poppy, who waited in the reeds. The stable fell into itself at last, sparks mushrooming into the ashen sky. Salem's hooves found purchase in the mud, and as his flanks rose out of the water, so too did a length of rope, tied around his left hock.

As the horse climbed the bank, the rope pulled taut, catching on the reeds. A moment later, Sara's hand flew to her mouth. A human body broke the surface of the water, its headless corpse bobbing in the early morning sun.

●●●

"I SHOULD HAVE warned him," Sara muttered, shivering. Her new dress, now ruined, stuck to her legs, algae and human rot clinging to her hair. Adam put his arms around her and she let him pull her into an embrace.

"This isn't your fault," he said.

"You don't understand."

They had pulled the headless corpse of Mr. Buchanan out of the reeds and laid him in the damp grass. Sara noticed the wedding ring on his swollen finger and wondered how she had never met his wife. She didn't even know her name. The stump of his neck wept, oozing water and blood, the arteries and tissues tattered already by blue crabs. She stepped away from Adam and wrapped her arms around herself.

Eva approached them from the stables, where fire investigators climbed across the smoldering remains, their heads bent. A uniformed officer strung police tape around a wide perimeter and tied it off around the willow in the front yard. The horses, thanks to Lucy, had been loaded up in the trailer and were being boarded temporarily at a local dairy farm in St. Helena.

"Can you ID him?" Eva asked her. She flipped open a black notebook, already filled with hurried writing.

"It's Jack Buchanan," she answered.

"You're sure?"

She couldn't very well tell her she'd heard his voice in a vision, so she pointed at the man's jacket. "The coat was a gift from my father many years ago. I saw him wearing it the other day."

"SOC found a hell of a lot of blood on the pier," said Eva. "That's where it happened. Rails are broken. Your horse must've plowed right through."

"I'll call the vet, have her check him over," Sara said, more a mental note to herself than to Eva, who she knew didn't care a bit about the health of her sister's horse.

"This asshole keeps changing his MO," she said.

"No he doesn't," Sara replied. "He's killing according to the stories. That's the MO. Cause of death isn't a factor in it at all."

She regarded her impatiently, and then said, "Do your stories say where the head might be?"

Adam rose, his stance threatening violence. He stood a full head taller than his superior, but Eva lifted her chin with a scornful smirk, unaffected.

"Stand down, Lieutenant," she commanded.

Annoyed by this display, Sara used the distraction to search the body for the killer's note. With a broken reed, she peeled apart the pockets of Mr. Buchanan's coat. They were filled with stones, presumably to weigh him, and subsequently Salem, down into the river.

"What the hell are you doing?" Eva demanded.

"I don't understand," Sara murmured, ignoring her. "He always leaves me a note. If the killer wanted me to find the body, why weigh it down? Why try to drown the horse?"

"I'm going to ask you to leave," Eva said, stepping nearer. "You're tampering with evidence."

"Maybe the note's with the head?" Adam suggested. "Can you tell which story this is supposed to be without it?"

"The Legend of Sleepy Hollow is my guess," she answered, standing. "The whole headless horseman thing is kind of hard to miss."

"I could just have you arrested," Eva said, and then turned to Adam. "And you written up for insubordination."

A horsefly landed on Sara's shoulder, but it spotted the corpse before she could brush it away. She chewed her lip, tasted the marsh.

"They never found his body," Sara said to herself.

Adam asked, "Whose?"

"Ichabod Crane's. I don't think we were supposed to find the body, just the head."

Eva shook her head, tucking her notepad into the back pocket of her slacks. "You two know I have to bring the Feds in, right?"

"Like hell," Adam replied. "If they boot Sara off the case, they'll never catch the son of a bitch."

"You have to give me something other than her wild suspicions. She's not exactly a reliable witness—" She turned to Sara "—Honestly, I'll settle for a partial license plate at this point."

"We're working on it, Cap. The guy's a ghost," said Adam.

"No, he's not." Sara wiped algae off of her cheek with the heel of her hand. "He's just a man."

"Well, I suggest you find him quick," Eva said. "We're running out of rope to hang ourselves. And for God's sake, shower. You both smell like ass."

John hailed Sara from the driveway, a canvas bag slung over his arm. She lifted her hand in reply as Eva returned to the stable.

"You do smell like ass," Adam whispered, stuffing his hands into his pockets.

"That's sweet," she replied without looking at him. "You too."

John was out of breath by the time he reached them. "I came to bring your things. Are you ok? Why are you all wet?" His gaze fell upon Mr. Buchanan's form beneath the plastic sheeting. "Oh my God."

Sara took him by the elbow and led him away from the corpse, and from Adam. When they were out of earshot, she scraped her fingers through her slimy hair to keep it out of her eyes.

"I owe you an explanation," she said. "I know."

"You don't owe me anything, Sara," he said, and slipped the bag off his shoulder, offering it to her. "I brought you some clothes from Savannah."

She accepted it with a frown, clutching it to her chest.

"You deserve better than how I've treated you, Johnny," she said.

He looked out across the marsh, squinting in the rising sun. "I know you're going through a lot right now, but I feel like I'm losing you." He met her eyes, but Sara looked away. "I am, aren't I?"

"Johnny..." but she didn't know where to start. "I'm not the person you think I am."

"That can't be true." He took her hands in his, turning her to face him. "You're intelligent and passionate and stubborn, and the best reporter I've ever known. That's who you are."

"No, that's who I want you to believe I am. There are things about my family that I can never tell you, things I've seen."

He released her hands, brow furrowing.

"I don't care about any of that. You've just lost your way. Do you remember what I always said when you were stuck on a story, when you'd follow the wrong lead or hit a dead end?"

"The path of error is the path of truth," she answered.

"Hans Reichenbach," he nodded. "You'll find your way to the truth, Sara. You always do."

"You don't understand." She turned away from him, stretching her hands and then closing them tight. Finally, she said, "I hear things sometimes, John. Things no one else can hear."

"What do you mean you hear things? Like voices?"

"I hear them before they happen."

"I don't follow," he said, frowning.

"I knew Mr. Buchanan was going to die. I heard the horse on the pier, heard the head hit the boards. I couldn't do a damn thing about it." Tears formed behind her eyes. "I'm sorry, I don't know how to explain."

John paused, cocking his jaw. After a beat, he asked, "Have you talked to anyone about this?"

"Adam knows."

"That's not what I mean."

Sara looked at him, mouth agape. "You mean a shrink?"

"I don't mean to offend you. It's just, you said it runs in the family—"

"You don't believe me."

"This is a lot to take in. I'm just trying to understand. You've just told me you saw this man's murder before it happened. I'm not sure what you want me to say."

She crossed her arms, Adam's words echoing in her mind.

I believe you. I've always believed you.

"I need to get cleaned up," she said without looking at him. "I'll call you later."

Leaving him without waiting for a reply, Sara trod across the lawn and climbed the porch steps, goosebumps prickling down her arms and back. She never should have tried to explain herself to John. What had she expected from him? He didn't have the faintest idea what this house held within its walls and was too pragmatic to even consider the existence of premonitions.

But, what if he was right? Maybe she *should* talk to someone, seek professional help.

No. Momma had sought help, and they plied her so full of anti-psychotics she could no longer recognize her own daughter.

Sara climbed the stairs to her bedroom, dropped John's bag on her bed, and peeled off her rancid clothes. The pipes banged and groaned when she twisted the shower knobs. Once the mirror clouded over, she let the near-scalding water wash the brine from her hair, her mind gratefully empty, until a familiar tune, played gently on violin, rose above the hum of the bathroom fan.

Mendelssohn's *Lieder.*

Sara closed her eyes and listened, trying to determine if this music came from within or without. It grew louder incrementally until she isolated the sound to the adjoining room. Cassie's room.

She left the shower running and dressed silently, the violin playing all the while. When she opened the door, her gaze fell immediately upon the bed. Mr. Buchanan's disembodied head stared back at her, bulbous eyes regarding her indifferently as his veins leaked fluids on the pillowcase. An old-fashioned smoking pipe, broken at the tip, leaned out of his bloodless mouth, propped against a swollen tongue the color of spoiled beef.

This, despite the horror it drew from Sara's throat, could not coax a scream from her lips. It was Cassie's teddy bear, slumped against Mr. Buchanan's crab-tattered ear, that finally tore it free.

She fled the room, slamming the bathroom door with her hand clamped over her mouth. With the steam-dampened door against her back, Sara shut her eyes tight, resisting the irrational need to rescue her sister's bear. *Lieder* ended, and then began again, emanating from Cassie's old CD player.

Adam knocked on the door a moment later, pulling another startled cry from Sara's lungs.

"Sadie?" he called through the door. "Are you ok? I heard you scream."

"No," she muttered, and he opened the door. Eva walked in behind him. It was just as well. Cassie's room would be a crime scene in a few minutes. Sara opened the bedroom door for them, but let the pair walk around her. She didn't need to see it again.

Amid the swampy scent of putrescence wafting in through the door, Sara recognized another smell. She knew it in her heart of hearts, where the aching lived. Daddy's aftershave. She shook her head, dismissing it as freshly upturned trauma.

"Son of a bitch," Adam said from Cassie's room, his voice low. Eva's radio crackled as she called up the forensic team.

"Is that a pipe?" she asked him.

"Looks like there's something stuffed into it."

Adam came into the bathroom a moment later and handed Sara a tiny scrap of paper.

"You were right," he said. "We were only meant to find the head. I think this is for you."

Sara read it silently.

He summoned up, however, all his resolution, gave his horse half a score of kicks in the ribs and attempted to dash briskly across the bridge.

"Is that from Sleepy Hollow?" he asked, and she could only reply with a nod. "Any idea what part of *A Study in Scarlet* that matches?"

"I can't just pull it out of my ass, Adam," she replied, but even as she said it, she knew with which chapter she'd begin.

"I'm sorry. You're right. Let's just get you out of here. We'll talk about it later."

"I need Cassie's bear," Sara said.

Eva lifted an eyebrow at her. "It's evidence. Sorry."

The stairs groaned, ushering up a team of crime scene technicians who flooded the room like swarming ants. Sara blinked back tears and walked into her own bedroom, Adam following. He shut the door behind them, so they had the illusion of being alone.

"Are you okay?" he asked again.

Sara sat down on her bed and picked up the copy of *A Study in Scarlet* off the nightstand.

"It doesn't even matter," she murmured, opening the book. What difference did it make if there was a connection to Sherlock Holmes? "It's all just a game to him."

"It does matter. Everything matters, *querida*. The more dots you connect, the better we see the big picture."

He sat beside her, waiting without speaking as she thumbed through the pages. She knew this book by heart, every line of dialogue and hidden clue. Her finger landed at last on a passage she had read many times before, but now it was black with rot.

And, flinging himself upon his horse, galloped furiously away, never even looking round, as though afraid that his resolution might fail him.

"I'll tell Eva," Adam said, reading to himself. "Good work."

"She thinks I'm a wackadoo. Am I really a consultant or is that just the name you've given me so I feel useful?"

He regarded her, surprise darkened by sadness gathering in the creases around his eyes. "Why are you talking like this?"

"Because a serial killer just walked up my stairs carrying a man's decapitated head, and then deposited it on my dead sister's pillow. How am I supposed to talk?"

On the other side of the door, Lieder still played, a soundtrack for the crime scene technicians. Adam drew a breath.

"Come stay with me tonight," he said.

"I don't think so."

"Well, you can't stay here, it's—"

"It's a crime scene. I know. There's a whole other floor and a west wing. I'll be fine."

Sara stood, collecting John's bag and carrying it to her dresser.

"Then I'm staying with you," he said to her back. Sara stiffened. "Don't think you're the only one who can be stubborn."

"Technically I can't stop you. It's your house too."

Sara opened the dresser, where she'd stashed the clothing Adam bought for her, then unzipped the bag. Johnny had packed all of her most loved articles, including the sweatpants and sports bras she lived in when no one else was around. Another pang of guilt touched her heart.

"I kind of expected more of a fight," Adam said. "Considering how much you hate being around me."

"I don't hate being around you," she admitted, and then regretted it. It was a confession she hadn't yet made to herself. His crooked smile only exacerbated the blush in her cheeks. "I have some errands to run. Call me when forensics is finished."

●●●

THE COUNTY ASSESSOR'S office, housed in a government building across the street from the cemetery, was as drab and lifeless in the lobby as it was from the perfectly manicured lawn. A single potted palm tree stood in the corner of the space, not a single frond unfurled. A man looked up from the reception area, a map of the county behind his bald head. He peered over at her from behind square glasses.

"Can I help you?" he asked.

"Yes, my name is Sara Wilde. I'm looking for the original plat to 131 Waterford Street."

"Are you the homeowner?"

"I am."

The secretary swiveled in his chair and began furiously typing at the computer. In a moment, he returned to the window with an expression of lament.

"Sorry, I can't help you."

"I'm sorry?"

"You'll need permission from the historical society to remove the plat from the premises. It's technically considered a historical document."

"I don't want to remove it. I just want to look at it."

"Ah. Why didn't you say so?" He stood up and vanished for a moment before appearing through a door to the left. "Come on back. The viewing room is through here."

She followed him to a small room, brightly lit by florescent bulbs. A table, adorned with a magnifying glass, reading lamp, and white cotton gloves, stood in the center of the space. Sara sat down in the only chair and waited for him to return.

Locating a forgotten family graveyard should likely not have been on her list of priorities. Still, she couldn't shake the feeling it was a strand of the web that ensnared her. If nothing more, her family deserved to be buried with their ancestors. With this task looming over her, Sara waited.

The man peered around the door, a faded document held carefully in gloved hands.

"The gloves, please," he said, and Sara slipped into the pair at the table. "Take your time. Let me know if you need anything."

Once he'd gone, Sara gently unfolded the plat and spread it open on the table. It had torn along the folds in some places, but she recognized the house in its original form, sitting alone on an enormous plot of land. A dotted line denoted the marsh on the eastern side of the house, and on the western side, where other homes now lined the street, there were only rice fields. She took note of the outbuildings, the privy, a feed storage building, the stable.

The stable.

It wasn't in the right place. In this plat, the building sat at the back of the house, not the side. Perhaps she was looking at it wrong. Sara traced her finger over the faded lettering, eyes turning to the place it ought to have been.

"Oh my God," she whispered. There, in the exact location of the stable's charred remains, was the family cemetery.

Chapter XIII

"NO WAY." Adam took a long pull from a glass of sweet tea and then shook his head. "Hell no."

Sara clenched her jaw, the kitchen chair hard against her back. Light from the setting sun bled through the windows, pouring itself across the table. She stabbed at the remains of egg fried rice with a chopstick.

"Someone just burned down my stable, which happens to sit right on top of the old family graveyard. You're telling me it's a coincidence?"

"No, I'm telling you you're going to have a hell of a time getting a court order to dig it up. Do you have any idea what I went through already trying to convince Eva to let you come back home?"

"You said forensics was done."

"They are, but this whole thing revolves around you and this house, and I can't seem to separate the two of you. Which means neither can the killer."

"If he wanted to kill me, he'd have done it."

"That's what worries me."

"I don't think this revolves around me at all," she said, shoving the take-out carton away. "Theodora Wilde is at the center of everything, I just can't figure out how."

"So your solution is to dig up her remains?" Adam finished his tea and pushed his chair from the table, busying himself with collecting the empty containers and dumping them in the trashcan beneath the sink.

"If she was at peace there, she wouldn't be trying to communicate with me. She's trying to tell me about her baby. I can't believe she drowned him. I just can't."

"Have you ever heard of *La Llorona*?" he asked.

"The weeping woman," she nodded. "Legend says she drowned her children after discovering her husband's affair. Now she lures other children to their deaths, crying."

"I think you may have yourself the genuine article here."

"Except she had the affair, not her husband. And I'm the only one who can hear her crying."

Adam shook his head, sitting at the window seat with his leg folded beneath him. He nodded to the place beside him, and she joined him. Outside, violet darkness descended upon Wildefell, and Sara felt it deep inside herself. She turned from the window, and he held her gaze, gently. The years between them fell away at last, leaving nothing behind but the breath of the house, and an old familiar sense of longing.

"We're going to have to talk about this," he said after a long moment.

"About what?"

"About whatever the hell this is." He waved his hand between them. "About this house. About your father."

"I don't want to talk about my father." She looked away.

"Well, I do."

"Adam—"

"You asked me what I wanted from you," he continued, taking her hand. "I want forgiveness."

"I can't. You don't understand." She withdrew her hand and held it in her lap.

"Then *help* me understand. You said you never wanted to see me again. That was the last thing you ever said to me."

"I was seventeen."

"So was I."

The air crackled between them. Sara picked at the hem of her tank top, tightness in her throat.

"I need to tell you what happened that night," Adam said, his voice raw, barely a whisper. He did not pause for her consent. "He didn't fall in. I did. I was fucking around, walking on the edge. I slipped."

"Stop."

"He dove in to help me, and he must've hit his head." Adam paused, swallowing hard. "He never came up. I couldn't find him, Sadie. He just disappeared in all that black water—"

"I know," she said. He lifted his eyes to hers, and then his lips parted as he realized the weight of what she had said.

"What?" he asked.

"I *know*. I heard it. Everything. The day before you went out with him."

"Why didn't you—"

"Stop you? Why didn't I stop you? What was I supposed to say? I thought it was a nightmare." She scrubbed her hand down her face.

"No," he said. "Why didn't you just tell me?"

"Because it was easier to blame you. It was easier to hate you all these years than hate myself. Sometimes I still hear you calling his name in the middle of the night, out there on the water. I can't forget it, ever."

The muscles in his jaw clenched tight, and when he closed his eyes, tears slipped between his eyelashes.

"Jesus, Sadie," he whispered.

"Then you shipped off to the Army, left me here to rot in this house. I thought I was in love with you, and you just left."

Adam stilled, but Sara couldn't look at him. She put her head in her hands.

"What did you say?" he asked.

"You *left*."

"You were in love with me?"

"It wasn't just a high school fling for me, okay?" She lifted her head to look at him at last. In his eyes, she saw all of the pain and loss she'd buried. "You were my best friend."

Adam's shoulders fell as he exhaled, and she searched his face for a reply, but he offered none. Her gaze fell involuntarily to his mouth, and the empty place inside her began to ache again, the place that remembered the brush of his lips against her skin.

She didn't stop him when he tucked her hair behind her ear, or held her face in his hands. And when he leaned forward, she could only wait, breathless. Adam hesitated. She did not.

With fifteen years of regret at her back, Sara kissed him.

A gentle sound passed from his mouth to hers, of relief, of breaking. The kiss deepened. Adrenaline poured into her blood, her longing shifting violently into desperate wanting. He raked his hands through her hair and pulled her against him, devouring her.

But then he pushed her away.

"What's wrong?" she whispered, covering her mouth with her fingers. His eyes lingered on her for a moment, and then he stood up.

"Where do I start?"

She'd made a horrible mistake.

"I should go to bed," she said to his back. He wouldn't look at her. Without another word, she fled the room and ran upstairs to her bedroom, locking the door behind her.

●●●

SLEEP TOUCHED HER only briefly that night. Plagued by nightmares, Sara tossed and turned beneath her blankets until the sky turned indigo. Voices reached her through the thick gauze of exhaustion, but she could not determine their origin until wakefulness broke over her with the dawn. Her eyes flew open.

A man's voice, speaking rhythmically. An incantation?

"Adesto itaque, Dux invictissime, populo Dei contra irrumpentes spirituales nequitias, et fac victoriam!"

The Latin continued, punctuated by many voices chanting in time, rising up from the front lawn. She rose, stumbling to the window. Beyond the glass, scores of people gathered before the house, arms outstretched toward heaven, toward her. Their candles flickered in the rising sun.

The doorknob rattled behind her.

"Sadie?" Adam called through the door. "We've got a problem."

Sara opened the door for him, and he walked past her to the window.

"A vigil?" she asked behind him.

"No," Adam whispered. "It's an exorcism."

"A what?"

"Goddammit," he ground out. "It's the church."

Sara remembered the last words Mrs. Wilson had said to her.

It's time this town exorcised its demons.

"You can't be serious," she said, folding her arms across her chest. "This is ridiculous."

"They look pretty serious to me." He closed the curtains and turned to face her; eyes underlined by swatches of dark. "At least they didn't bring their pitchforks."

Sara knotted a hand in her tussled hair. "What the hell am I supposed to do?"

"Come on."

He walked out of the room with violence in his eyes, and Sara followed him down the stairs, and onto the porch. Fifty pairs of eyes regarded them, but the priest continued on with the ritual.

"She's coming!" someone called. They turned toward the pair of them as one entity, and Sara stepped backward. Mrs. Cunningham moved out of the crowd and motioned for Adam to join them.

"Come away from her, young man," she said, her long fingernails catching the bloody rays of sunrise.

"He's spent the night with her," an older woman said, pointing at him. "He's already lost."

"What the fuck is wrong with you?" Adam cried. Gasps and murmurs answered him. Still the priest spoke his Latin to the house. Inside, Sara heard a glass shatter in the kitchen.

"None are lost, friends," Mrs. Cunningham spoke. "For where two or three are gathered together in my name, there am I in the midst of them!"

The crowd shouted, "Amen!"

"What is it you plan to do?" Sara yelled to them, her courage mounting into anger. "Burn me at the stake?"

"That's enough," Adam said under his breath. He walked down the stairs in his bare feet, toward the tangled knot of the priest's congregation. Sara couldn't stop him. Pain bolted from her spine into her eye so violently she fell to her knees.

"Let the Lord into your heart," Mrs. Cunningham implored, but the words crumbled against Sara's ears, rusted iron on stone. "Freely and of your own will."

The hush of the congregation passed away, like the echo of a bat on the dark side of twilight. Fog poured into the windows, blinding her, creeping through the fractures in her consciousness until only footsteps on gravel remained.

A jay shrieked in the distance. The porch boards hardened to stone against Sara's back. She waited as the footfalls fell silent, unable to draw breath into her lungs.

A muffled murmur, the sound of waking, and then a scream.

Please, a voice said. *Please don't.*

Lucy.

"No!" Sara cried, but her legs would not carry her. A hideous, wet sound silenced the screaming, followed by the hollow pound of a hammer. The pain became too great. Sara tore at her hair, trembling, as the priest spoke his prayers over her body.

- - -

LUCY WASN'T ANSWERING her phone. Sara redialed, sliding into the Mustang and slamming the door. Adam's number appeared on her screen, and she answered before it could ring.

"Did you find her?" she asked.

"She's not at home, not at the school. The principal said she didn't show this morning. Did you try Blackbird's?"

"I'm just leaving. They haven't seen her." She turned the key and the engine roared to life. Unsure where to go next, she let it idle in the parking lot. Anger prickled along her arms. She'd woken from her episode with the fearful faces of Mr. and Mrs. Cunningham's flock staring down at her, Adam hurling curses at them as he knelt over the unmoving body. It took a full half hour to disperse the crowd, and even longer for her to gather herself enough to articulate anything but Lucy's name. If they'd only left her the hell alone, they could've been out searching sooner.

"I put a BOLO out," Adam said. "Every cop in this city will be looking for her." He sounded out of breath, as if he'd been running. "She's probably just out shopping or something."

"We both know that's not true."

"I can't believe you this time, Sadie. I can't."

Sara couldn't reply to this. She shifted into drive and backed out of the lot.

"Just keep your phone on you. Go back to Wildefell. If she's in trouble, she knows she can find us both there."

He ended the call with a muttered good-bye, and Sara headed toward home with tears in her eyes.

"Lucy," she whispered. "Where are you?"

Her phone rang. She answered it without looking at the screen.

"Lucy?"

An eternal pause stretched across the line, and then, "It's John."

"Johnny, this is a really bad time." The tears spilled over, the remnants of her hope dwindling away.

"I've been thinking a lot about what you said yesterday," he said. "I want you to know that it meant a lot you trusted me enough to tell me those things."

"I really can't do this with you right now."

"I found someone who I think might be able to help," he continued. "His name is Dr. Walsh. He works at a place called Saving Grace."

Sara squeezed the wheel, clenching her teeth until her jaw ached.

"We're done, John. Don't call me again." She threw the phone onto the passenger seat with a cry that only made it as far as her teeth. The phone rang again. It was Adam.

Sara leaned over and snatched up the phone as she pulled into the drive of Wildefell, dread catching hold of her heart.

"Adam?"

He took a shallow breath, and then said, "I found her."

- - -

THE RUINS OF the Old Sheldon Church, a stone structure that had only partially withstood the fire of two different wars, stood tall with oak branches for a roof. Spanish moss hung down across the windows, phantom curtains against a steady drizzle of cold rain. Cracks cut through the mortar like fault lines, waiting only for a final tap of pressure to send the stones tumbling over one another. Its steadfastness did nothing to calm the horrible pounding in Sara's chest, or the suffocating tightness in her throat.

There's a churchyard on the hillside...

Theodora's voice moved over the lyrics in her mind, over and over, until her gut churned with the rhythm.

Through the hollow threshold, the remains of the altar jutted out of the mossy earth, and on it, a sacrifice.

Adam knelt before the altar, unmoving, his shirt soaked to the skin. He'd turned to stone, it seemed, as if he had glanced upon a gorgon. Sara was not so lucky. No shock dulled her senses or stopped her from staring at the grotesque sight before her. She heard every cricket, every sparrow. Jasmine and honeysuckle perfumed the air, but beneath their sweetness lurked the bitter tang of blood. What she saw, however, paled her other senses to trifles.

Lucy's body draped the altar, tied down with a length of rope. A wooden stake protruded from her chest. Her arm hung limp over the stone, blood and rainwater dripping from her fingers. The life had been drained from her body, let onto the cool earth which drank it up. All Lucy's loveliness had come back to her in death, and she appeared not as a corpse, but as a woman asleep.

"Adam?" Sara whispered, and when she approached, she saw his shoulders tremble.

"She's gone, Sadie," he said, his voice cracking apart as he spoke her name.

Sara touched his shoulder, and he covered her hand with his own.

"Backup's on its way," he said, and sirens wailed in the distance as if he had conjured them. He wiped his eyes with the back of his hand and walked toward the street, leaving Sara alone with the empty vessel of her sister's best friend. She collapsed inside herself, the grief and guilt overpowering her.

"Lucy, Lucy," she whispered, and she watched as if from above as her hand brushed the damp hair from Lucy's face. Tears spilled down her cheeks. Behind her, Eva's voice broke through her grief.

"Get her away from the body," he said.

"Leave her alone," Adam replied. The voices grew nearer, along with a great number of footsteps, but Sara found herself unable to move. Rain fell in sheets, pouring down her nose and pasting her hair to her cheek.

"Lucy," she said again, drowning. Tears smeared all the world's edges. She felt hands on her shoulders, not Adam's, drawing her away. She resisted, bowing over Lucy's body.

"Please," she pleaded.

"You can't touch her," Eva said.

"Let her be," Adam said, but still the woman tried to remove her.

"I'm sorry," Sara wept. She had to tell her. She pulled against Eva, who now had both her arms in her grasp. "This is all my fault. I'm so sorry."

"I said let her be," Adam commanded, grabbing Eva's shoulder. Sara looked back at them.

"Touch me again and I'll have your badge. She's compromising evidence."

"Fuck the evidence," he retorted. "Back off."

"Get your head right, Lieutenant."

No one else touched her. And then, something metallic caught her eye, beneath the slick of blood on Lucy's fingers. A wedding band encircled her ring finger.

"That's wrong," she murmured. "This is wrong." Sara inhaled, resuscitated.

"What is it?" Adam asked, appearing by her side.

"She's wearing a ring."

Eva bent to examine it, still bristling. She snapped on a latex glove and gently lifted Lucy's hand. Tucked into the underside of the ring was a folded slip of blood-soaked paper. She extracted it, unrolled it, and read:

"*There was undoubtedly something, long and black, bending over the half reclining white figure. I called in fright, 'Lucy! Lucy!' and something raised a head, and from where I was I could see a white face and red, gleaming eyes.*"

Chapter XIV

*S*ARA SHIVERED as she climbed the porch steps, skin chaffing against her soaked jeans.

"Coffee?" she asked, though she barely spoke loud enough for Adam to hear.

"Please," he answered behind her. His boots scuffed against the slick wood, but he otherwise made no sound. Sara recognized the all too familiar varnish of shock over his eyes, but because she could scarcely see through her own, she could make no effort to comfort him.

Her fingers trembled as she attempted to unlock the door. She struggled, unable to steady her hands in order to insert the key.

"I'm sorry," she said, pouring herself into the words, hoping his forgiveness for this small matter might pardon her from all the rest.

"Don't." Adam placed his hand over hers. He unlocked the door, the warmth of his body at her back. When Sara let her weight fall into him, desperate for a safe place to rest, he slid his arms around her waist and held her.

Then he brought his lips to the curve of her neck. Rainwater fell from his hair onto her throat. She reached for him, palm brushing across the stubble on his chin.

Sara believed, even as she leaned into this embrace, that none of this was real. In only a moment, she might wake, alone in her apartment in Savannah. When Adam turned her to face him though, this conviction wavered. A brief moment of indecision passed between them, and then the amber in his eyes caught fire.

Adam pushed her hard against the door and kissed her.

He tasted of rain, of the night, and Sara made no effort to resist it. A sound akin to agony rolled deep in his throat as he pressed the length of his body against her. He reached around her and opened the door without ever taking his mouth from hers, and they stumbled into the dark.

Stop.

The door closed behind them, somehow.

Sara slipped her hands beneath his shirt and lifted it over his head, frantic, desperate for him. Her fingers found his belt buckle.

Stop.

She shut her eyes and tried to turn away, but the action occurred only in her mind. Her tank top was on the floor. He slipped his arm around her, the warmth of his skin pouring heat into her blood.

This wasn't real. None of this was real.

"Stop," Adam said for her. With a growl of frustration, he took her by the shoulders and pushed her away.

"Jesus Christ," he breathed, the spell broken. "What the hell was that?"

Sara wrapped her arms around herself, feeling exposed.

"Something we were about to regret."

She found her shirt, and then his, and tossed it to him. Adam clicked on the table lamp, the light casting long shadows across his face and darkening the swell of his lips, red from her kisses. The mourning returned to his eyes, chased away only momentarily by some kind of shared madness.

Sara turned away from him and slid back into the damp tank top, trembling as much with cold as with her bitter longing.

"Sadie," he said behind her. She turned to face him. Her eyes fell to his bare chest, and then to his unbuckled belt, and all the heat in her body flooded into her face. "I'd never regret being with you. I never have."

She could not reply to this. Instead, she walked to the linen closet at the bottom of the stairs and grabbed towels scented with mothballs and lavender fabric softener. Adam's shirt remained balled up in his fist, and Sara wished he'd put it on. She pressed the towel to his chest and then walked quickly through the dining room.

"Do you still want coffee?" she called, drying her hair as she went.

"I want to run from this as much as you do," he said after her. "But I can't be your mistake. It took me too long to get over you."

He followed her into the kitchen, and when she couldn't bring herself to look at him, he took her by the wrist.

"I won't be the other guy, Sadie. You're with someone," he said.

She closed her eyes. "Not anymore."

"What?"

"I ended it with John." Sara pulled away from him and occupied herself with the coffee maker. Adam walked to the window but didn't look out. She felt his eyes on her all the while.

"What happened?"

"He called me while we were looking for Lucy... he wanted to give me the number for a psychiatrist."

"Ouch."

"It was Dr. Walsh."

"Damn."

"He had no way of knowing Dr. Walsh is my mom's psychiatrist. He was just trying to help, but... I couldn't. Maybe I was just looking for a reason."

"Did you love him?" Adam asked.

"Does it matter?"

A pained expression sketched lines around the edges of his eyes. "It matters to me."

"We met at work," she said instead of answering. "He got a job with the paper about two years ago. My editor put us together so I could show him the ropes."

"That wasn't all you showed him, then." He said this matter-of-factly, without judgement.

"It's not any of your business, but no. We haven't— I couldn't—" He held up his hand and waved the rest of her sentence away. "He's a good man. He's kind and supportive, and *normal*."

"Sounds boring." Adam crossed his arms over his chest, dropping both the damp towel and his shirt onto the kitchen table.

He was right. Johnny was an empty, quiet place where she could mold herself into whoever she wanted to be. But he was dreadfully dull, as mild-mannered a reporter since Clark Kent, without the exciting secret identity.

"You haven't answered my question," he said.

"No," Sara answered, surprised to feel angry tears rolling down her cheeks. "I should be so lucky to love a man like him, but I don't. I can't, and I don't know why. There's something broken inside me."

"That's not true," he whispered.

"You know it is." Sara brushed away the tears and lifted her chin, jaw set. "Are you satisfied?"

He shook his head, just once. "God, no."

Adam closed the space between them, took her face in his hands, and kissed her again.

Translating the emotion searing through her as panic, Sara pushed him away and slapped him hard across the cheek. He clenched his jaw and shut his eyes, his face turned from her.

"Adam, I'm—" Her handprint blossomed across his face. "I'm so sorry, I didn't mean—"

He lifted his eyes to hers, the intensity of his gaze singeing the edge of her sentence into nothing but vapor, a breath.

"I deserved that," Adam said with gravel in his voice. Sara pressed her palm to the mark she had left, and he closed his eyes again, leaning into her touch.

"You didn't."

Another breath.

Sara kissed him the way she'd struck him; violently, and without restraint. Adam groaned into her mouth. His hands slipped down her back, landing on her hips, the rhythm of the kiss revealing his intention. The lights of the old house flickered as he lifted her onto the counter, the eaves and rafters echoing with rain. It blew in through the open window at Sara's back and she shivered. Her body hummed, the stroke of a bow across a violin, the heavy throb of a bass guitar.

Adam pulled away.

"Not like this," he breathed against her lips. "Not here."

He lifted her off the counter, and carried her upstairs. Not to her bedroom, but to his, the guest room he'd claimed as his own those many years ago. It was the room she'd crept into when she was seventeen, careful to avoid the creaking boards so her parents wouldn't hear.

When Adam laid her down on the bed, she remembered the night she gave everything to him. She remembered his trembling hands and how they fumbled for the buttons on her nightgown. Tonight, he trembled still, but there was no uncertainty in his eyes. Only want.

The power went out as he peeled off her top for the second time.

"Damn house," she murmured. "I'll get the flashlights." But Adam pressed his mouth to the hollow in her throat.

"Later," he said, and slipped his fingers into her hair. The rain lulled, wind whispering through the reeds as Sara closed her eyes and let his hands recall her memory. No one touched her the way he did, with as much tenderness or urgency. She hadn't let anyone. It was as if she'd been waiting half her life just to feel him again, to let him heal the wounds she could no longer suffer alone.

He lowered himself onto her, the darkness complete but for the silver glow of his watch. Sara traced her fingers down his back and felt him shiver.

When she gave herself to him at last, she did it wholly, instinctively. Damn the consequences. And as he moved with her, his fingers entwined with hers, she felt something rise inside of her, like the pulling of a wave toward the beach. It crested over her, wonderfully, fearfully, and she held her breath when it at last collapsed, taking her up in its current and under. Sounds dulled, her vision blurred and then clarified to crystal. When she reemerged, she saw Adam, his chest heaving, face buried in her shoulder. He emptied himself into her with a muffled cry, and held her there beneath him, spent.

"*Querida*," he said, his voice either breaking her heart or making it whole again. She hummed a foggy question mark, but he didn't answer.

- - -

DAYLIGHT FRACTURED THROUGH warm rain droplets on the guest room windows, dappling tussled sheets. Adam's chest rose and fell beneath Sara's cheek, lulling her into a kind of reverie as he ran his fingers along her arm. The power had yet to be restored, and the morning's heat gathered already in the room.

"Do you remember our first kiss?" he asked.

"Yeah, you bit me."

"I didn't bite you," he replied, laughing. "I just didn't know what to do with my teeth."

She looked up at him, and he gathered her close. "You're better at it now, at least."

"Yeah?" he said against her mouth, and she nodded, but turned away when he moved to kiss her. Adam fell back against the pillows, sobering.

"What's wrong with us?" she asked.

"That's a loaded question."

"We shouldn't have done that," she said.

"Which time?" When she didn't reply, he sighed, and said, "I know."

"It's just... Lucy."

Sara knew first hand grief could manifest in unexpected ways, but *this* had never been one of her coping mechanisms.

Adam smiled sadly, and looked down at her. "Can you imagine the look on her face though if she found out?"

"She'd probably be dancing for joy."

"She and Miss Connie were… they always thought we—"

"Belonged together," she finished, and he pressed his lips into her hair.

"This one time," Adam began after a moment. "Lucy found a kitten in the field behind our house. She brought it home and fed it, put it in one of her doll's sweaters. She just… absorbed it into her life. She was like that. It didn't matter if it was inconvenient or crazy. The thing could've been rabid, but she didn't care. She just rescued it and loved the wild right out of it."

"Is that what she did for you, too?" Sara asked.

"What, love the wild out of me?" She nodded. "Maybe she tried, but I was too angry to notice. When my mom died, it felt like everything good in my life was gone. They sent me away to live with Tia Teresa and Lucy was there waiting for me with a homemade apple pie. She was just… sunshine." His voice wavered as tears slipped down his face, but he didn't try to hide it or wipe them away.

"We have to stop him, Adam," she said.

"We will," he answered immediately. He pressed another kiss into her hair, and rose in search of his jeans. Sara took the opportunity to admire him.

"If you want to get out of bed today, don't look at me like that," he said, turning back to grin at her.

She bit down on her lip, playfully averting her gaze with a laugh. Soon, however, the creeping sensation of suffering crawled back inside her. What right did she have to laugh, to feel any fleeting happiness whatsoever? Adam must have perceived this change, because he ran his hand across the back of his neck and sighed.

"I'm going to check in with Eva, see if they figured out where that wedding ring came from."

"I think I might have some idea," Sara said, and grabbed her phone off the night table, gathering the sheets around her chest. "The quote on the slip of paper was from Dracula."

"I figured." He paused, looking at the floor with his jaw cocked. "Hey, Sadie…"

"Yeah?"

"You heard everything, right?"

She nodded.

"Was it quick?"

Sara swallowed the acid in her throat. "Yes," she lied.

He accepted this without pressing her further, and Sara returned her eyes to her phone. She pulled up an online edition of *A Study in Scarlet*.

"Lucy Ferrier," she muttered.

"Who?"

Adam waited silently as she searched the document, scrolling until her eyes stung. She was going to find the link, for all the good it did. Sherlock Holmes would have solved this by now. He would have considered it analytically, looking at the end result and deducing all of the events preceding it, observing all of the menial details and forming them into a seemingly miraculous conclusion. Sara, despite her efforts, had not mastered this skill. Still, she'd kept a copy of this novel beside her bed as a child, as reverently kept as a family Bible, so it was only a matter of time before the right passage appeared to her.

"Got it," she said, and then read, "*He walked up to the silent white figure, which had once contained the soul of Lucy Ferrier. Stooping over her, he pressed his lips reverently to her cold forehead, and then, snatching up her hand, took the wedding-ring from her finger.*"

"White figure," Adam mused. "That same phrasing was used in Dracula, right?"

"Sure was, why?"

"Makes me think of your *Llorona*."

Adam's phone rang somewhere downstairs, and he left to search for it. Sara untangled herself from the sheets, dressed quickly in her own room, and followed. She found him in the kitchen, phone pressed to his ear.

"Contreras," he answered, meeting her eyes. "Shit, already?"

"What happened?" Sara whispered, but he waved her off.

"Yeah, she's here. I'll tell her."

He ended the call. "Feds are here."

"What? What does that mean?"

"It means we have two hours to gather everything we have on this case."

"And then what?"

"We hand it over."

Chapter XV

RMED WITH the now dog-eared copy of *A Study in Scarlet*, and a pocketful of notecards, Sara parked the Mustang in a visitor's space at the precinct and took a steadying breath. Adam, who had gone before her to collect the case files from the office, came out of the double doors with a visitor badge. He tapped on the passenger window.

"Are you coming?" he asked, voice muffled by the glass.

"No," she answered, but he didn't hear her. Sara opened the door and stepped out onto the asphalt with her heart in her throat.

"You'll do fine," he assured, handing her the badge.

"They're going to have me committed."

"Just leave out the parts that sound crazy," he said with a grin, and led her toward the door with his hand on the small of her back.

"It's *all* crazy."

They walked inside together, and Sara recalled with no small amount of misery the last time she'd been in this building; the smell of burnt coffee, Adam's glassy stare as the officer asked them questions about her father. Where did you last see him? Was alcohol involved? Could he point out where he'd fallen overboard?

It didn't make any difference. They never found his body.

Adam guided her through the security gate and down the hall, the eyes of uniformed officers and plainclothes detectives alike on her back. In a large conference room, Eva sat at the head of an oval table, the other seats filled with only a few people she recognized. Dr. Delacruz, the M.E., and the young man from the forensics team sat together. When she and Adam settled into a pair of chairs beside a woman in a burgundy blazer, Eva rose from her chair.

"Hi, everyone," she said. "We have a couple new faces here, so I'll make some introductions. Ms. Sara Wilde, consulting with Lt. Contreras," she motioned toward her, and Sara lifted her hand in an awkward greeting. "And Special Agent Charlotte Grant, from the Behavioral Analysis Unit at the FBI."

The woman in the blazer stood up, and despite her relatively petite form, her posture revealed that she was not to be trifled with. Auburn hair framed a kind face, and freckles dotted a delicate nose, but her eyes sparked with ruthless intelligence. No one moved.

"Thank you, Captain," she said, her voice warm. She addressed the group, "I know I don't have any fans here, so before I launch into this, I want you each to know I have no intention of taking anything from you. I'm here to help solve this case, and to offer whatever resources I can. You're all obviously very capable. This bastard is just slippery."

Sara saw Adam lift his eyebrows in surprise. Similar expressions volleyed around the table, until Agent Grant smiled.

"Now that I have that out of the way, I've put together a preliminary profile based on the details Captain Mauk shared with me prior to my arrival. I've made myself as familiar with this case as possible off site, but I'll need you all to stop me if you hear anything that doesn't sound right."

She paused, waiting for a response. When no one moved, she opened a folder and removed a black and white image. Sara recognized it as a still from Benjamin Herman's security tapes.

"Okay, then. Here we go," Grant began, passing the photo to Sara, who handed it to Adam without looking at it. "CCTV footage obtained from one of the scenes shows a white male of above average height, perhaps with a leg injury. No facial features were visible. Based on the information I've received, it's clear our perp has knowledge of literature, specifically gothic, so we're likely looking for a scholar of some kind. Maybe a professor, or a writer."

She paused briefly to consult her files, and went on. "The circumstances of each killing are manipulated to coincide with the stories. The time required for these plans means he probably has a 9-5 job, one that leaves evenings free, or he's perhaps taken a leave of absence. This is probably someone who is active in the community, someone who is aware of the local population. He'll go to dinner parties and HOA meetings. He may even hold a position of authority. These are not crimes of passion, or of revenge. They're a message. But, with no true identifiable pattern in the timeline, location, or victimology—"

"Agent Grant," Sara interjected. Grant lifted her chin toward her, waiting. "I don't think it's true there's no pattern in victimology. That would imply the murders are random, and they are absolutely not."

Grant gave a little bow of the head. "Perhaps you can explain?"

"First, I believe there is a pattern in the location."

"Wouldn't that be you?" Eva piped in. Sara pinched her lips together.

"Yes," she answered. "Yes, the murders seem to be centered around the vicinity of my family estate."

Adam added, "They were all committed within a five mile radius of the property, and often, on the property."

"The victims are also chosen specifically for their likeness to the characters in the literature," Sara said.

Agent Grant nodded, thumbing through the files. "Why don't we segue to the literary connections. Ms. Wilde, could you help us with that?"

"Yes, of course," she replied, and Grant sat down. Where would she begin? She couldn't mention Theodora Wilde, because aside from her own strong conviction, she had no evidence to indicate her ancestor was in any way connected to the terror befalling this town. She took a breath, and removed the copy of *A Study in Scarlet* from her back pocket.

"I'll start at the beginning," she said at last. "My sister, Cassandra, and grandmother, Constance Wilde were the first victims, as you know." With a carefully contrived clinical tone, she described the scene of the crime, and its relation to *Murders in The Rue Morgue*.

"And you discovered the bodies?" Agent Grant asked, once she had read Poe's passage.

"Yes."

"You were in Savannah that night, and you drove down after your sister didn't reply to your messages." This was not a question, and so Sara didn't reply. Agent Grant continued after consulting her notes. "The next murder, Elisabetta Amello. You made a connection to *Rappaccini's Daughter*?"

"Correct. We found an ivory pill box in her mouth, which contained a single pill. The M.E. can confirm the cause of death was poisoning." Sara turned to Dr. Delacruz, who nodded.

"There were copious amounts of Bella donna, in tablet form, forced down her throat," Delacruz said. "That's the confirmed cause of death."

"However, the pill in the box was 'entirely harmless,'" Sara said, and then held up the book. "This is a reference to the Sherlock Holmes story, *A Study in Scarlet*. I believe each of the murders is connected not only to gothic literature, but also to this story. Adam, could you read the passage on this page?" She handed him the book, the quote marked with a Post-It tab.

He read, "*Of the two pills in the box, one was of the most deadly poison, and the other was entirely harmless.*"

"Inside the pill box," Sara continued, "was a note that read, '*She herself had become the deadliest poison in existence. Poison was her element in life.*' This is a passage from Hawthorn's *Rappaccini's Daughter*."

She lifted her eyes from her notecards to find Agent Grant leaning toward her with her fingers tented on the table, listening intently. This gave her courage.

"The next murder was modeled after *The Picture of Dorian Gray*."

Adam, taking his cue, read, *"There's the scarlet thread of murder running through the colorless skein of life."*

"And from Dorian Gray," Sara went on. *"He was trying to gather up the scarlet threads of life, and weave them into a pattern to find his way through the sanguine labyrinth of passion through which he was wandering."*

Agent Grant interjected, "That brings us to John Buchanan, then. The body was found headless on your property, is that correct?"

Sara answered, "He was chased down by one of my horses and then beheaded. We found his body in the marsh."

"Was there evidence to indicate he was chased?" an officer asked.

"Yes," the M.E. answered, lifting her hand to indicate the question was hers. "The autopsy confirmed cause of death was actually a heart attack. It appears his heart gave out before he was beheaded."

Sara went on. "We found a note inside a broken smoking pipe, which is a passage from *The Legend of Sleepy Hollow* by Washington Irving. I'm sure you all know the significance of the pipe if you've ever seen any Sherlock Holmes movie, but a *broken* pitch pipe, specifically, was also found among the effects of Ichabod Crane in *Sleepy Hollow*."

Adam flipped to the next tab in the book, and read, *"And, flinging himself upon his horse, galloped furiously away, never even looking round, as though afraid that his resolution might fail him."*

"And in Sleepy Hollow," Sara said, "'*He summoned up, however, all his resolution, gave his horse half a score of kicks in the ribs and attempted to dash briskly across the bridge.*'"

Agent Grant shook her head and then folded her arms over her files, as if everything contained therein was no use to her. "You've done a hell of a job putting all of this together," she said, motioning to them both.

Unsure how to reply to this compliment, Sara continued on, eager to be through.

"Lucy Contreras is the latest victim," she said, and Adam clenched his jaw. "It was staged to reflect Dracula. The passage found at the scene is as follows: '*There was undoubtedly something, long and black, bending over the half reclining white figure. I called in fright, 'Lucy! Lucy!' and something raised a head, and from where I was I could see a white face and red, gleaming eyes.*'"

When she'd finished, Adam said, "Sara paired this one also with Sherlock Holmes." He peeled off the last Post-It tab, and read, "'*He walked up to the silent white figure, which had once contained the soul of Lucy Ferrier. Stooping over her, he pressed his lips reverently to her cold forehead, and then, snatching up her hand, took the wedding-ring from her finger.*'"

"The murder weapon was an iron stake?" Agent Grant asked, seeming to accept the evidence before her as valid. No one called Sara crazy or made under-breath references to her mother. Despite the morsel of pride budding in her chest, her stomach still roiled.

Delacruz answered Grant's question, "From a preliminary investigation, yes, but I can confirm once I've finished the autopsy. Her blood was drained through a small cut in her wrist, so I'll need to determine which came first."

"And this woman was a close friend of yours?" Grant asked Sara. She could only nod.

"She's my cousin," Adam added.

"Were the other victims known to either of you in any way?"

"The first two were my grandmother and sister, and Mr. Buchanan has been our stable hand for thirty years. I didn't know the others." After a pause, still unsure if she'd gotten her point across, she added, "Agent Grant, not only is the killer repeating the death scenes in gothic literature, he's directly linking them to the only detective worthy of solving them."

"Sherlock Holmes," Adam finished. "He's writing a new Holmes story."

"Exactly."

Grant nodded slowly, lips pinched downward. "And you're sure the killer is working only with *A Study in Scarlet*?"

"Fairly," she answered. "So far."

Exhausted, Sara dropped back down into her chair.

"Can we use that to determine which story comes next?" Eva asked, and Sara turned to her, surprised.

"That's likely a question only Ms. Wilde can answer," Agent Grant said.

"There are hundreds of gothic novels," Sara replied. "It would take months to cross reference them all."

"We've already determined you and Wildefell are at the center of all this," Adam said, "It stands to reason he would only select novels you know well, right?"

"In my mind's attic," Sara mused to herself.

Upon Adam's curious glance, Agent Grant clarified. "Sherlock Holmes believes the mind is not limitless. A person can only fit a certain number of facts into it. Ergo, the killer can only select from books Ms. Wilde already knows."

Sara lifted her brow with a smile, glad to have found a kindred spirit among the horror.

"I did my undergrad in English literature," she explained.

"What about all of the other Sherlock stories?" Eva asked. "Why isn't the killer pulling from those?"

"Sherlock Holmes isn't technically a Gothic character," Sara answered. "Doyle wrote during the Enlightenment period, during the Scientific Revolution."

Adam asked, "Then, he's trying to enlighten us?"

Agent Grant shook her head. "It's a weak motive, but we'll have to run with it until we learn more. Let's adjourn for now. We'll meet again in a couple of days. Sooner if our perp continues to escalate. I'm looking forward to working with you all."

The members of their grim team rose and filed out the door, but Agent Grant stopped Sara with a hand on her arm.

"Can you hang back for me?"

Feeling a little like she'd been asked to the principal's office, Sara waited until the others had gone. Grant closed the door and sent her a tight smile.

"Take a seat," she said, and Sara returned to her chair. The agent sat down again at the head of the table and tapped her fingers on the stack of files.

"Did you have more questions?" Sara asked.

She frowned, and then asked, "You and Lieutenant Contreras are involved?"

"I don't know how to answer that."

"You don't have to. Listen, can I call you Sara?"

"Sure."

"I have a lot of questions. Questions I think frankly should've been asked from the beginning."

"I don't know what you mean."

"Lieutenant Contreras and your sister, Cassandra, were also involved at one time, weren't they?"

Sara, becoming increasingly disturbed by this line of questioning, narrowed her eyes. "That's right."

"And she left her half of the Wildefell estate to him."

"She did. Agent Grant, I'm not sure what you're getting at."

"I'll be honest with you, Sara. The Bureau already has a suspect."

Sara straightened, waiting. Then it came, as blinding as a flashbulb.

"Adam Contreras is our number one person of interest."

She sat, stunned, and after a moment managed, "That's ridiculous."

"He has motive, opportunity, and means." The agent counted these items off on her fingers as casually as a grocery list. "He hasn't followed protocol with the investigation, and we believe his reason for including you in it is some kind of fantasy fulfillment for him."

The mordant laugh building inside Sara died in her throat.

"I'm sure he has an alibi," she said.

"Not one we can verify."

"Why him and not me?"

"Because we've confirmed your presence in Savannah during the first murders." When Sara couldn't reply, she added, "We'll be keeping a close eye on him, and on you. If you see anything, I expect you to let me know."

Sara accepted the proffered business card, still too flabbergasted to be angry.

"You're asking me to spy on him?" she asked.

"Not at all. I'm asking you to remain vigilant, as you have been. I appreciate the time and effort you've devoted already to this case." Agent Grant rose with a professional smile, and left the room. Sara stared at the table, unable to move.

So aside from me, who else has been in your life long enough to know how important those two things are to you?

Adam's words came to her mind. They'd darkened somehow, the spore of doubt encrusting them until they became something else altogether.

"Are you all right?" Adam said, peeking his head through the door. "What did she say?"

Sara's lips parted so she might tell him the agent's outrageous theory, but something else came out of her mouth.

"Nothing. It's not important."

Chapter XVI

ℋER PHONE was ringing. Again.

It vibrated in her back pocket, but she ignored it, focusing instead on the sound of her pumps on the sidewalk. John had included them in the bag, and despite her falling out with him, she was grateful to walk again in the shoes she'd worn as a successful reporter, when she was free.

She could do it again. She could run, build a new life. She'd done it before.

The door to the Beaufort County Times was heavy. It resisted her.

Once inside, Sara expected nostalgia. She had prepared herself for a flood of old memories, for the smell of the newspaper to launch her into grief or reverie, but the lobby had been so heavily renovated she didn't recognize it at all. Only its bones remained. The pillar in the center of the room, wallpapered with articles and the faces of missing persons, brought forth a few vague memories, but none she could land on. Since everything had been digitized, the only smell she noted was a lingering perfume and a microwaved lunch.

Reporters sat at desks laid out in rows, and to the right, an elderly secretary answered phones. Sara approached her and waited. She felt no sense of belonging, no pride that this all now belonged to her. Instead, a heavy sinking sensation pulled at her chest. What was Grammy expecting her to do with it? She sure as hell couldn't run it.

"Hi there," the secretary said, smiling warmly after hanging up the phone. She tucked a pen into a poof of white hair, and folded her arms across the desk. "What can I do for you?"

"My name's Sara Wilde," she said. The woman's smile fell. "I'd like to look at your archives."

"We're working on digitizing everything. You can probably find what you're looking for on our website," she answered with frost in her voice.

"I'm looking for articles from the late 1800s. Are those available?"

"That far back?" She lifted her thin eyebrows, rose from the desk, and waved Sara into a narrow hallway. Flickering fluorescent lights dotted the path. "We've only made it as far as 1952. It's a work in progress. You'll have to look at the microfilm. I'm Aggie, by the way," she said over her shoulder. Sara paused.

"Aggie Barlow?"

"The one and only." The woman turned with a tight smile, and shook her hand. "Our secretary is on maternity leave." She sobered even further, the wrinkles on her neck smoothing slightly as she lifted her chin. "I haven't told them yet, you know."

It took Sara only a moment to understand her meaning.

"You know me, then."

With a nod, she answered, "Mr. Delaney called me as a courtesy. I just want you know this paper is everything to me. I met my husband here. It's my home."

"I know it is. I don't have any interest in taking it from you."

"Well, dear, it's a little late for that. It's already yours." She turned around and continued walking before Sara could offer any more assurances. "Archives are this way."

Once Sara was settled in a musty room, an ancient computer before her, Aggie Barlow shuffled back down the hall, mumbling what sounded like a prayer.

Sara did not have room in her heart for the guilt swelling inside it. She had fully intended to sell this paper to the first person who would take it off her hands, but now, she felt compelled to maintain it as Grammy had, as the woman behind the curtain. She shook her head, clearing these thoughts in order to focus on what brought her here.

Theodora Wilde, and her baby.

Sara consulted her phone, where she had recorded the dates of Clementine's letters, and the letter from Theodora's lover. She also saw Adam had called three times, but she couldn't bring herself to speak with him, not until she could figure out how she felt about Agent Grant's accusations.

As she scrolled through the microfilm in search of the recorded dates, her mind conjured Adam like a specter. She saw him on the pier the morning after she discovered Cassie and Grammy's bodies, felt all of the anger and the pain anew. She watched him swim through the rank water of the marsh to come to her aid. And she witnessed him collapse under the weight of Lucy's death. There, surely, was evidence enough he could not be capable of these horrible things. His pain had been genuine. Hadn't it?

He'd been with her all night and all morning that day, until they discovered Lucy's body.

Until *he* discovered her body. Alone. The pit in Sara's stomach hardened to granite.

A headline on the screen caught her attention, pulling her gratefully away from these encroaching thoughts. The article was from 1893, written by a Grace Holmwood.

ABANDONED IN THE COLD!
Newborn Girl Left on Steps of Lochcrest Orphanage

BEAUFORT, March 17
   This Tuesday last, Sister Agnes Clairmont discovered the half-dead body of an infant on the steps of her orphanage. The baby, swaddled in blankets but abandoned on the stone

without even a pillow for its head, rose the Sister from her slumber with wretched cries.

Grave fears for its welfare have been allayed by Dr. Grimson, of the Beaufort Hospital, who reports that the child is in good health. No progress has been made on the discovery of its parents, and the child is currently a ward of the kind sisters at Lochcrest. May the Lord continue to keep the innocent children under His mighty wing.

This investigation is ongoing.

Sara leaned back in her chair with her fist to her lips. She checked the dates on her phone. The obituary of Theodora and the unnamed child appeared just two days before this article. She scanned the microfilm, discovering both the obituary, and the article on Theodora's death in the same edition of the evening paper.

"Did you save her?" Sara whispered. If so, only Theodora's body would be buried in the family cemetery. The absence of the child's remains would prove her theory. She dialed Adam.

"Sadie? Are you okay?" he answered on the first ring.

"I'm fine, I was wondering if you've made any progress with that court order?"

"To dig up the cemetery? No, but there's no one stopping you from tearing down the stable and coming upon it accidentally."

"You make a hell of a point," she replied, eyebrows lifted.

"Listen, I've been trying to get ahold of you. Where are you?"

"I'm at the paper. I found something interesting."

"Okay... I'll meet you at the house?"

"No," she said more insistently than she meant to. "No, I uh— I'm going to grab some dinner. Just let me know if you hear anything back, okay?"

"Sadie, if this is about last night..."

When she didn't reply, he said, "Okay. Well, forensics is done with the wedding ring, and they found an engraving inside. I wanted to run it by you, see if it means anything."

"Go ahead."

"It says, 'Grander than the sea—1979.'"

Sara's blood turned to icy sludge, polluted by grief as much as anger. *Our love is grander than the Sea.*

It was Momma and Daddy's motto. Her parents spoke it to one another every time Daddy went out on his boat, or left to cover a big story.

"Does it mean anything to you?" Adam said.

"It's my mother's ring," she answered.

"What? How?"

"You heard them say that phrase a hundred times." This partially formed accusation left her lips in a hurry.

"It sounded familiar," he said. "That's why I called. What are you getting at?"

Sara's eye caught another headline of interest.

BEAUFORT COUNTY TIMES
SOLD TO BENNETT WILDE!

"Can I call you back?" she asked.

A pause, and then, "Sure. Hey, you haven't seen my badge at the house, have you?"

"No. Did you lose it?"

"Apparently."

He bid her an awkward goodbye, but she was already in another era, one where Theodora Wilde's recently widowed husband had sought revenge.

BEAUFORT, April 17

An anonymous source reports that the recently widowed Bennett Wilde has threatened Mr. Mauk into selling this paper. This has not yet been substantiated, but it is the opinion of this writer that Wilde is a desperate man with nothing more to lose, which makes him a most dangerous villain indeed. Our respectable Mr. Mauk surely had no choice but to bend to the will of a man more powerful and cruel than he. I am, no doubt, destined shortly to seek employment elsewhere and I ought to speak frankly, ought I not?

Rumors around town speak of an affair, between Theodora Wilde and another man here in this very town. There have been whispers that the child did not belong to Bennett at all, but to him. Could this be the cause of Theodora's steady decline into lunacy, and Bennett's mad desire to ruin our honorable employer?

We can do little but speculate and mourn the loss of an innocent babe, and, for those who worked under the employ of Mr. Mauk, our livelihoods.

Sara stopped reading, her fingers over her mouth. This article had been written only two weeks after Theodora's suicide.

"That's why you bought the paper," she said. "To ruin Thea's lover?"

She felt his shame and hatred inside herself as she stared at the microfiche. He must have allowed the murder/suicide suspicion to stand, perhaps even furthered it, in an effort to preserve the family name. Somehow he had discovered the affair, and the child it had wrought, and took his revenge with the only weapon he had: his money. But, what had happened to the child?

Sara's back straightened, bracing her against a singular suspicion. The idea collapsed upon her like a derelict building.

"Holy hell," she murmured, rising from the chair so quickly it fell backward and crashed on the floor.

●●●

GRAMMY'S ELEGANT HANDWRITING filled each page of the address book in Sara's hands. She thumbed through it, fingers tracing the names of friends long forgotten.

"It has to be here," she said, flipping the pages back and forth, unable to recall the name of the family contractor after so many years. Finally, a set of worn business cards dropped from the book onto the kitchen table, as if tossed there by a guiding spirit. The third name in the stack was Peter Wallace, owner of Wallace Contracting. She didn't even know if he was still alive, let alone running his business, but she needed someone she could trust to be discrete. She dialed the number.

"Wallace and Family," a woman answered.

"Hi, my name is Sara Wilde. I'm looking for Peter."

A pause over the line revealed what she suspected. "He, um—he passed away last year. I'm his daughter, Elaine. I run things now."

"I'm sorry to hear that, Elaine."

"Thank you. What can I do for you? Your name sounds familiar."

"Your father was our contractor for many years. I'm looking for someone to take up a concrete foundation. There was a fire in my stable and I want to tear it down."

"Oh," she answered. Even before the woman's sharp inhalation, Sara felt the jolt of realization across the line. "Oh my God, I'm sorry I only just now realized who you were."

Sara interrupted her before she could launch into condolences.

"I'm just trying to move on from it all. Can you help me?"

"Of course. Yes, I can send someone out to do an estimate tomorrow."

"I don't need an estimate. I'd actually like it to be done today."

"Today?" she repeated, stammering. "We're booked solid through September."

She did not have time for this. Blood must out.

"I'll pay double the rate, plus a thousand dollar bonus if it's hauled away before nightfall."

"That's—this is—" Elaine exhaled, and Sara heard the clicking of a keyboard. "Well, I'm sure I could find a cancellation."

"Perfect."

Sara rattled off the address with a nagging scummy feeling in her chest. She'd never used her family's money so flagrantly. In fact, she'd scarcely used it at all. It was blood money, and although she had no physical evidence of this fact, she could think of no other logical reason for the family to have been so monstrously cursed. She wondered as she ended the call if succumbing to the use of it would add her name to the long list of Wildes who'd met an untimely end.

As the house folded quietly around her, its dark eaves and shuttered windows listened as she sat in the sweltering stillness. Last night's storm sent a tree crashing onto a nearby transformer, and the power company had yet to restore power to the neighborhood. In the absence of air conditioning, the scent of blood and bleach rose up out of the swelling floorboards. Although nearly unbearable, Sara had nowhere else to go. She removed the copy of *A Study in Scarlet* from her bag, and fanned the pages.

Theodora hadn't appeared to her in days.

Perhaps all her spirit needed was someone to say her name, someone to substantiate the fact she had existed at all. But, even after arriving at this acceptable conclusion, Sara felt alone, unsettled.

She thumbed through the pages again, listlessly, the images of the tale long gone, replaced by patterns in sentence structure until it remained nothing more than syntax. An unsolvable math problem. Inside her heart, where she'd always held the story close, it began to curl into itself like an oak leaf in late September. The more she read, the more it died.

Sara closed the book and pushed it across the table, toward the chair Cassie had occupied in life, and the chair Adam occupied only a short while ago. She did not expect to feel his absence so aggressively. It was as if the house, which so often made its presence known by the slamming of cabinets or the flickering of lights, mourned his loss in devastated silence.

Was he indeed lost? Had he done these things Agent Grant insinuated?

He has motive, means, and opportunity.

Sara mulled over this, chewing her lip until it was raw. Motive.

She had lied to him for years, let him believe she blamed him for her father's death. Let him believe she hated him. Had he spent the last fifteen years devoting himself to revenge?

Sara froze in the chair, her fingers splayed on the table.

The words, "Oh my God," cracked through the ice in her blood, and she snatched up the book.

"'Again, however, his active spirit shook off the lethargy which springs from despair,'" she read aloud, no one listening but the spirits of her long dead ancestors. "'If there was nothing else left to him, he could at least devote his life to revenge.'"

Another moment dripped away. Her heart thundered in her ears. "Frankenstein."

A knock sounded at the door. Upstairs, the house answered with a knock of its own, as if angry to have been awoken. She rose, her eyes on the staircase. No spirits looked down upon her from the rails, but she felt them all the same.

Adam smiled tightly at her when she opened the door. She was about to tell him he didn't have to knock, but his haggard appearance gave her pause. His eyes were so bloodshot it looked like he'd spent the last two days on some kind of bender, and his hair hadn't seen a comb in just as long.

His Carhart jacket, threadbare at the elbows and stained with what appeared to be motor oil, hid most of a 9mm handgun holstered on his hip. She'd never seen him wear a weapon, even at the crime scenes. Under his arm, he held a folded newspaper. Sara opened her mouth to tell him of the connection she'd made to Mary Shelley's famous tale, but ultimately held her tongue. Maybe it would be best to tell Grant instead.

"You look like hell," she said instead.

"My cousin was murdered by a serial killer and the woman I just slept with is ghosting me. So, I'm doing great, thank you for asking."

Sara pinched her lips together, but had neither time nor space in her heart for guilt. She drew a steadying breath, and then asked the question she'd been holding inside.

"Did you take my mother's ring?"

"What? No, it's in evidence."

"I mean when you went to visit her. When you told her about Cas and Grammy. Did you take her ring?"

Adam's eyes widened.

"I already told you I hadn't been to see her," he replied, lips moving slowly over the words, an expression of suspicion tilted his head to the side. "Is that in question again?"

"Did you take it, or not?"

"Of course I didn't," he replied. "What is it you're really asking me, Sadie?"

Sara could not elaborate. Grant's theory bored such a deep cavity into her heart that speaking it aloud would gut her. Adam only cocked his jaw, nodding. Then he handed her the newspaper.

"I came over to show you this. I thought it'd be better to do it in person."

As Sara unfolded the newspaper, Adam turned and walked quickly down the porch steps with his hands in his pockets. She saw the front page headline before she could call him back.

POLICE HIRE PSYCHIC TO TRACK SERIAL KILLER
BEAUFORT, SC – August 30
By John Warren

Local police have brought on self-proclaimed psychic, Sara Wilde, to help solve a string of murders plaguing the quaint seaside town of Beaufort, SC. In an interview, she claimed she "heard things before they happened" and intimated that she often witnessed spirits in her childhood home, Wildefell Manor. Coincidentally, the manor housed the murderer's first victims, her grandmother and sister, and Wilde has since attempted to assist the police in subsequent killings. Unfortunately, however, she has to date been unable to offer any actual assistance to the BPD in either locating the killer or preventing the presumably foretold murders from occurring.

Already limited police resources have residents concerned at this seemingly flagrant waste of funds. Additional investigation into Wilde's past revealed two worrying details, the first being a family history of mental illness (her mother, for example, is institutionalized), and a romantic relationship with the lead detective on the case, Adam Contreras.

Thankfully, Agent Charlotte Grant of the FBI has now taken over the case, so locals might yet have a hope of walking the streets of their dear town in peace. For now, the killer is still at large. Who will his next victim be? And will Sara Wilde, the town pariah, be able to stop him? This investigation is ongoing. Updates will be reported as available.

Sara crushed the paper in her fists, the ink of this betrayal darkening her fingers as much as her heart. Heat burned in her cheeks as she dialed her editor. He answered on the fifth ring, his voice gentler than usual.

"I was wondering when you'd call," he said.

"How could you print this bullshit?" she demanded, angry at herself for the knot in her throat.

"Whatever happened between you two messed him up bad, honey. He went over my head and sent it to the owner."

"It's yellow."

"I know." After a pause, he added, "You've got to get me that story, kid. Let me run it, clear your name."

"I'm trying. I've linked the murders to my heritage piece—"

"You what?" he interrupted.

"They're connected. Whatever happened to my ancestor and her child is directly related to these murders, I know it is. I just have to prove it."

The editor sighed, and then said, "I can get you a few more days, but you've been discredited. My word you're not crazy will only get you so far."

✝ H.B. Diaz

Sara leaned against the wall and looked up at the vaulted ceiling as the open front door creaked on its hinge. "I'm used to being the pariah, Chief. This doesn't change anything."

Chapter XVII

*N*IGHT DESCENDED like a cloak over Wildefell Manor, spewing shadows into the raw scar of earth once cradling the stable. True to their word, Wallace Contracting had completed the work before dusk, and accepted the extra zeroes on Sara's check without complaint. Now, Sara stood at the hole's edge, her boots caked with crumbling mud. The handle of the shovel cooled her palm as she surveyed the work yet to be done, her father's propane lantern casting ghostly light into the gaping maw.

The final resting place of Theodora Wilde, and the supposed body of her infant child, stood just beneath her feet. She drove the spade into the soil. Again. Again. She dug until the skin pulled away from her palms and sweat poured into her eyes. A barn owl, her only witness, stood guard near the pier, hooting into the darkness.

At last, when the moon shone high above her, the shovel struck stone.

A headstone.

Dropping onto her knees, she cleared away the caked earth, but the years of neglect had worked their evil. Only the date was legible. 1824. She heaved it up over the edge and went back to work.

Two more tombstones met her shovel, and while she couldn't read the inscriptions, their presence proved without doubt she had indeed located the family plot. This drove her on, until at last, her shovel cracked through rotted wood, and struck bone.

"Sara? The hell are you doing out here?"

Sara gasped, her shovel dropping with a thud onto the earth. Adam peered over the edge of the ever growing hole. She hadn't heard him approach.

"I could ask you the same," she answered, wiping the back of her hand across her forehead.

"I just came to get my toothbrush," he said. "I guess I should've worn my grave-digging boots."

Sara rolled her eyes, then dropped to her knees and cleared the earth away with her hands.

"I think I found something," she said. He didn't reply, just shook out of his jacket with a sigh and slid down into the hole. Sara extracted the remains of a human hand, strung together with crackling webs of sinew. Golden rings hung loose on the desiccated bones, falling to the cold ground and glinting in the frail light.

"Stop," Adam said. "Let me call a forensic anthropologist. There's a procedure for these kinds of things."

"What's this?" Sara said, ignoring him. She swept soil from what first appeared to be another headstone. She unearthed it. It wasn't a headstone at all, but a small marble casket. A coffin made for an infant.

"Can you hold the light down here?" she asked, and he rose, collected the lantern, and held it to the stone.

Clementine Wilde

Of this mortal coil but a short while

Dormiens cum angelis

"It's her," Sara whispered, as if she might wake her. "It's Theodora's baby." She ran her fingers over the name. Adam crossed himself.

"What are you doing?" he asked as she clutched the lid. "You can't open it."

"I need to know."

"You're desecrating a grave."

"What is it you think I've been doing all night?" Without waiting for him to stop her, she lifted the heavy lid. Earth crumbled onto the silk inside.

The coffin was empty.

"Adam," she whispered. The lamplight wavered as he knelt down beside her, the empty casket between them. He did not reply. She continued, "If Clementine survived, and had children of her own…"

"There would be another lineage," he finished, knowing her mind.

"Another heir. And another suspect."

All at once, the scent of death overwhelmed her. She turned her face from the casket, covering her nose with her arm. "I need to get out of here. I can't take the smell."

"What smell? There's no body."

The acrid scent of ammonia swallowed up the putrescence, and Sara gagged, stumbling backward. A saw screamed to life somewhere far away as the pain cut into her eye.

Then a woman screamed, too.

"No, no," she muttered, pressing her palms to her eyes. She didn't recognize her voice. Each time she spoke the word, the other woman's voice sounded in her ears. She felt Adam's hand grasp tight around her arm, but then there was nothing but the black of night and the guttural, hideous cries of a stranger.

The saw whined at a higher frequency than a chainsaw. It made contact with something wet, and then the frequency lowered.

A bone saw.

The screaming intensified. The saw bored through marrow. Sara smelled it, the heavy dust of the woman's flesh. She called out for her mother, and then fell quiet.

A drawer slid open, releasing cold air soured by bleach.

Sara felt the earth beneath her knees. She drove her fingers into the soil, grasping for reality so she might escape this torturous death.

"Sadie!" Adam called from far away. She heard her own voice again, screaming. Her ears throbbed with the sound of it, her throat burning.

"The M.E.," she said, gasping. "Call the morgue."

Adam wrapped his arms around her, pulling her to her feet. She clung to him, breathing him in as he slipped his cell phone out of his back pocket. Still holding her, he dialed Dr. Delacruz and waited. A man's voice answered. He put the call on speaker.

"This is Lt. Contreras. I need to speak to Karla. Who is this?" Adam asked, stiffening.

The man at the other end of the line exhaled a trembling breath. "I'm Jimmy, one of her techs. Oh my God. You, uh... you better get down here." Sara heard a gagging sound, and then the man vomited.

"We're too late," she muttered. "How are we too late?" Her eyes fell to Adam's chest, focusing on a splattering of reddish stains beneath his collar. She pushed away from him.

"Is that blood?" she demanded, stumbling away, the bones of her ancestors beneath her. Adam looked down at his shirt.

"Looks like."

Sara's fingers fell upon the shovel, and she grasped it instinctively.

"Where were you?" she asked. "What have you done?"

"Sadie," he began, his eyes falling to the shovel. He held out his hand to stay hers. "I must've cut myself shaving. I've been here with you. You just heard another murder, right?"

She could only nod.

"It's not possible for me to be here, and at the morgue. I don't know what you heard, but you always hear it before or during the murder. Never after."

"Maybe I didn't want to see this time."

"Think about what you're saying. You just discovered there might be another heir to the Wildefell fortune. My family came here in the 70's. What you're saying isn't logically possible."

"Agent Grant disagrees," she retorted.

"I already own half the house. What else could I hope to gain?"

"Adam, tell me you didn't do these things," Sara cried, tears burning down her cheeks. When he met her eyes, the depth of his devastation crushed her like a stone.

"If I have to tell you that," he whispered, "we don't have anything left to say."

He climbed out of the grave, and then turned back to look down at her.

"You'll be wanted at the morgue."

- - -

"I HOPE YOU haven't eaten anything," the forensic technician said. A set of blue scrubs hung limply on his thin frame, his face a shade too pale.

Sara pitied the man, who looked no older than twenty-five, as they stood around the autopsy table, its contents mercifully covered by a plastic sheet.

"Intern?" Adam asked beside her, and the man nodded.

"I've only been here a week," he answered, and his cheeks and neck paled to a sickly shade of green. An older man entered the room, and beneath his surgical mask and goggles, Sara found his eyes kind, and they crinkled around the edges when he smiled at them. He patted the intern on the shoulder, who wasted no time in fleeing the scene.

"I'm Dr. Sloane, the assistant M.E.," he began, but Agent Grant walked through the door, passing the intern as he fled. She held up her badge and introduced herself.

"You weren't going to start without me, were you?" she said, her good humor somehow unsettling. "What do we have here?"

"I've never seen anything like it," Sloane answered. "Except in the movies."

He pulled back the sheet. Sara turned away, her empty stomach churning up acid into her throat.

"*Puta madre*," Adam muttered.

"This is where we found her—them." Sloane inhaled, exasperated, then concluded, "It."

Sara, daring another look at the gruesome creature, released a noisy breath and wondered if the hideous, naked thing was even real. The head of Mr. Buchanan, with pallid flesh and bulging eyes, pale blue and terror stricken, was sewn carefully to a body that was not its own. The stitches, thick and blatant and black, pierced through the ashen skin of the neck and affixed it to a woman's torso, cut at the shoulders like the Venus de Milo. It was the limbs though, asymmetric and irregular, that made the scene truly grotesque.

The arms, clearly female, were delicate and wan, stretched to fit the empty shoulders and stitched with less obsessive regularity than the head. The thread had torn through the skin in some places, leaving jagged rips as if the killer had been rushing through the creation of some sort of macabre suit. The right arm, an ill shade of olive, was slightly longer, the fingers more graceful than the left arm, which was almost the same hue as the pale blue gowns Dr. Sloane extended toward them as they peered down at it.

Sara slipped her arms into the crinkling fabric, unable to move her eyes from the beast, only vaguely aware forensics was now milling about, snapping photos and holding tweezers ready to pluck up evidence from the scene, sorely unused.

The legs belonged to two different men; the first short and stubby, covered in thick, dark hair. The second was long and muscled, perhaps that of a hiker or an athlete. A man, a human, had beauty of its own right, a cohesive piece of creation whose parts functioned uniformly. But this, though made up of man, resembled nothing of the sort. The killer had created a monster, a horrible, maligned simulacrum of humanity.

"Any ID yet?" Grant asked, leaning closer to inspect the stitches.

"You're not going to like it," Sloane nodded. "The head and left leg belong to James Buchanan. The torso—" he cleared his throat, and then averted his eyes, which had begun to seep. "The torso belongs to Dr. Delacruz. She was working late tonight. The right leg belongs to Benjamin Herman. The rest of his body, sans the leg, is still in cadaver drawer two." He motioned to the open drawer behind him, a detective from Baltimore hovering over it with a camera.

"The right foot belongs to Lucy Contreras." Adam closed his eyes as Sloane continued on. "The left arm belongs to Elisabetta Amello. The right belongs to—"

"Cassie," Sara finished. She recognized her fingers, and a memory, unwelcome and painful in comparison, emerged behind her eyes. Sleepovers and manicures. Sara painting Cassie's nails pink. Pretty in Pink. She remembered the name from the bottle.

Sloane hummed a note of affirmation. "Their remains are also in their respective drawers. We will get to them in time."

"Where's the rest of Karla's body?" Adam asked, his voice hollow.

"We found it cleaned in drawer seven."

"The killer cleaned the body?" Grant asked, eyes leaving the body for the first time to meet Sloane's.

"As thoroughly as if I'd done it myself," he replied.

"And her effects?"

"Still missing. There is one more thing, though."

Sara, at this moment, could no longer bear the sight of this macabre creature, so she averted her eyes to the floor. Something gold caught her attention beneath the table, and she bent to retrieve it.

It was Adam's shield.

Goosebumps prickled down her arm as she closed her fingers around it, unwilling still to accept the implication of this discovery. She stared at his name, emblazoned in gold across the face of the badge, and the malformed tissue holding her heart together split apart. Her gaze rose, distorted by tears. No one had seen her. Sloane lifted one of the creature's arms, revealing a series of letters carved into the flesh over the ribs.

R A C H E

"Could the killer have been trying to write the name Rachel?" Grant suggested.

Sara laughed. She couldn't help it.

"Is something funny?" Grant asked, her voice scalpel-sharp.

"Rache is the German for revenge," she said. "Don't lose your time looking for Miss Rachel." And then she took the shield in her hand, and shoved it hard into Adam's chest. "I think you were looking for this."

It fell into Adam's hand, and he paled.

"Where did you find that?" Grant asked.

She answered, "Under the table," but did not look away from Adam. This appeared to be the final piece of evidence Grant was waiting for, because she sent her a solemn nod, and then removed a pair of handcuffs from her back pocket.

"Lt. Contreras," she began. "I'm placing you under arrest."

"You're what?" he cried, but did not resist her when she stepped behind him and pulled his hands behind his back. "This is a mistake. Sadie, tell them."

But Sara could not speak.

Chapter XVIII

HE CLOCK downstairs tolled three, its bell pealing into the shivering silence of the sleeping house. Sara listened, her comforter pulled up around her chin, a candle guttering on the night table. The others were listening, too. She could feel them all around her, waiting for the very witching hour of the night.

As the last chime faded away into the mouse holes and the cracks in the stone, her sister's door creaked down the hall. Footsteps sounded above her in the attic, and below, a child's voice sang a hopscotch rhyme.

They were restless.

Sara closed her eyes, swollen from crying, as a worm of panic bored into her chest, spilling adrenaline into swiftly pumping blood. Before, when she was a child, Grammy kept these shades at bay. With smudging sage and firmly spoken incantations, her grandmother maintained control over the groaning spirits of their long-dead kin, but she was gone. She was one of them now.

Sara drew a breath, conjuring courage. She opened her eyes as the doorknob rattled.

"This is my house!" she yelled, sitting up and tossing the blankets aside. She ran to the door and threw it open, but the hall was empty except for a shimmering band of moonlight. Stepping into the light, this small square of safety on a worn carpet, Sara listened.

Tap, tap, tap.

A shadow moved across the window at the end of the hall, like a great bat flapping its leathery wings against the glass. She took a step toward it, and then another.

Tap, tap, tap.

Now within arm's reach of the window, Sara saw it was only a tree branch, Spanish moss fluttering in the gusty breath from the sea. The ghost of the little girl downstairs began to sing again.

Miss Lucy had a baby.
She named him Tiny Tim.
She put him in the bathtub
To see if he could swim.

Sara stumbled backward to the staircase, catching herself on the banister and running down the dark steps.

"This isn't real," she whispered, but this possibility was perhaps more terrible than the alternative. *A history of family illness*, John had called it.

Adam had seen them, too. Hadn't he? Was he just playing along to humor her, to build her trust in him? She reached the bottom of the stairs. The girl's footsteps padded across the oak, the flash of her hair catching the moonlight as she disappeared into the dining room. Sara followed, but the room was empty.

The table gleamed in the silver light, shadows settling into the many indents and scratches. At her left, something stirred inside the fireplace.

"Rats," she assured herself, but a puddle of darkness crept toward her feet, glistening. There, draped across the iron grates, was the echo of Cassie's mutilated corpse. Blood reached Sara's bare feet, but she could not move.

Sara, her sister said, her broken jaw hanging slack. *Don't you know him?*

"No," she whispered, backing away. Her bloody feet left prints on the floor, but they weren't right. They weren't hers. Boot treads formed in the stains, appearing silently one by one until they disappeared into the foyer. Sara followed them to the front door, grasped her fingers around the cold knob, and peered into the night, the silence even thicker than the dark.

Nary a cricket chirruped in the bushes, but the air swelled as if the earth drew in a trembling breath. Her hand tightened around the doorknob.

A moment passed, and then two.

And then the door slammed shut with such force that it dragged her along with it, fingers still clenched around the brass. Her shoulder met the solid wood with a thud. She wiggled the knob, which turned freely, but no matter how hard she pulled, the door would not open.

Sara! a voice called behind her.

Sara! one called from the kitchen.

Sara! Sara! came from the sitting room, where the clock chimed no hour at all. It's bells rang throughout the house, maniacally, drawing the grandfather clock upstairs into its horrible chorus. She felt its tolling in the very marrow of her bones. Sara spun toward each call of her name, but found she was alone. She tried the door again, a cry of fear humming in her throat, and when her efforts failed again, she fled to the sitting room. The windows, too, stood firm against her assaults. Although their locks moved freely, she could not open them. Frigid air poured from the walls. It spilled out of the fireplace and drove its icy tendrils into her lungs.

As she pounded on the glass, Sara became conscious of a cracking sound deep in the bowels of the house, like an oak splitting at its center. A jagged scar ran up the wall, the wallpaper ripping as if sliced by a rusted scalpel. Plaster fell from the ceiling.

Sara ran from the room with her arms over her head. The back deck, her last shred of hope, beckoned her with its single, inexplicably flickering light bulb. The electricity had not yet been restored.

Miss Lucy had a baby.
She named him Tiny Tim.
She put him in the bathtub
To see if he could swim.

She couldn't reach the door, for the child appeared before her. She regarded Sara with a curious expression. Her silver hair hung limp across vacant eyes as she tilted her head, the song caught inside her open, cavernous mouth.

"Let me out," Sara commanded, but the child only pressed her finger to her lips.

He's very angry, she whispered finally, and then turned away, her apparition dissolving like nothing more than a breath of fog.

Sara did not move. Behind her, the house had fallen quiet. Even the clocks ceased their relentless ticking. A presence at her back drew up the hairs on her neck. A horrible melancholy of spirit fell over her, and when she turned to face it, even her fear had been squelched.

He stood before her, as flesh and blood as she. His great coat hung to his knees, and in one hand he supported himself with an ivory handled cane. In the other, he held a pistol.

You have ruined us all, he growled. His mouth did not move beneath the shock of white whiskers over his lip, and when he lifted the gun, he did so a thousand times at once, like a stop-motion film set at triple speed. She stepped backward, her back hitting the glass doors of the porch.

Sara knew him by his eyes, for they were so like her own.

Bennett Wilde.

Out of the silence came a *click* as the cocking mechanism engaged.

"Out," she whispered, but she heard her grandmother's voice. "Get out! This is my house."

He opened his mouth, and out of the black came a hideous, livid moan. Marley's Ghost would have fled this sound, his ponderous chains dragging behind. Foul wind came at her from all sides, collecting debris and strips of wallpaper. Silk flowers from the vase on the table stuck to her cheeks. She sank to the floor with her hands over her ears, eyes shut tight. Books and trinkets tumbled from the shelves, and upstairs, the portraits in the hall crashed to the floor. And then, Cassie's voice drifted down the stairs.

You know him, she said again.

Sara lifted her head, these words lingering in her heart. Ruddy, glorious dawn splintered through the windows. Bennett Wilde was nowhere to be seen. The house went back to sleep, taking with it all evidence of her visitations. The flowers returned to their rightful place in the crystal vase. All of her mother's figurines were placed just as they'd always been on the dusty shelves. The wallpaper, however, lay about the room like the tattered sheets of an ill-used novel. On the wall, the missing pages told stories of bygone eras; Fleur de Lys for the survivors of The Great War, when the house served as an impromptu hospital. Ivy from the Progressive Era, and beneath still, black roses for mourning.

Sara rose and walked into the sitting room. While the plaster appeared intact, the wallpaper here too had been ripped, from the crown molding to the ceiling. Sara touched the wall with her fingers, the only one of her senses she could not doubt.

It did not heal at her touch. Her vision did not blur, nor did the old familiar pain shoot into her eye. Sara, despite the aching dread growing still inside her stomach, felt the relief of a smile.

Her mother's madness had not touched her, after all. It was real.

•••

MR. DELANEY REGARDED the flayed wallpaper in the sitting room as he tipped a tea cup to his lips.

"Strange goings on," he muttered, narrowing the space between his eyebrows.

"You have no idea," Sara answered, and then returned her gaze to him. He settled himself more comfortably into her mother's favorite armchair, tugging at his sweat-dampened collar. Sara needed him to leave. She had to talk to Adam.

"So, what did you need to discuss with me?" she asked.

"Well, I've heard the news. I'm at a bit of a loss, to be frank with you. If Mr. Contreras is incarcerated, he of course forfeits his rights to the Wildefell estate. Mind, I'm sure this is all a mistake. We both know he could never do the things they've accused him of in the news."

"It was a mistake," Sara said, recalling with a pang of misery the last thing he'd said to her. She *knew* him. What had she done?

"I just can't believe it."

"Neither can I," she said. She crossed her legs, and uncrossed them again, and then stood up to pace the room, having no other outlet for the nervous energy coursing through her. The clocks, somehow exhausted by their danse macabre with the dead last night, had stopped working altogether. Only Mr. Delaney's wristwatch kept the time. 9:00 am. Adam would be awake by now, perhaps eating a sloppy meal of gray eggs and toast.

"We will cross that bridge in time, I'm sure," Delaney said, setting his cup on the round table beside the chair. "I came by with an ulterior motive, unfortunately."

"Yes?" she urged. What now?

"I've come to attempt to convince you to sell the estate."

"I'm sorry?"

"To me. And my wife." He continued on before she could reply. "See, as I've said before, we've been dreaming of running a bed and breakfast all our lives. Now that the kids are grown, and it's high time I retired, we have our eyes on this place." He looked around the room with a smile on his face, as if it were full of happy memories, as if it already belonged to him in some way.

"Mr. Delaney—"

He held up his hand, and then opened up his brief case, which had been resting on his lap. "Before you answer me, I'd like to present my offer to you."

He extracted a single sheet of paper, stood, and handed it to her. She glanced at it, her mouth falling open. He hovered close above her, his thin frame somehow vaguely threatening. She took an instinctive step backward.

"Mr. Delaney, this is easily double what it's worth."

"You can see then how desperate we are for it. We're also willing to partner with you on the bed and breakfast, if you wish. Twenty percent."

"I can't accept this." She handed the paper back to him.

"Is it not enough?" His countenance fell. Gone was the perpetual smile, and the expression of cheer. Sara suddenly pitied anyone he might cross in the courtroom. A hardened lawyer, and not a family friend, stood before her.

"It's more than enough," she answered. "But you of all people know I can't sell it. You've known me a long time."

Sara stilled.

He'd known her a *very* long time, since even before she'd fallen in love with all things gothic. She remembered how impressed he'd been with her article on Sherlock Holmes all those years ago. He'd asked for a copy of the paper.

"I was afraid you'd say that," he said. He reached into the pocket of his pants. Sara stepped back still, until her calves met the clawfoot sofa. Delaney removed only a ballpoint pen. He scratched through the number on the page, and scribbled a new one, more outrageous than the first.

"How—?" she stammered.

"You underestimate me, young Sara," he said. "We've been saving all our lives for this house. I'm afraid I won't take no for an answer. Name your figure. Our minds are made up."

"So is mine." She held the page out to him, but he did not take it.

"Very well. Perhaps you need time to consider."

Mercifully, a knock sounded at the door. Sara left to answer it without another word, and listened to his footsteps behind her.

Eva Mauk was waiting for her on the porch.

"Excuse me," Delaney said, brushing past Sara and walking out the door, leaving Eva bewildered and still outside.

"Do you need something?" Sara asked her, no longer in the mood for niceties. Eva looked after the lawyer for a moment, and then turned back to Sara, a picture of fury.

"Do I need something?" she repeated, smirking. "I sure as hell do. You made a joke of my precinct. My best detective is in jail, someone is still murdering people in my town, and the press thinks we have our heads up our asses. So, I need you to stay the fuck out of my way."

Sara, taken aback by the assault, could not reply. Eva, apparently, took this as an invitation to continue.

"My grandpa was right, you know. You Wildes are a bad lot, ever since Bennett Wilde murdered James Mauk."

"What?"

"He shot him in the head with his old pistol. You haven't heard the story?"

"I—"

"Of course you haven't. They probably told you he paid a fair price for the paper, but that's a lie. James Mauk was murdered in cold blood, even after he complied to all your ancestor's demands."

"That wasn't reported in the paper..." she said, mostly to herself.

"Of course it wasn't. Bennett owned it by then. You think he'd write up a confession?"

"Were these claims substantiated?"

"How could they prove a thing like that? The Wildes had money. The Mauks—" she set her hand over her chest "—lost everything."

"It was over a century ago..." she said. "You're holding me responsible for these things?"

"I'm holding you responsible for what's happening *now*. And I'll be damned if I'm going to let you all get away with it a second time."

With that, she turned, and stormed down the stairs, leaving Sara alone. Exasperated, she closed the door and slid against it, her head toward the ceiling. With Eva's words ringing in her ears, she slid her fingers into her hair, unsure now where to turn. Did the killer want revenge for the sins of her ancestors? Was he the long lost heir, come to claim his inheritance?

Sara closed her eyes, a new possibility emerging. Maybe the killer didn't want any of that at all. Maybe he only wanted what was rightfully his all along. The newspaper.

Chapter XIX

*A*GENT GRANT had left Adam in a holding cell at the Sheriff's office, under FBI custody. When Sara arrived, checkbook at the ready, it was Grant herself who greeted her at reception. She smiled piteously, an expression Sara had grown to resent.

"I need to see him," Sara blurted out.

"I can't allow that."

"You can't stop me." She attempted to stride past the front desk. The officer manning it rose to his feet, but stood down upon a motion of the agent's hand. She stepped in front of Sara with her arms folded behind her back.

"We have physical evidence linking him to the scene of the crime, Ms. Wilde," she said slowly. "Thanks to you, he'll be going away for a very long time."

"Either you get out of my way, or my lawyer will bury you under a wrongful arrest suit until all you have left is your ugly blazer. I don't have anything left to lose."

Grant rose her eyes to the officer, who waited for instruction.

"I suppose you'd like to pay his bail," she asked Sara without looking at her.

"I would."

"Very well." She met Sara's eyes, her gaze as sharp and cold as onyx. "I don't need to tell you what happens if either of you leave town."

Sara slipped by her and pushed open the door leading to holding. Adam was the only prisoner. She found him sitting on a cot, elbows on his knees, and looking rather like he hadn't slept in weeks.

"Couldn't sleep much last night?" she asked. He drew a sharp breath as she looked through the iron bars, but did not stand to greet her. Instead, he tented his hands and held them to his lips, a seething storm cloud gathering between them.

"Could you?" he replied. When she didn't answer, he said, "I've been doing this a long time, Sara. If you think I'm stupid enough to leave my badge at a crime scene, you have another thing coming."

"I know."

"I'm being set up," he continued. "We were getting close."

The uniformed officer appeared behind her with a set of keys attached to a lanyard. She stepped aside as he unlocked the door. With a look of suspicious surprise, Adam rose.

"I paid your bail," Sara said. "We have a lot to talk about."

On the way back to Wildefell, though, the conversation stopped and stalled like traffic down Main Street. Adam had fallen to brooding. Sara had so much to say she didn't know where to start. *I'm sorry* didn't seem adequate, so she said nothing at all. When the tension between them filled up the Mustang as if it were sinking underwater, Adam rubbed his eyes and turned to her.

"I need to ask you a question," he said. She could only wait, tapping the breaks to stop at a traffic light. "And if you can't give me an honest answer, I'll get out and walk." He waited for her to nod, and then asked, "If there's any part of you that believes I'm responsible for these things, I need you to tell me now."

"That's not really a question," she answered. The light changed, so she guided the car down the street, slowing to turn toward home. Rain speckled the windshield. The wind ushered dead leaves along the gutters, gathering them into storm drains like a mother hen in preparation for another storm.

"I just spent the night in a holding cell," Adam said. He turned away and looked out the window. Sara saw his grim reflection in the glass. "I am not in the mood for this."

"I know, I'm sorry. You had nothing to do with this. I know that now."

"What changed your mind?"

"The house," she answered, but did not elaborate. She remembered her sister's voice. "I know you," she added. "The way only kids do."

In the window, the reflection of a smile broke the brooding misery in his expression.

"Eva came to see me," she said, and he lifted his eyebrows at her. "She accused Bennett Wilde of murdering her ancestor, James Mauk. I think he was the man Theodora had the affair with."

"Who is Bennett Wilde again?"

"Theodora's husband. I think Eva is telling the truth."

Adam hummed a low tone of unease. "Do you understand what you're saying?"

"I did some research. The paper was owned by James Mauk before Bennett bought it. James' brother, Richard, was Eva's great grandfather. She came to tell me off, said she wouldn't let me get away with it 'a second time.'"

Sara guided the car through Wildefell's gates, the wipers struggling to keep up with the deluge. Adam shook his head.

"I don't like it," he said above the rain. "I don't like it at all."

"I'd thought Bennett just bought the paper out from under Mauk as a way to get back at him for the affair, but to murder him in cold blood?"

"People have been murdered over less. Maybe once he had the paper, he found it wasn't enough. Theodora belonged to another man. That kind of thing wears you down."

The weight of this last sentence fell squarely across Sara's chest, and she felt it wriggle into her heart, as intended, as she shifted into park. The weak shadow of Wildefell draped over them, settling in the spaces between their conversation.

"There's obviously no way to prove Bennett murdered anyone now, but I looked into it, and found missing persons notices in a few of the papers around Beaufort. I think that's why Theodora killed herself, she couldn't carry the weight of her lover's death. Guilt is a powerful thing, too."

"And you think Eva is the heir? You think she's related to you?"

She shook her head. "No, she's all Mauk. Maybe we were on the wrong track with the heir. The point is Eva holds my family responsible for the ruin of the Mauk family. That's a motive."

"I can't just accuse my superior of being a serial killer, Sadie. And why now after all these years? We need more."

"There is more, but not about Eva."

"What now?"

"Mr. Delaney came to see me, too. He tried to get me to sell the house to him for an ungodly amount of money, said he wouldn't take no for an answer."

"You think your family lawyer is a suspect too?"

"You didn't see him," she said, unbuckling her seatbelt. "He scared me. I've never seen the look on his face that I saw yesterday. He's known me long enough to know all about my lifelong fangirl affair with Sherlock Holmes and gothic stories."

"You've been busy." Adam turned to her. "I was away for less than 24 hours and you already have two new suspects? Were you playing detective while I was gone?"

She shook her head and lifted her shoulder. "Investigative reporter. There's a difference." With an ornery smile, she added, "A big difference."

Sara nodded to the windshield as the rain let up and set her hand on the handle of the door. He shot her a now's-our-chance look, and they leapt from the car as swiftly as if it had been choreographed. On the west side of the property, cold rain pooled into the graves she'd opened. She imagined the tiny marble casket filling up with water and disappearing beneath the mud.

The house huddled around them as they tramped through the door, gathering them close into its stillness. Adam shook the rain from his hair, but did not speak. Their footfalls returned hollow echoes to them, sounding somehow as if they belonged to more than two people. The air conditioner hummed, dispelling some of the foulness.

"Finally," Sara breathed, and flicked on the light. "Hey, did anything ever come of the boot prints?"

Adam answered, "Nothing concrete. Dockers, size 12."

"Dockers?"

"Yeah, does that mean anything to you?"

"Daddy wore size 12 Dockers."

Adam ran his hand down his face and walked past her toward the kitchen. "I need a drink."

She followed, and found him bent over the liquor cabinet, a bottle of Scotch already in hand. Two tumblers clinked together as he retrieved them from behind the glass.

"It's impossible, right?" Sara asked as he poured himself a couple fingers of her father's favorite whiskey. "He's dead?"

He inhaled, releasing it slowly as he poured her drink.

"I think we're being conned," he said. "The killer's trying to make you believe he could be anyone, everyone, so you have no one left to trust, not even the memory of your dad. It's fucking cruel."

"He *could* be anyone," she said, accepting the glass he offered. She tipped it back, but didn't taste it.

"Let's focus on Delaney for a minute."

"And Eva. You know she's always hated me. Both have motive, right? And means. They both have fairly easy access to the house. What about alibis? Is that what you look for next?"

"I can't ask the police captain if she has an alibi, Sadie," Adam answered, refilling his own glass and leaning against the counter. "That's not how it works."

"But you could just ask her casually, couldn't you? Off the record?"

"Like you asked me?"

Sara stood before him, inside his shadow, and wished for all the world she had never come back here. Generations of Wildes had wrought little but suffering to anyone foolhardy enough to come into their orbit, and Sara was no different.

"You deserved better than that," she answered. "I'm sorry."

"Are you?" He swallowed a gulp of the whiskey her father would only sip.

"What does that mean?"

Adam only shook his head and reached for the bottle again. She set her hand on his.

"If we could just solve this," she said. "If we could end all of this. I really believe we—"

"Will you just stop?" he said, pulling away.

"What?"

"Just for five minutes, could we stop talking about this case?"

She wasn't sure how to reply. "I'm sorry, I—"

"I was arrested, Sadie. Do you understand what that means? I'm not on the case anymore. I'm probably not even on the force. There's nothing we can do now."

"You don't believe that."

"You can play armchair detective all you want, but I'm out. I've had enough."

"I know things aren't going how we planned, but—"

"And how did we plan them? We've lost everything. It's just us. And I don't even know what *us* is." He dropped down in a nearby kitchen chair and pinched the bridge of his nose, the whiskey glass clenched tight in his other fist. "I'm just so damn tired of this."

"Of what?"

He looked at her, exasperated, as if the answer was obvious. "Of pretending this is all fine, of pretending *I'm* fine. I spent most of my life believing you hated me, and you *let* me. You actually thought for a minute that I was a serial killer, and despite all that, I still—" Anguish stayed the remainder of the sentence. She could see it in his eyes, in the tendons of his neck and the bulging muscle in his jaw. When he spoke again, his shoulders fell in defeat. "I still love you."

The words hung between them like spider's silk, and Sara could neither reply nor breathe, for fear they might be blown away.

"I used to think it was this house," he said, sliding his glass onto the table with the remainder of his energy. "Maybe I'd left some part of myself here that could never leave again."

"Adam," she managed. He lifted his eyes to hers, the intensity of his stare holding her hostage as he stood up, so close she could smell the whiskey on his breath.

"I was wrong, Sadie. It was you I left myself with. It's always been you. I'm just another one of your ghosts."

Sara lifted her hand to his cheek, and although he leaned into the touch initially, each passing moment brought greater anguish into his features, until he appeared as though he might split down the center. He pressed his forehead to hers and the tension in his brow passed through her as his hands slipped into her hair.

"Haunt me, then," she whispered. She tasted his name on her tongue, but could not speak it again. Adam's chest heaved as if he were battling a great monster inside himself, his fingers tightening in her hair, his mouth only a breath from hers.

When he at last surrendered to their kiss, he did so not with a cry of passion, but of agony. It raked through her, throbbing in her bones and pulling taught the sinews holding her together. Drawn here by the reaching clutches of death, she could not extricate herself from him, couldn't tell his misery from her own. Tears fell down her face as this kiss deepened, and Sara felt as if she were at the edge of the world, with only darkness beneath.

Adam, at last, pushed her away, trembling. Moisture gathered at the edges of his eyes.

"I *can't*," he ground out, and before she could reach for him, he fled. The front door slammed behind him, and Sara found herself, again, quite alone.

- - -

THE WORDS WOULDN'T come. Sara sat at her father's ancient computer, her fingers poised over the keyboard. Her bitter retort to John's article was on the edge of her tongue, at the tip of her fingers, but she could not articulate it. Disgraced by her ex, and resented by Adam, Sara had resolved to write her way out of this grave, but her mind ricocheted to Adam's kiss.

Wildefell's darkness had sewn the two of them together imperfectly, the stitches swollen and painful, so they could be neither together nor free. She had never felt a kiss so laden with desperation and grief, and wanting.

She lifted her fingers to her lips.

I still love you.

His words lingered, netting across her mind and gathering bits of memory and raw feeling. She'd let her hatred ruin him. And now, despite all her efforts to convince herself of the contrary, it was impossible to hate him. As if through an old phonograph, Sherlock Holmes spoke to her as he had in the days of old, before the pages turned dark with mold.

Once you eliminate the impossible, whatever remains, no matter how improbable, must be the truth.

If she couldn't hate him, there was only one other possibility, only one other explanation for the violence of emotion throbbing in her chest, filling her to bursting.

Sara set her fingers on the keyboard and began to type. At first, she sought only to distract herself, but the words coalesced into something discernible, and so she pressed on.

In the end, when the sun began its descent toward the swamps and her eyes burned, it wasn't at all what she had set out to write. Her wounds had not bled into it, had not stained the words with her grief or spoke to her brokenness. A triumphant smile lifted the edge of her lip as she watched the article print.

This was her story, and she was taking it back.

THE SCARLET THREAD:
The love affair that inspired a serial killer
By Sara Wilde
Beaufort, South Carolina—
August 31

Poison was her element in life.

These words, written on my grandfather's typewriter, sat on the tip of Elisabetta Amello's tongue. Moments earlier, before a killer's hands drew bruises from her neck and forced poison down her throat, Elisabetta had been tending to her plants. Perhaps she had been dreaming of owning her own garden store, or attending the local university to obtain a botany degree.

She would not have the opportunity to tell us what she wanted out of this life, for her killer put other words in her mouth. Too much of a coward to speak for himself, too inadequate to use his own words, the killer plagiarizes those who have seen the success he will likely never glimpse. You see, although I do not know his name, I know him quite well. He has left himself plainly at crime scenes all across town, and while his victims can no longer speak, I have heard them crying out.

I am listening.

So that I may become a mouthpiece for those who have lost their lives, I am going to tell you a story, dear reader. It is an old one, full of scandal and sacrifice. It is the story of my great-great grandmother, Theodora Wilde, the man she loved, and the daughter who survived it all.

Theodora, married to a cruel man named Bennett, likely lived a cloistered life within the walls of Wildefell Manor, spending her days living in fear of the man to whom fortune had bound her. In the summer of 1886, Stephen Wilde was born (from whom I hail), but even the baby could not bring joy into a loveless marriage. I can only imagine the loneliness Theodora felt in those bleak and bitter winters. With Bennett managing their vast estate and many of the properties in greater Beaufort, he spent little time at home, leaving her to tend to the child with a housemaid whose name has been lost to time.

Then, when she had all but lost the will to go on, she met a man. It is unclear where they first met, perhaps a spring gathering or a dinner party, but letters to her closest friend, Clementine, reveal the intensity of the impression he made upon her. A passionate affair soon developed, and in the Winter of 1892, Theodora's son wrote to Clemmy that she was with child.

This man was James Mauk, owner of the Beaufort County Times.

Before the child came into the world, Bennett must have discovered the affair. Scandal tore through the quiet town. The Wilde family name tarnished under the light of allegations both true and alleged. Bennett made a decision. He used the weapon he wielded best: his money. He purchased The Times from the Mauks, and although many claim he threatened the family until they agreed, the property records indicate a fair price was paid.

But, in the eight month of Theodora's pregnancy, James Mauk went missing. Rumors abound concerning this man's fate, the most popular that Bennett Wilde dispatched him with all the cruelty he was known for, and the pistol he wore always on his hip.

Unable to bear the absence of her lover, she drowned herself in the murky waters of the marsh, unborn child in toe.

At least, that's the story Bennett Wilde had printed in his new paper.

But, it's not the truth.

There was another story printed about a nun who discovered an infant abandoned on the steps of her orphanage. I believe Theodora's last act was to save her child. I know firsthand the weight of the Wilde name. It was indeed a kindness, the last act of a desperate mother, to rescue her child from a life within the walls of the house which had held her prisoner.

I will let you draw your own conclusions, except to say that another branch of the withered Wilde family tree had sprouted, and if it exists still, there is yet another heir to the fortune, the property, and the newspaper.

It is my belief that this heir may in fact be the killer who has been plaguing our town, and taken the lives of my family. Could he, upon discovering all I have heretofore uncovered myself, believe he is owed what was taken from the Mauk family all those years ago? Does he seek justice for the murder of James Mauk, or does he seek revenge by destroying the Wilde family line?

There are many unanswered questions, but blood will out. It always does.

In the words of Sherlock Holmes, "There is the scarlet thread of murder running through the colorless skein of life, and it is our duty to ferret it out, and to expose every inch of it." I have gathered lengths of this tattered thread the whole of my life. It is no longer enough to expose it to the light. It is time I burned it out.

Readers may contact Special Agent Charlotte Grant with information pertaining to this unknown heir. Members of the Mauk family are encouraged to speak out with additional details. The Wilde family is offering a reward of $5,000 to anyone with information which leads to the apprehension of the killer. This story is developing, and the investigation is ongoing.

✝ H.B. Diaz

Sara read through the article one last time, and then attached it in an email to her editor. Her cursor hovered over *send*. No, this article belonged to her. It belonged in Beaufort. She typed in Aggie Barlow's email address with a short note, and sent it to the Beaufort County Times.

Chapter XX

*A*DAM ANSWERED the door with a beer in his hand, clad in only sweatpants. When he saw Sara standing on his porch, he laughed.

"Who's haunting who now?" he said, and then finished his beer.

"Can I come in? It's almost dark."

Darkness had never frightened Sara. She had borne it, and the entities it enshrouded, for so long she scarcely felt its coming at all, but tonight was different. There was nothing waiting for her in the dark of Wildefell except the livid phantom of Bennett Wilde, and a host of entities all trying to speak to her at once. Sara could not suffer another night like the last. It was this, and only this, she assured herself, that drove her to Adam. She had nowhere else to go.

Adam's bare chest rose and fell. He wiped his forehead with the back of his arm, but he did not let her in.

"Are you drunk?" she asked.

"I'm working on it," he answered, and then stepped aside at last. "Was about to switch to Jim Beam."

He left only enough space for her to brush by him. She felt the heat of his body in her cheeks. He closed the door behind her and she turned to find him leaning against it, as if he couldn't come any closer to her.

"I need to tell you," she began, but he shook his head.

"Don't, I've had enough. *Ya no puedo más.*"

"Adam, I'm sorry." She tossed her messenger bag on the couch and tried to meet his eyes. "You're the best man I know, and I've treated you— I'm just *really* sorry, for all of it. I know that's not enough, but it's all I have."

Adam heaved himself off of the door, and set the empty can on the coffee table before dropping down onto the couch. The table was bare except for a pamphlet from a funeral parlor and a lawyer's business card. He nodded to the place beside him. The springs of the sofa creaked as she sat, the sagging cushion bringing him a margin closer.

"No," he said quietly. "It's not enough."

Sara's heart fell. He had no reason to accept her apology.

"I shouldn't have come here," she said, but when she tried to stand, Adam took her hand.

"It's not enough because I want everything," he said, brushing a lock of hair behind her ear. "I want what you can't give me. I know that."

Sara wanted to tell him he was wrong, but she couldn't speak at all. He withdrew, her silence his confirmation.

Adam reached for the pamphlet on the table, and handed it to her. A smiling couple, photographed in front of a sparkling lake, stared back at her, and it gave her the creeps.

"Do you think she would like it there?" he asked. "Lucy."

"It looks nice," she answered, but only to humor him. She knew all too well the dead do not stay where they are buried.

"I thought she'd like to be near the water."

Sara considered this for a moment, and nodded. "Do you think she'd like to be buried with Cassie... at Wildefell?"

Adam turned toward her and looked at her, for the first time, like she was actually insane.

"In the graveyard you just excavated with your dad's rusty shovel?"

"I'm going to have the remains identified and reburied with headstones... in case anyone wants to leave flowers. They're my family. We should know their names. Maybe they can't move on because they were all forgotten. Someone built a horse barn on top of them."

"That would make me pretty cranky, too," he joked, and she leaned against him. He stiffened but did not shy away.

"I just want them to be at peace. *I* want to be at peace."

The conversation settled into quiet. Sara chewed her lip.

"My arraignment is Monday," Adam said at last. "If things go south, I need you to promise me something."

"Don't talk like that," she said, but he took her hand.

"Promise me you'll sell the house."

She looked up at him, stunned. "What?"

"Get out. Go home to Savannah and live your life."

Sara looked at her lap. She had no life in Savannah, her bridges burned to ash. All she had left was Wildefell. And Adam. His shoulders sagged as if he had heard this inner dialogue, and then he put his arm around her with a sigh. Exhausted, she nestled against his chest.

His heart beat strong and steady in her ear, and she closed her eyes.

"Would you like to stay tonight?" he asked gently, but she didn't hear him.

● ● ●

A CROW CAWED once, and then again, waking Sara from a sleep disturbed by strange nonsensical dreams. When her eyelids scraped against her eyeballs, all she could make out in the sandy haze was a ceiling fan.

The crow called once more, drawing her up at last into wakefulness. A blinding ray of sunlight sliced through the slats in half-open wooden blinds, and she rubbed her eyes.

"Are you okay?" Adam asked.

She scrambled off the bed, taking the sheet with her. Adam sat up, his chest bare, blinking in the sun.

"Oh, shit," she muttered, leaning against the windowsill. She looked down at herself. Still fully clothed in last night's jeans and tank. "Did I—did we?"

He swung his legs over the side of the bed with a smirk. "You'd remember that, I promise." Then he sighed and added, "No. You fell asleep and I didn't want to sleep on the couch again."

"Oh."

"You still talk in your sleep, you know," he said, and he grabbed his t-shirt off the floor and pulled it over his head.

"Do I?"

"You kept saying, 'It's time to come home.'"

Sara could not reply to this but for a nearly imperceptible shake of her head, which Adam didn't appear to see.

"I've got to make a phone call," he said, heading toward the living room. He added over his shoulder, "There's a fresh towel in the bathroom if you want to shower."

She didn't have time to shower. If Adam's arraignment was on Monday, she only had two more days to stop the killer, and then it would be too late.

"It's Contreras," she heard Adam say into the phone. "I know, and I wouldn't be calling you if it wasn't important. Please, Eva, just hear me out." A pause, and then, "Could you look into Delaney for me? The Wilde's lawyer."

Sara held her breath, listening.

"It's a good lead," Adam continued. "He wants the house, and has means and opportunity. You have to know Grant is wrong about me. We went to high school together. You know I didn't do this."

Adam sat down on the couch and sighed. Sara had a phone call to make of her own. She fished her cell out of her pocket. A notification hovered above the email app, and she tapped it, opening a message from Aggie Barlow.

Welcome aboard, it read. *This will run with the next edition. Contract to follow.*

She smiled, and then dialed Agent Charlotte Grant. If Adam couldn't get the dogs on Eva's scent, she would.

"Special Agent Grant," she answered.

"Agent Grant, this is Sara Wilde." A long pause stretched between them, and Sara wondered if she had hung up on her.

"Ms. Wilde. How can I help you?"

"I have information pertaining to the case." She explained how Eva had come to visit her, her veiled threats, and her family history, nearly all in a single breath. And then she waited.

"Tread lightly," Grant said at last. "These are serious accusations."

"More serious than arresting the wrong man?"

"I will look into it," she said, ignoring this. "I would suggest you keep this to yourself. And leave the investigation to me, please. You've done enough."

Sara lied that she would, and then joined Adam in the living room. He looked even more exhausted than he had last night.

"When was the last time you ate?" she asked him, and he frowned.

"There's something bothering me, Sadie," he said, leaning his elbows on his knees. "I saw the look in your eyes when you came over last night. You were scared."

"I was," she nodded.

"Why? You grew up in a haunted house. Nothing scares you."

"Everything scares me." Sara sat down in an arm chair across from the couch, focusing on the geometric pattern of the throw rug. "I saw Bennett Wilde."

Adam only lifted an eyebrow.

"His spirit appeared to me, and he—he ripped the wallpaper. He physically tore it down the wall. The entities that appear to me affect only my perception of things, never the physical world. If his spirit is powerful enough to do something like that—"

"You're afraid he'll come after you."

"I'm exposing his greatest secret. The shame of the family. I think he'll *kill* me to keep it safe."

"Why the wallpaper?"

"Does it matter?" she asked.

"Everything matters. Everything is a communication."

Sara drew in a deep breath, and there in that quiet space before the exhale, it dawned upon her.

"The wallpaper," she whispered. "The Yellow Wallpaper."

"I thought the paper was blue?" Adam asked.

"No, no. Perkins' *The Yellow Wallpaper*. That's the next murder." She sprung up from the chair. "I need my books."

Outside, a brief rainstorm left the sidewalk slick and gleaming. Steam rose from the concrete, caught in the early morning sunlight, assuming the form of strange beings. Trolls guarded the crosswalks. Slinking beasts kept watch behind the tree-lined street. Sara ran.

Tourists and locals alike regarded her curiously as she sped toward Wildefell. Their dogs sniffed the air, ears pinned back. Adam kept pace behind her but did not call out for her. He would know where she was going, where she would always go. Her heart pounded in her ears as she rounded the corner and approached the gates. Rain dripped from the reaching branches of the willow, the wind drawing it aside like a curtain to let her pass. She stumbled up the porch steps and threw open the door.

The moment she crossed the threshold, the house ripped her down the center. Deep, gnawing pain bored into her eyes, and she collapsed to her knees with a cry of agony. Adam's hands landed on her shoulders but could not keep her there. In a moment more, the black drew her into its arms and held on so tightly a constricting snake might have wrought its muscled scales around her. Out of the gelatinous, suffocating darkness came a sound she knew too well.

Her mother was weeping.

Why have you been away so long?

Momma's voice, as dry and withered as an autumn leaf, shook with effort, and with grief. No one answered her, but Sara felt a hand on hers. She recognized the weight of it, somehow knew it apart from all others, and yet she could not recall to whom it belonged.

Momma knew. Sara felt her certainty in the naked center of her heart, and in the blood of her ancestors pumping fiercely through her veins.

Daddy.

Then, Sara heard him speak.

Happy birthday, Imogene. Did you think I forgot your gift?

Sara knew these words. She had heard them many times before, but it was just so dark. She couldn't see where she'd left them last, couldn't remember under what circumstances they'd been spoken. The memory crept behind the walls inside her, slinking along the floor, rattling the iron bars, its unblinking eyes everywhere and nowhere. She couldn't see it.

"Daddy?" she whispered, her own voice underwater; under a million gallons of brackish marsh. Momma sobbed, and Sara felt the roughness of a rope slip across her throat.

Oh, yes, Momma whimpered. *Yes, I suppose it's for the best. Let's be together again, my dear.*

"No!" Sara cried. The rope tightened as she fought through the dark, clawing and kicking until her face broke the oily surface. The pain subsided, and the ink dissolved until her eyes perceived Adam, always Adam, cradling her in his arms.

"Who?" he asked, and her vision faded again, drowned now by the saltwater of her own tears.

"Momma."

Chapter XXI

*M*OMMA WASN'T breathing. Sara watched the nurse perform CPR, her mother's lifeless body laid on the hard floor. A cord of rope, cast to the floor, twitched and wriggled like a snake as the feet of the staff trampled it.

They wouldn't let her in the room. She tried to shove her way through the door, but another nurse, assisted by Adam, held her back.

"Give them time, Sadie," he said in her ear, but she could barely hear him over the sound of her own hoarse voice.

"Momma!" she cried, straining against them. They were too late. They couldn't be too late.

Over the loudspeaker, someone paged security, and on the table, her father's voice played and replayed from the crackling speaker of an old video camera.

Happy birthday, Imogene. Did you think I forgot your gift?

The video looped again and again. Her mother's face smiling as Daddy held the camera.

Sara remembered the bitter morning in early February, before Momma let the voices inside. He had built her a greenhouse so she could grow her plants all year round. Only its leaning wire frame remained, its tattered plastic shell flapping like a vulture's wings every time it rained.

A noise slipped from between Momma's lips; not a moan, or even a gasp, but a sound like wind through dried cornhusk.

"Her throat," Sara muttered, and then louder, "Momma!"

She broke free, launching herself into the room and shoving the nurse aside, who stumbled against the bed frame with a cry. Sara tore the CPR mask off of her mother's face and opened her mouth. Inside, partially blocking her airway, was a crumpled slip of paper.

The nurse, having recovered herself and observing why Sara had assaulted her, hooked her finger into Momma's mouth and extracted the sopping note.

Adam relieved her of it as she continued CPR, and in a moment, Momma gasped, her fingers flying to her throat.

"It's all right, Ms. Imogene," the nurse soothed. "Your daughter's with you. You're going to be ok."

"Cassandra?" Momma breathed as Sara took her hand.

"Who did this to you?" Sara asked, clutching her, tears of relief and anger streaming freely down her face.

"Sadie," Adam whispered behind her. His hand fell upon her shoulder.

"Momma, who did this?" she repeated.

"What have you done?" Momma asked, wrenching her hand away. "I wanted to see him. Take me back! I want to go home."

She strained against the nurse's steady grasp, clawing at her own face with animal violence. As Adam led Sara from the room, her mother's curses followed her into the hall. Sara covered her ears and sank to the floor, her wretched sobs lacking only sound.

"*Querida*," Adam whispered in her ear. He gathered her into his arms.

She saw the note crumpled in his fist.

"What does it say?" she said, wiping her nose with the back of her hand.

"I think you were right," he said, unwrapping it. Sara read the killer's note to herself, her mind filling in the blanks where the ink had smudged.

It is stripped off—the paper— in great patches all around the head of my bed...I never saw a worse paper in my life. One of those sprawling flamboyant patterns committing every artistic sin.

Someone closed the door, but Momma's hideous screams bled through the walls, rattling against the wire-lined window panes. It might have been a mercy if they'd been five minutes too late. She tried to banish this thought as Adam helped her to her feet.

"She's been suffering so long," she said. "What kind of life is this?"

Adam didn't reply, but led her down the hall into the lobby where the cries weren't so heart wrenching. They sat down on a bench beside the automatic double doors, two wilted ferns standing guard.

"What can I do?" he asked, and Sara shook her head.

"I shouldn't have left her here. I should have known he'd go after her."

"Don't do this," Adam warned. "Don't go down this path again."

"This is all my fault." She buried her face in her hands. Adam slid off the bench and knelt before her, taking her hands in his own.

"Sadie, we had a victory today. We beat him. *You* beat him."

She felt no sense of accomplishment or victory at all, not with Momma screaming down the hall. She could only shake her head.

"Listen to me. Just me." Adam took her face in his hands. She met his eyes, and his own tears glistened in the harsh florescent light. "We can stop this."

Moved by the strength of his emotion, Sara drew a trembling breath, and then reached for her bag. Inside, the battered copy of *A Study in Scarlet* caught the light, its glossy cover glinting. Satisfied he had gotten through to her, Adam rose and kissed the top of her head.

"I'm going to get us some coffee," he said, and she watched him until he disappeared into the elevator.

Momma's screams ceased abruptly, though their ghosts still echoed inside Sara's mind as she removed the book and flipped through the pages. She read for nearly a quarter of an hour, lamenting how dearly she once held this tale, and how desperately she now loathed it. Her phone vibrated inside one of the pockets of her bag as she found what she sought.

A vulgar flaring paper adorned the walls, but it was blotched in places with mildew, and here and there great strips had become detached and hung down, exposing the yellow plaster beneath.

The phone continued to vibrate long after it should have, which meant whoever was trying to reach her wouldn't take no for an answer. She dug it out of the bag and stared at the letters on the screen for a long while.

Johnny.

Her finger hovered over IGNORE as it rang and rang, but in the end, she answered, intent on closing this chapter of her life once and for all.

"Hello, John," she said into the phone.

"Sara," he breathed. "I wasn't sure if you were going to answer."

"That makes two of us."

"I read your article," he said. "Bold move, sending it to the Beaufort County Times when you're under the employ of another paper. You may as well have sent in your resignation."

"The story belongs in Beaufort, John," she answered.

"You're right. That's why I'm calling. I shouldn't have—what I mean to say is— Sara, I reacted very poorly."

Sara leaned her head against the cool wall and lifted her brow.

"Which time?" she asked bitterly. "The time you referred me to an actual lunatic asylum, or the time you defamed me and my family in the newspaper with quotes I said in confidence?"

"I deserved that."

"I didn't. You betrayed me."

After a pause pregnant with tension, John sucked in a loud breath, and said quickly, "Let me take you to dinner tonight."

"I don't think that's a good idea."

"Please, Sara. I need to see you, just once more. To give you a proper apology, and to say goodbye."

Sara rubbed her eyes, the residual pain still blurring her vision. They had been part of each other's lives for a long time. Perhaps it would do her well to see him in person. At least she could slap him if she still had a mind to, after everything he'd done to her.

"Fine," she said at last. "Where?"

"Do you know the lighthouse on Huntington Island?"

"Of course I do, but there's nowhere to eat nearby."

"I'll make my chicken parmesan."

Sara laughed. "It's open to the public, John. And there's nowhere to sit."

"I'll take care of everything, just trust me."

"Trust you?" she repeated automatically, which left him silent, perhaps wounded. "I want to make something clear, John. We aren't together anymore because I *can't* trust you. I'm accepting your invitation because I need closure. Is that clear?"

"I understand." And then, "Do you regret it? Us?"

"We aren't on the same path, John. We never were."

"The path of error," he mumbled, and as he spoke, the phrase she used to find encouraging became somehow grotesque. The words decayed, leaving only memories strewn with regret.

- - -

THE WATER SCALDED Sara's shoulders. Steam swirled around her, filling her gasping lungs as she leaned against the cool porcelain tiles, her chest heaving. None of this was supposed to happen. She covered her face with both hands, a vain attempt to dampen the sound of her panic so Adam, who waited in her bedroom, wouldn't know.

"I'm sorry, Momma," she whispered amid sobs. The doctors said Momma would be all right. Her bruised neck would heal, and the psychiatrist could work her through the trauma, but Sara had already lost her. Momma would never forgive her for saving her life. It was the same look she'd given Adam all those years ago when he'd returned home without her father.

Momma wanted to die.

The sobs wracked her body, until she could no longer bear her own weight and she sank into the tub. Hot water stung her eyes, the steam so thick she could barely breathe. Adam knocked on the door as she drew her knees to her chest.

"Sadie? Can I come in?"

Sara inhaled, wiping her eyes and standing too quickly. The room spun, black fungus speckling the edges of her vision.

"Yes," she answered, afraid she'd lose consciousness. She closed her eyes. The door opened, ushering cooler air into her lungs, but the darkness spread. She grabbed the shower curtain to steady herself.

"Help," she murmured. At this plea, Adam drew the curtain gently back, and leaned in to catch her as she collapsed in his arms.

The fungus cleared as she clung to him. He stepped into the tub and held her until her heart found its rhythm, until the panic subsided, and then took her face in his hands, the pad of his thumb brushing her cheek.

"I need you to believe none of this is your fault," he said. Her lip trembled, and he pressed his forehead to hers. "None of this is your fault."

Sara's shoulders fell as she surrendered. Inside, she knew she had been the victim of a great and terrible plot, and she was not to blame for the outpouring of tragedy it had loosed upon her home, but this took all the power from her. It took everything.

"I should have let her go," she said, giving as little voice to the thought as possible. "I should have let her go to Daddy."

"Sadie."

"I should have let you go, too. I ruined your life. You should just go."

Adam's expression darkened.

"I'm not going anywhere," he said.

"Yes, you are. You're going to leave me like everyone else. You have to. But I can't bear it. I can't survive it." The tears stung her eyes, and she became conscious again of Adam's body, and of her own nakedness. She folded her arms across her chest and stepped backward. Realization dawned across his face, as if she had told him outright she still loved him, too.

"I'm not going anywhere," he said again, and with the dark and grieving cousin of a smile, he kissed her. Water poured down over them, his soaked shirt warm and soft against her breasts as she slipped her arms around his neck.

Sara closed her eyes, savoring the sensation of his hands on her back, his mouth on her neck, but the water began to cool and then she smelled the sea.

His body stiffened against her, but she didn't open her eyes. She didn't want to see.

"Sadie," he said, her name pulled taught. The water fell sluggishly, denser, slimier. He pulled her out of the spray with a disgusted cry, repeating her name. Sara opened her eyes at last. Black algae gathered around their feet, clogging the drain. Filthy water pooled at their ankles.

"What the hell?" Adam cried, and tore the shower curtain back so they could stumble onto the cold tile. Sara shushed him.

"She's coming," she said, and clutching him by the shirt, she pointed as they stood together before the mirror. "Watch."

But Theodora did not appear in the fogged glass. The hideous water poured from the sink faucet, alive with the wriggling bodies of maggots and slugs. Adam's fingers tightened around her arm as his eyes rose.

Gray steam rose and fell as if sentient, gathering from the corners of the room into a cloud that swelled against the plaster ceiling. Slowly, it coalesced into a human form, the form of Theodora Wilde.

Her features united and then came apart, undulating in and out of existence. Crystalline moonlight rippled across her face, her dark hair a writhing shadow in the strange light. Sara had never noticed the delicate curve of her nose, so like hers.

The moonlight passed again over Theodora and shone upon the blanket she clutched to her chest. In a halting, unnatural motion, the apparition tilted her head and then opened her arms. The blanket slipped across her hands and flickered out of existence, and then something crashed to the floor with a hollow splash. Sara heard Adam cry out. The water around their ankles began to recede.

As Theodora's manifestation fell apart, wisping away like bog mists, Sara prepared herself for the horrible scream that usually punctuated her visitations. Instead, her ancestor hummed her lullaby, and then vanished.

The sink and bathtub drained silently, and the pool on the floor seeped into the stone, leaving behind only a small, rusted tin box.

Adam stood against the wall, his mouth agape. He had seen her. A part of Sara still believed Theodora was only in her head, and this corroboration of her existence both relieved and disturbed her at once.

"*Dios te salve, María, llena eres de gracia,*" he mumbled, and moved to cross himself but his arm fell back to his side, as if he realized the futility of it. When Sara turned back to the tin, it was gone.

She wrapped herself in a towel and flew down the hall, throwing open the door to Grammy's bedroom. Adam's bare feet padded behind her as she grabbed the tin from the old rolltop desk and dumped its contents onto the floor. The broach tumbled out, Theodora's hair shimmering in the dim light.

"What are we looking for?" Adam asked, and knelt to help her rifle through the papers and photographs, his soaked clothes dripping onto the carpet.

"I don't know, but there's something here we missed."

Sara opened every envelope and read the inscription on the back of every photograph, pausing only at Theodora's memento mori to remark to Adam how beautiful she must have been in life.

"There's nothing else here," she said at last, rocking back on her heels. "Why would Thea show me the tin?"

She took up the empty box and ran her fingers over its sharp edges, and along its center. The bottom bowed slightly and gave a little when she pressed it.

"It's a false bottom," she said, and wedged her fingernail beneath the tin until it bled. Finally, the panel popped off and clattered to the floor, revealing an envelope, addressed to her in Grammy's hand, and five bullets.

Adam picked one up and inspected it, whistling low.

"These are from a Colt pocket revolver," he said. "An old one."

Sara lifted the letter from beneath the ammunition and slid her finger beneath the seal, leaving a stain of her blood.

Dear Sara,

I hope you never find this. I hope its edges yellow, and time works upon it until all that remains is dust. If all my efforts are in vain, however, and you have discovered this blasted little tin, it means that I am no longer with you in body. It means you have come looking for answers. I am here to give them to you.

You no doubt know now that another heir to the Wildefell legacy still lives. The child, supposedly drowned by Theodora, your 2nd great grandmother, survived. Her name was Clementine, the namesake of Thea's very closest friend and confidant.

Clementine the elder was the sister of James Mauk, Thea's lover, and ultimately the ancestor of our prodigal heir. This was, at the time, quite the scandal. Clementine and Theodora parted ways, never to speak again, but I believe Thea hoped she would forgive her for drawing her young brother into sin, and so she gave her daughter her best friend's name. Clementine lost her only brother, her best friend, and her niece in the span of only a handful of days. She believed until the end that Bennett murdered him, though they never found his body. I have been unable to prove or disprove this accusation, but if what I have seen of Bennett reflects him as he was in life, I don't doubt him capable of cold blooded murder. His spirit lingers here, angry. We keep him at bay, but his rage makes him strong.

I digress. You'll be wanting to know what on earth ever happened to little Clementine, and I'll tell you. She was adopted by, in so far as we know, a church-going family who later relocated to Athens, Georgia. In her early twenties, she married and it is said she had a child, but we cannot locate the birth certificate. This is where the trail grows cold. We do not know the identity of the child, but be assured the progeny of this line will come to claim their birthright should it ever be made known to them. By then, Theodora's tragic history, and the tale of her daughter's survival, will have faded into obscurity. Only the Wildes knew the story, and when my father passed on, eventually your mother and I were the only ones left who knew the truth. And now you know it, too.

We have kept Bennett's favorite pistol (and what I believe to be the murder weapon) hidden away all these years to protect our family name. You will find it in the attic, in a large music box carved with a cameo of Theodora. The weapon has been cared for by me, polished and cleaned weekly to appease Bennett's spirit. He remains protective of it to this day. Be careful should you seek it out. These bullets belong to it. I leave them to you now so that you may either maintain our hold on this secret, or out the truth. This is your decision, and I will not attempt to sway you. I am simply too tired.

You always were a cunning little sprite, and I know the house will guide you down the right path. You mustn't let Wildefell fall into the wrong hands. It is your duty now to keep it, and to continue our endeavors to bring peace to the spirits that lie within. Someday, it will show you how it all came to be, and you will understand why we are this way, but that is a story for another time.

Although this story was passed down to me, and to my father before me, I had hoped you would not inherit it as I did. You mustn't be angry with me for keeping it all from you. I was only trying to protect you, trying to ensure this house remained in our possession, for the Wildes are the only steward it will accept. Even if you should marry, you will always be a Wilde. You must keep the name as your mother and I did, so it may be passed on to your children. The house will not suffer any man unwilling to submit to this condition.

The house chose you, my child. You must choose it above all else. I believe in you, baby doll. Do not fail us. And always remember, I am with you. Wildefell is my home and I cannot leave, even in death.

All my love, Grammy.

Sara held the letter in her hands, her tears smudging the faded ink. She hadn't noticed Adam reading with her until he set his hand on her arm.

"Sadie," he said gently.

"She knew," Sara whispered, wiping her nose with the back of her hand. Her soaked hair dripped down her back and she shivered, so Adam took the quilt off of Grammy's bed and draped it across her shoulders. "She knew there was an heir, and she knew Bennett was a murderer, and she did nothing."

"She did what she thought was right."

Sara picked up the old bullets and rolled them in her palm. "I need to find the gun."

"Why? What good would it do even if we could prove Bennett did it?"

"It would be fitting, wouldn't it? To end it this way."

Adam narrowed his eyes on her, his expression revealing that he caught her meaning, but believed he'd interpreted it wrong. She clarified it for him.

"I don't care about Bennett," she said. "He's gone. We're here, now, and so is the bastard heir."

"That isn't justice."

"Of course it's not. It's revenge. As vital to me now as breath or food."

She met the intensity of Adam's gaze with her own.

"Do you hear yourself?" he asked. "You sound like him."

This barb caught against her heart, but the anger and the grief had fashioned such a callus she barely felt it at all but for a slight twinge inside her chest.

"If you're suggesting I take the moral high ground, I can't. He's taken everything from me."

"Not everything. Not yet." He waited for this to weigh upon her, and then added, "If you do this, he wins. You're just another one of the monsters in his story."

"I have to stop him." She turned away from him, her eyes falling on the wallpaper and following the curling, wilted vines that climbed in faded ink up the wall.

"And we will. The weight of a man's life is heavy, Sadie. Trust me. I know."

Sara released a long breath, and then let him take the bullets out of her hand. She caught a glimpse of his wristwatch.

"I'm late," she said, standing. She shed Grammy's quilt and turned to leave the room.

"Where are you going?"

"To tie up a loose end. I'll be back soon. Find the gun."

Chapter XXII

*A*S THE rising moon dragged the angry sea back into itself, Wildefell pulled at Sara. She stepped on the gas pedal, and her father's mustang—her mustang—lurched forward across the bridge as if struggling against the unseen force.

Although she had driven this same road many times in her life, she had the uneasy sensation she'd made a wrong turn and was going the wrong direction. The sign for Huntington State Park rose up in murky dusk, dispelling her uncertainty, but none of the ill-ease. The ever-lingering scent of Cassie's perfume gathered close around her, so she lowered the window and drew a breath laden with both the ocean and the forest. Beneath the record-scratching of locusts in trees smeared by speed, the sea snarled. Hurricane season was coming, and Sara felt it deep within. The air carried a dampness that spoke of rain, and of violence.

She turned on the radio to drown out the fierceness, scanning the stations. Between five second samplings of Patsy Cline and Johnny Cash, Robert Johnson played his old familiar tune.

I can tell the wind is risin', the leaves tremblin' on the tree—

Sara hit the dial, and the ocean reigned once again.

By the time she pulled into the parking lot, a poorly paved square of gravel canopied by pin oaks and pines, she had pulled out her phone to call John and cancel this good-bye dinner altogether. Adam's arraignment was tomorrow. She hardly had time to humor this kind of thing. Maybe all she'd needed was a quick drive, some time away from Wildefell to clear her mind. She ought to head back.

Her finger hovered over John's name on the screen, but she did not make the call. Here before her was a rare opportunity for some small amount of closure. It felt selfish to want it, to need it, given everything at stake, but she was already here. She would give him half an hour to speak his mind, and then return to Wildefell, and to Adam.

The area was deserted. A few crows cawed in a maple, its leaves already dying, but the tourists had all packed up their beach umbrellas and gone home. Her shoes ground into the crushed gravel pathway, the gathering of trees eventually opening to a grassy field, which led in turn to a narrow beach. The gray ocean gnawed at the sand, foaming and rabid like a ravenous dog. Above all, stood the lighthouse, unchanged over the last century but for the salt which encrusted it. As the sun bled upon its façade, it appeared more like a corrupted memory, or a fever dream.

When she approached, a woman in a park ranger's uniform smiled widely at her.

"Are you Sara?" she asked. Sara nodded. "Go on up. Everything's ready for you. You're a lucky gal. I can't even get my boyfriend to buy me flowers on my birthday."

The woman laughed, but Sara could only feign a smile. A falling sensation in her stomach heightened her uneasiness. Something wasn't right. She clutched the cool iron railing and looked up into the center of the spiral staircase, feeling for all the world she had wandered too far from home and lost her way.

She did not heed this internal alarm, but instead set her foot on the first step, and climbed. It was just dinner, after all. What would it hurt?

Sara ascended the dizzying staircase, her footsteps rattling against the iron. When she at last arrived at the top, where the lighthouse's overlook opened to a 360 degree view of the state park, she found a table set for dinner.

"John?" she called, assuming he'd gone round to the other side, but he did not answer. She stepped up to the table, its checkered cloth flapping in the wind. On one of the place settings, lit as much by the dying sun as by an overly dramatic candelabra, was a paperback book.

The Strange Case of Dr. Jekyll and Mr. Hyde.

Sara's mouth went dry as she swept her fingers over the cover.

"No," she whispered. A napkin had been tucked between the pages, and she opened to the place with the wind's aid. It snuffed out the candles as she read the underlined passage.

*"Did you ever remark that door?" he asked; and when his companion had replied in the affirmative, "It is connected in my mind,"
added he, "with a very odd story."*

"No," she said again, backing away from the table. Sara knotted her fingers in her hair, a thousand encounters coalescing and then splitting open.

The path of error is the path of truth.

"Reichenbach," she muttered. Her back hit the window, and she flew toward the staircase. As she descended into the center of the lighthouse, she had the distinct feeling she was still back at Wildefell, and she'd never left at all. She smelled the musty carpet in the hall upstairs and heard the creaking of the pull-down ladder leading to the attic. Pain cracked across her skull and tore into her eye, and she collapsed onto the steps, vaguely aware she was falling, but unable to draw herself out of the churning darkness.

The ladder creaked and groaned, footsteps echoing inside her, and then she was in the attic. She knew it by the smell; black mold and mothballs, and a century of unwanted heirlooms abandoned under blankets of dust.

Sara knew the man who climbed the ladder. She listened to him walk across the creaking attic floor and recognized the hitch in his gait.

Adam.

He didn't see the shadow, didn't feel the shift in the air, but Sara felt it. She tried to cry out to him, but her voice would not come.

A sickly *crack* filled up the space in her mind, the sound of breaking bones, and the *drip, drip* of blood falling to the floor. Adam grunted.

You? he said, and then spat, but there was no reply. Another blow made contact, bursting open flesh and shattering bone. And then another.

Sadie, he whispered, her name thick with blood. *You need to come home.*

John's voice sliced into the center of her skull as her head struck concrete.

She can't hear you, you fool.

Consciousness waned. The taste of blood filled her mouth. She fought the darkness, clawing her way toward the sound of her name.

"Sara? Ms. Sara?"

Her body tensed and then fell slack again. Slowly, gnawing pain drew her up and out of the mire. Her eyes flew open, and she gasped.

"Adam," she breathed, and tried to stand, but her knees cracked hard on the concrete.

"Wait, wait," someone said. "I called an ambulance. You fell down the stairs and hit your head. You shouldn't move."

The park ranger hovered over her, a radio cracking on her hip. Night had collapsed onto the park, lit now by a jaundiced yellow streetlamp and the watery glow of a crescent moon.

"Call 911," Sara said, and stumbled to her feet. Vertigo knocked her legs out from under her, but the ranger grabbed her by the arms and helped her stand.

"I did," she answered.

"Not for me." Sara couldn't gather her thoughts enough to explain. She pushed the ranger aside and began to run. Pain screamed through her arm when she reached for her cell phone. The splintered end of her ulna pressed up against the underside of her skin, scratching to be let out, but she did not break stride. Adrenaline dripped like morphine into her blood, and even as she pulled open the door of the

Mustang and folded herself into the seat, she felt only the throbbing of her own heart.

"I'm not too late," she muttered to herself. "I can't be too late."

With her broken arm cradled against her side, she wiggled her phone out of her pocket. The screen had shattered during her fall. It wouldn't turn on.

Come home.

"I'm coming," she wept, thick dread welling up inside her lungs, drowning her. She threw the phone into the footwell of the passenger side and navigated the winding forest road through burning tears.

How could she have been so blind?

"This isn't real," she said, blinking. "How can this be real?"

An ambulance, the one meant for her, sped past, the afterimage of its whirring lights echoing across her eyes for miles.

Sara thought back to the day Mr. Woodward walked into her office with a lanky, mild mannered man in tow. Had there been something familiar about him then, some spark of recognition, some *knowing*? She'd so obstinately denied her heritage and intuition that she led him right to her family. She let him in.

The gates of Wildefell came at last into view, the dark iron gleaming in the moonlight. Her brakes squealed as she parked in front of the dark house, the only light shining from the window in the attic. She stumbled out of the car, holding her useless arm close.

Somewhere far away, a fox screamed.

By the light of the moon, Sara climbed the porch steps. The door opened at her touch.

"Adam?" she cried, but stillness reigned inside the house. Her swift footsteps sounded across the foyer, and up the stairs to the second floor. She lifted her eyes to the trap door in the ceiling, to the ladder swung down beneath it. Dark blood snaked down the rungs, dripping onto the floor and pooling against the baseboard.

"No," she murmured, flinging herself up the ladder. Her right hand would not close, though she felt no pain, so she let it hang useless at her side as she hoisted herself up into the attic, its rungs slick.

Sara breached the opening and peered into the attic. Adam was unconscious, perhaps worse. His body had been tied to an overturned chair, the wire biting into his wrists and ankles. An open wound in his skull bled freely into a black pool beneath him, and his splintered collarbone jutted through the fabric of his shirt. He might have been mauled by a wolf, and not a man.

"Adam," she breathed, hoisting herself up, and then falling to her knees beside him.

She'd come too late.

Sara reached for his hand, but did not take it. Three of his fingers were broken and set at unnatural angles, the fingernails ripped from their beds. If she touched him, she could no longer deny reality. It would still be a nightmare, a horrible vision, so long as she didn't prove he was truly there.

Her lip trembled as she extended her hand to find his pulse. Her fingers met his skin, and she closed her eyes, collapsing under grief so intense it shuddered inside her bones until she felt she might crack open.

"No, no, please," she whimpered. "I still love you. Please, don't."

Behind her, someone began to clap. She turned.

"So touching, so genuine. I don't even have any notes."

She recognized his voice before the tears cleared from her eyes.

"John," she said, standing. She turned her back to Adam, her stance wide so as to protect him, although it mattered little now. John sat in a chair beneath the only window, the moon alighting on half his face. He opened a book, and with a grotesque smile, began to read.

"The Boots pointed out the door to me, and was about to go downstairs again when I saw something that made me feel sickish… From under the door there curled a little red ribbon of blood which had meandered across the passage and formed a little pool along the skirting at the other side."

Sara swallowed the bile in her throat, grief crystalizing to anger as sharp as flint.

"You son of a bitch," she spat. "You tortured him."

"Well, obviously. The brutality of it is the whole point. Didn't you read the book?"

John stood slowly and set the dog-eared copy of *A Study in Scarlet* on the seat of the chair, his movements as casual and disarming as ever. Sara's arm throbbed. She'd lost feeling in her fingers.

"When did you know?" he asked, stepping toward her.

"Reichenbach," she answered.

"Ah, so you caught that, did you?"

"It's the place Sherlock Holmes dies. Did you think I wouldn't put it together?"

"A little too late if you ask me," he said, nodding toward Adam's lifeless body. He stood only inches from her now, so close she could feel his sour breath in her hair. Adam hadn't gone down without a fight. John's cheekbone had been crushed, changing the structure of his face. A crescent shaped stain of purple pooled below his eye, and blood still slithered down his neck from a notch in his ear, giving his whole aspect the impression of indistinguishable deformity. Sara lifted her chin and met his eyes. How could she not have seen the monster in him?

He bent and retrieved a cane from beneath one of the old dining chairs, its ivory handle flecked with blood and bits of tissue. Sara recognized it as her father's, the one Grammy had given to him as a wedding gift. It had belonged to her father, Stephen, and to Bennett.

"Do you remember when you told me about this cane?" John asked. "A family heirloom. What was it you said?"

Sara remembered that night. They'd gone to the company picnic together. John had brought a blanket, and they shared watermelon and childhood stories, but she wondered now if any of his had been true.

"No? I'll remind you," he continued. "You said that sometimes you imagined he was John Watson, and the two of you would play at solving mysteries. I knew then. This—" he motioned with the cane, pausing at Adam "—was all your idea."

"You bastard," she muttered, but he only smiled again, blood from his split lip staining his perfect teeth. Sara kept her eyes on the cane, which he clutched tighter.

"Accurate enough," he shrugged. "Our paths are intertwined, Sara. This, all of this, is how it was always meant to be. And to think, if that adoption certificate hadn't been passed down, generation by generation, until I found it in an old family album, I might never have known. I might never have traced that orphan baby back here, to Theodora Wilde, and to you. What I'm trying to say is, look at everything that had to align to bring us here to this moment. Isn't it remarkable?"

"It's insane. You're insane."

"Says the woman so desperate to believe in ghosts she couldn't see I've been here all along? Every creaking floorboard I stepped on, every time I bumped a table or stubbed my toe, you blamed the house." He laughed and set his free hand on his forehead. "I mean, my God, it was just so easy."

"They're real," she whispered. "I've seen them."

"Of course you have. God, it's just so deliciously gothic. You must be in heaven."

"The word you're looking for is hell."

"Oh, come on. Hasn't it been a thrill, living out your very own Sherlockian mystery?"

"What do you want?" Her throat tightened around these words, so they scarcely made any sound at all.

"That's the question you've been dying to ask, isn't it?"

"I never wanted Wildefell. You could've had it." She would have given anything to have Cassie and Grammy and Lucy with her again. Her legacy, her home, everything, but he scoffed at her.

"I don't want this old pile of rocks and bones. I want what Bennett Wilde took from us. The newspaper, back in the hands of a Mauk. It's my birthright." He smirked. "I think journalism must run in our blood, cousin. But that isn't important right now. What about the question you've been afraid to ask?"

"What?"

"What do *you* want? Deep down you must have known who I really was. This is what you wanted, someone to take it all off your shoulders."

"That's not true."

John lifted his hand to her face and brushed his fingers across her cheek. She gritted her teeth but could not move.

"Do you know how easy it was to manipulate you?" John said in her ear. His fingers moved down her neck. "How quickly you let me in to fill up the emptiness inside you?"

Sara slapped him hard across the face, and although her palm stung with the force of it, he appeared to feel no pain at all. He smiled at her, stepping backward. If she could keep him talking longer, she could come up with some way to get out of this, some way to call for help or find Bennett's gun. He wouldn't know it wasn't loaded.

"Why Sherlock Holmes?" she asked.

"It was the only thing in the world that made you feel alive, and now I've taken it from you."

"So, what? You're going to kill me and claim your fortune?"

"Before the sun comes up," he began, waving the cane toward the window, "I'm going to walk out of here and explain everything to Agent Grant. When you didn't show for our date, I came to Wildefell and found you beating Contreras here with Daddy's cane. Wildefell belongs with a Wilde after all, and you couldn't allow the detective, the outsider, to taint the legacy. Unfortunately, I'd arrived too late to save him."

"That's never going to work," Sara said, but he didn't appear to hear.

"I'll admit, I didn't expect your sister was fucking him too, and that she'd leave her part of Wildefell to him. Quite a plot twist, that. I had to rewrite a few pieces, but I adapted, as you can see." He nodded back to Adam.

"And you're just going to announce to everyone that you're the long-lost heir?"

"I'm going to tell them that you and the detective discovered my identity, that you manipulated me to get close to me in Savannah, and then planned to kill me so I couldn't inherit Wildefell. I created a crime only Sara Wilde could execute. It was always you. The detective was just the lover doing your bidding. Poor chap."

"Why kill him if you already framed him? His arraignment was tomorrow."

"I didn't kill him. You did. Half the town already believes you're insane like your mother. It won't take much to convince them that you roped him into your scheme and then murdered him. I framed you both, see?"

"And my father?"

John looked down at the cane and tapped it against the floor-boards. "Clever, eh? Just a little something I thought up to, ah, distract you while I worked. You all have so many home videos stashed away up here. It wasn't difficult to become him from time to time."

Out of the corner of her eye, Sara spotted the cameo of Theodora described in Grammy's letter. Bennett's chest sat atop a sewing table draped in white. John looked over his shoulder, and then reached behind his back and removed the weapon from his belt.

"You're looking for this? The detective was too."

Sara's heart dropped into her stomach. There was no plan B. Then, John actually handed over the gun. She took it cautiously, and then narrowed her eye on him.

"It's not loaded," he assured her. "This must be a precious family heirloom. You should have it."

"You wanted my fingerprints on it," she said, understanding.

"It's kind of poetic, that you would try to use the same gun on me that Bennett used to kill my ancestor. People eat that up. It's going to be a hell of a headline."

Sara looked down at the gun, her hope waning. She tucked the weapon in the pocket of her jeans, and another long shot sprung up into her mind.

"You're going to kill me now, then?" she asked.

"It's about that time, yes."

Sara lowered her head. "Can I say goodbye to him?"

"I'm not a monster. Take your time."

Sara turned from him and knelt beside Adam. She brushed his hair off of his forehead, and his right eye fluttered open. Her heart surged. He was alive! Every ounce of energy she possessed, she used to suffocate evidence of her joy. Tears sprung into her eyes.

"Right pocket," he wheezed, and she leaned to his ear.

"I love you, Adam," she whispered. "I always have."

Sara fished the bullets out of his pocket and loaded the gun.

Then, she spun on her heel, aiming the weapon at his heart.

She fired once, but the shot went wide and blasted a nearby tiffany lamp into glimmering shards. A fraction of a second behind the blast of old Bennet's gun, she heard another, though she was certain she hadn't pulled the trigger. This phantom shot met its mark, the force of it knocking John backward against the windowpane. The antique glass shattered, and as he crashed through, his eyes focused on a place behind her, his expression the very image of horror.

Sara turned.

Theodora Wilde stood behind her. She held her husband's pistol, aimed at John. Even as Sara held the very same weapon in her own trembling hand, Theodora fired again. John fell at last through the window, his bones cracking on the stone below.

When she looked back, Theodora was gone.

Chapter XXIII

Two weeks later...

*S*ARA TAPPED gently on her mother's door, Brian the nurse looking on with an encouraging nod.

"Momma?" she said, and then stepped hesitantly inside. Restored to her home in Wayview Psychiatric facility, Imogene Wilde sat in her usual chair with a blanket wrapped around her shoulders, looking out the window toward the sea. It had always been a nice view. Sara wondered if it made her happy sometimes.

Her mother turned, her eye clear and quick as it had been when Sara was a child. Recognition dawned across her features, and aged her, as if all the years had fallen upon her at once instead of over time.

"How are you, Momma?" she asked. Her mother turned back to the window, smiling.

"Quiet," she answered. "I can hear you this time. They were all so loud last time you came to visit, I could hardly hear you at all. Pesky bastards."

Sara smirked. "They are that, it's true."

"Doctor Walsh says my new medication should keep them quiet sometimes, but who knows. They always come back, don't they?"

"Yeah." Sara sat down on a creaking wooden hope chest, one her mother had insisted on bringing with her when she checked into this place. It had been so long since Momma had looked at her and really seen her, even longer since she'd smiled at her. Sara blinked back cautiously hopeful tears, reminding herself this moment could not last.

"Does it hurt much?" Momma asked, setting her long fingers on the plaster cast around Sara's wrist. She didn't ask how it had happened.

"Not much," she answered.

"That's good."

Momma turned back to the window, the smile falling away. A long moment dripped by, time kept by the ticking clock and the sun hanging high over the water.

"He's not coming back, is he?" Momma asked.

Sara swallowed, her gaze landing on the still ocean.

"No, Momma. He's gone."

"They're all gone?"

"Yes."

Momma nodded, her finger tapping out a rhythm on the arm of the chair. Then she turned toward Sara abruptly and took her hand.

"My beautiful baby girl," she said, her lip trembling. "I don't know how much quiet I have left today. It's so good to hear your voice. I want you to know something."

"Yes?"

Her mother looked at her, a troubling desperation in her eyes. It was a moment of horrible sanity, stripped bare by years of anguish and loneliness.

"They're not all in your head," she said at last, eyes gleaming. "The voices. We're not crazy."

Tears stung Sara's eyes. Her mother's features blurred.

"I know, Momma," she answered. "I know that now." She sniffed, and wiped her cheek with her sleeve. "I think I can get you out of here... if you wanted."

"I belong here now," she answered, patting her hand. "You're stronger than me. You know how to tell them apart from each other. You know what's real. I never did."

"I don't always know what's real," Sara said. "There's no proof."

Momma reached up and brushed the hair from Sara's face. She closed her eyes, the touch a comfort and an agony all at once.

"You must trust yourself, baby. That's all we have."

"How do I know any of this was real?" She didn't explain what she meant, but her mother's smile led her to believe, somehow, she already knew what had befallen her. She rose from her chair and motioned for Sara to stand.

"I have something I've been meaning to give you."

Sara frowned, folding her arms across her chest as her mother opened up the hope chest, her shoulders stooping, white hair cascading toward a stack of neatly folded blankets.

"The story of how this came to be is very important to our family, but I…" She removed a moth-eaten baby blanket, as blue as the sea, and held it to her chest. Tears glistened in her eyes. "I think it belonged to my great grandmother, but I'm sorry, I can't remember her name, or why I have it. I'm so sorry, I don't know the story anymore. But maybe it's… maybe it's the proof you're looking for."

"Theodora," Sara whispered. "Her name was Theodora."

Her mother didn't ask how she knew it, only handed Sara the blanket and sat back down. She sighed, and returned her gaze to the sea. Her shoulders straightened as if the giving of this gift had relieved her of a great burden.

"Thank you, Momma," she whispered, but began to tremble. When the sobs wracked through her, she had no more control over them than she did the tide. Her mother's hand fell upon her shoulder, and then she embraced her, the sensation so foreign to Sara she stiffened against it.

"Hush," Momma whispered. "It's over now." Sara allowed herself to rest her head on her mother's shoulder, grief washing over her anew that this moment would not last. The voices would return, sending Momma into spiraling madness, and Sara would be an orphan again. But for now, she clung to her blouse and breathed in the familiar scent of her apricot hand cream, the baby blanket between them. Momma pulled her back and wiped the tears from her cheeks as gently as if Sara were only a child, frightened of the things in the dark.

"My precious baby girl," Momma said, Sara's face cradled in her delicate hands. The smile reached her eyes. "Here we are. The last of the Wildes."

Sara gathered herself, squeezing her mother's hands. "Here we are."

- - -

COOL WIND FROM the sea gathered up a handful of scarlet leaves and laid them gently to rest on the gravestones in the Wilde family plot. Sara placed a daisy on the bare earth, kneeling.

"I hope you can find peace," she whispered, and traced her fingers over the letters carved into stone. The land beside her was still an open wound, gridded and marked with flags by the Beaufort Historical Society. Thus far, with the assistance of a forensic anthropologist from the University of South Carolina, they had positively identified Theodora, Bennett, and their son, Stephen. Their grave markers, though now little more than index cards covered in plastic, held fast to the soil despite the threatening wind. Sara wondered how many more bodies lay beneath the surface, and how long it might take to restore them to their rightful graves.

The funeral yesterday had been quiet, the bodies of her family, blood or otherwise, laid to rest alongside the others, where they belonged. No one ever left Wildefell.

"Sadie?"

Startled, Sara looked over her shoulder, and then sent Adam a reprimanding smile. He balanced a to-go tray of coffee against the sling preventing his clavicle from disarticulating again.

"You're supposed to be resting. You've been out of the hospital all of three days and you're traipsing all over town already?"

He grinned at her. "Good morning to you, too." When his eyes fell on the headstones, the smile fell. "How could we have lost them all?"

Sara returned her gaze to Cassie's grave, situated between Grammy and Lucy so she might never feel alone.

"Do you think they're happy?" Sara asked.

"Are you kidding? They're probably already overthrowing heaven."

Sara smiled, the idea of this warming her heart, though she didn't think she believed in heaven at all. They walked together through the tall grass. Sara shivered as the wind whipped through her hair. She wrapped her arms around herself, the cast on her arm digging into her chest.

"I stopped by to check on the horses this morning at the boarding stables," Adam said. They reached the driveway and skirted an open storage pod before walking up the porch steps. "They're both doing fine, though Salem is getting into trouble with the mares."

Sara shook her head as they walked inside, and Adam lifted his chin to sniff the air.

"Did you smudge the house again?" he asked.

"I can still smell the blood," she answered as they made their way past towers of boxes, labeled with both her handwriting and his, and stepped into the sitting room. Adam removed a book from his back pocket and extended it to her.

"By the way, this is from Eva," he said. "She asked me to give it to you."

Sara furrowed her brow, reading the cover. It was a book on spiritualism, first published in 1925. A note bookmarked the copyright page.

"What's this?" she said to herself, and opened the small envelope.

I know this isn't the same book as the one I ruined back in high school, but I hope you can see it for what it is. I was wrong, Sara. I hope you can forgive me. We're practically family, after all.

"Wow," Sara muttered.

"What is it?" Adam asked.

"An olive branch."

The edge of Adam's lip shifted upward. Sara tucked the note back into its envelope and set the book on the end table.

"That reminds me," Adam said. "She wanted to know if you were going to press charges?" He eased himself into her father's chair. Sara settled in front of a box labeled OFFICE and slit the tape with a box cutter.

"Charges?" she asked.

"For the church congregation."

"Oh my God," she said, leaning back on her heals. "I forgot about that."

"That's a no, then?"

"I probably scared the hell out of all of them."

"I'll explain everything on Sunday."

"You think they'll let you in? You're with a pagan now. I might as well be dragging you around on my broomstick."

Adam laughed in his old way, until it reached his eyes. "Unless I burst into flames when I walk through the door, there's not much they can do to keep me out."

"Your faith has always astounded me."

"It keeps me grounded, just like yours."

Sara opened the moving box and lifted out her grandfather's typewriter, a mordant smile creeping across her lips.

"Glad Grant let you have that out of evidence," Adam said. "It'll look nice on your desk at The Times."

"John had it in his hotel room," she replied, shaking her head and setting the heavy piece of machinery onto her lap. "Just sitting on the desk plain as day. He didn't even imagine someone might come looking for it."

"Arrogant bastard," he muttered.

"Well, along with a nice little library of gothic fiction, and every newspaper article I ever wrote, it wrapped up Grant's case pretty neatly."

Adam frowned as she set the typewriter aside and removed a table lamp cloaked in bubble wrap.

"I'm worried about Grant, Sadie," he said. "If they trace those bullets to Bennett's gun, it could make things… complicated."

"There were no bullets."

"What?"

"I missed," she said, but continued unpacking.

"I don't understand. You shot him."

Sara shook her head. "Theodora shot him. I saw her behind me. I watched her pull the trigger, saw John get blown back by the force of the bullets, but when I asked Grant, she said the M.E. didn't find them. There weren't even any wounds. Official cause of death is injuries sustained during the fall."

Adam leaned back into the chair and smiled. "I'll be damned."

"I can't prove it happened that way."

"You don't have to. Theodora showed up at the final hour to protect her family."

Sara bowed her head, an unexpected wave of emotion crashing into her.

"I thought..." she breathed, and she heard him rise and limp to her side. "You were—I couldn't find your pulse."

"I'm ok, Sadie," he whispered, and sat down beside her on the floor. She shook her head, dropping a smaller box of office supplies to wipe her eyes.

"Are you sure you want to move in here with me? With a girl who sees ghosts and hears voices?" Sara laughed, but it was false.

"I read something the other day," he said without answering her question.

"Oh?"

"A Scandal in Bohemia."

She smiled. "That's one of my favorites."

"I know, and it made me realize something. John set out to make you into Sherlock Holmes, but I think he was wrong. I don't think you're Holmes at all. Maybe *I* am."

"Oh really?" she replied, forcing lightness of heart into her tone, though the mention of John brought acid into her throat. "Who am I then?"

The grin fell from Adam's face. He met her gaze, the amber in his eyes melting to sweet syrup.

"You're Irene," he answered softly. "You're *the* woman."

Understanding fell over her gracefully. Somewhere upstairs, a door slammed soundly shut. Sara smiled. It was only the house, after all.

That damned northerly wind.

THE END.

Made in the USA
Columbia, SC
19 October 2024

44399024R00133